Yell

A tale of life an ʊve in a hi-vis vest

Dave Thompson

Yellow is a work of fiction. Any resemblance to actual persons or events is purely coincidental. Stories about famous performers in this narrative are entirely fictional.

First and foremost,
to Lorraine,
who always said I had a book in me and kept
encouraging me to write one.

Also,
to the good people of Eventsec.
None of you made it in here whole,
but we're all in here somewhere...

1. Tiered seating and tight trousers

The caramel square on the table between us was hardly touched. I was hungry, but I knew that saying to a client, 'Have you finished with that?' was highly unprofessional. As was not really listening to them, which I confess I had been doing for several minutes. It had been a long week, with a number of similar conversations. Opposite me, Paul, slouched in his chair and still in his work overalls, kept talking.

'I mean, it's not that the job is hard. I mean, I can cope with the work. It's just, I mean, getting up early to start at eight, and not finishing until four, it takes it out of you, so it does.'

I took a deep breath and tried to hold back.

'Well, it should, that's what work is all about. You put energy in, and they pay you for that. If it didn't take effort, it wouldn't be called work.'

'Aye, aye ... I hear what you're saying,' he replied, giving every indication that he didn't. 'I'd just like something different ...' Paul tailed off as someone on the other side of the coffee shop caught his attention.

I took another deep breath and tried to keep my voice even.

'You've had seven different jobs in as many months, Paul,' I said, 'You're twenty years old, and you've never stayed in the same place for more than ten days.'

'I was in Screwfix for a fortnight,' he said earnestly.

'Ok, I'll give you that one,' I conceded, 'But you've formed a habit. What I really think you need is just to get used to the world of work. Get yourself into a routine. Stick at it ...' Paul sucked in air through his teeth and pulled a face. 'Then maybe look around and see what else is out there.'

I usually tried to help a client come to their own conclusions, but Paul and I had been down this road before, and much as he was a good kid at heart and very likeable, it was time for a more direct approach. Besides, the big clock on the coffee shop wall was ticking dangerously close to five.

'Do you know what I would *really* like?' Paul said, leaning forward. I groaned inwardly.

'What would you *really* like?'

'I'd like to work in a snooker hall, taking the money, handing out the balls and that wee triangular rack. I mean, that would be a cushy job.'

I tried hard not to sigh too loudly.

'Paul,' I said slowly, 'Maybe that's the dream job, but while you're waiting for an opening in the snooker trade, the best thing you can do right now is to stick with the storeroom you've got. It's good money, weekday hours and nice people. Promise me you'll stick it out to next week.' I didn't normally beg clients, but I was desperate for him to commit, for his own sake, if not for my sanity.

'I'll see, Robbie,' he replied, 'I'm going in tomorrow anyway.' My heart sank. The best predictor of future behaviour is past behaviour and it looked very much like Paul and I would be back to looking at job adverts this time next week.

I glanced at my wristwatch; I had just less than an hour to get home, changed and across town.

'I hate to run off,' I said, 'But I've another appointment, so I'm going to leave you to your caramel square.'

Paul pulled another face.

'Not feeling it,' he said, 'Something's not quite right about the toffee.'

*

It didn't take long to get home, but time was still tight. I shaved quickly and ran my hand over my face to check for rough patches. Taking in my reflection in the mirror I concluded that my face was getting bigger. Fatter cheeks, eyes with bags and I was starting to develop the under-chin skin of a basset hound. On the brighter side, I could still see traces of the twenty-something who was still alive and well in my head. At fifty-two my younger self was still recognisable, even if a touch overcooked.

Shirtless, I looked down at the couple of inches of stomach hanging over my belt. Park Run every third week wasn't keeping it at bay, but I refused to admit to myself that I was bigger than I used to be, despite the need to buy larger trousers.

A small fleck of red appeared to the right of my Adam's apple. I watched it thoughtfully in the mirror, predicting it wouldn't develop into a trickle, but I gave it a few seconds of close attention to make sure; it wasn't worth risking my new shirt.

6

I sat on the edge of the bath. It creaked and I glared at the taps. I looked back in the mirror. This is what other people would see tonight, except with a shirt. Not unfriendly, no threatening tattoos, no piercing stare, no facial scars. I considered my resting face to be passive and open. Vacant, was how Shirley had often described it, though she hadn't meant it unkindly. Vacant, as in without guile.

Smiling, I picked up my mustard-yellow polo shirt by the tail end. I examined my neck for any further blood flow, and happy the tiny fleck had dried, pulled the shirt on over my head and smoothed it down. It was a perfect fit; tight enough to not make me look even bigger and loose enough not to accentuate the moobs.

Downstairs, I put on my freshly polished black shoes and mustard fleece. I checked my watch. A little ahead of schedule perhaps, but without much to spare. I hovered between the fruit bowl and the biscuit cupboard, weighing up between Mars bar and apple. The Mars bar won. 'I'll probably walk it off,' I mumbled to myself as I locked the front door.

*

The drive to the Belfast Auditorium was slow but steady; it helped to be driving into town from the east when most of the traffic was heading out of the centre. The news item on Radio Ulster was too intense so I flicked the stereo to CD and Springsteen's 'Born in the USA' album. The stereo was knackered,

7

and the CD had been jammed in it for the last two years. Still, it was an outstanding album, and you could be stuck with worse.

I glanced at the clock. I was still on time. I tapped my fingers on the steering wheel to 'Glory Days', channelling my adrenaline. I was a little nervous, but I'd had new jobs before, so I knew this wasn't something to sweat. Tony loved it – and never shut up about it – and besides, while it would be helpful, I knew I wasn't depending on it. Worst case scenario, I still had four days a week covered, this would just give me a little leeway in the budget.

It seemed simple enough. You submitted your availability through the company app, they offered you the stewarding shifts they had available, and you committed to the ones that suited. Sometimes you'd get to see a bit of a gig too; what could be better?

*

I swung the car into the car park, catching sight of two or three other yellow-shirted stewards making their way into the building. I cut off 'My Hometown' in its prime, locked up and walked towards the entrance.

Stepping inside, I took in the expansive foyer of the Belfast Auditorium. I'd been to one gig there before, and, being slightly the worse for wear, hadn't really taken it in. Four staircases led to the floors above and a ring of enormous pillars made it an impressive space. Too impressive for tonight's act, a reformed boy band, desperate for cash to pay off their divorce settlements and rehab bills.

'Robbie!' My cynical reflections were interrupted by a man of similar age, build and hair cut hurrying towards me.

'Tony! How's it going?'

'At this point it's all fine, but it'll go tits up later. Have you signed in yet?'

'No, just about to.'

'Ok. Get that done; always sign in first.' Tony gestured to the line of stewards across the foyer. 'I've made a wee swap, so tonight you'll be on tiered seating with me.'

'Take it easy on me, now, Tone.'

'Ha! There's no rest on tiered seating! It's a good workout though.' He glanced at his wristwatch. 'Supervisor's meeting, I'll see you shortly.' He spun round and hurried off.

'Here, where do I go after sign in?' I called after him.

'Top of the stairs,' Tony called back, 'Directly above. You'll see the others standing about.' He disappeared into the melee of workers criss-crossing the foyer.

I joined the back of the sign-in queue and looked around me. The mustard yellow shirts were queueing here, but there were others in white shirts and black ties, black polo shirts, black t-shirts with drinks logos, white t-shirts with stripy aprons and hi-vis fluorescent yellow coats all milling around. It had never occurred to me that so many people worked here.

'Name?' asked the twenty-something girl behind the desk.

'Robbie McKittrick.'

'Rabbie, right,' she replied in a broad Belfast accent. I found my name on the list and scribbled my signature.

'One shot?' the girl said.

'Sorry?'

'One shot?' In her accent, I heard this as 'one shat?' and fleetingly thought, *is she asking me if I've had a shit*?

'I'm not sure what that is,' I replied.

'You new?'

'No, I didn't know.'

'Are ... you ... new?' the girl asked slowly.

'Yes.'

'A one shot is a two-pound car parking ticket for staff. It's cheaper than paying at the end of the night. You can buy it now. Do you want one?'

'Yes,' I replied, squeezing two pound coins from my pocket.

With my 'one shot' safely tucked away, I climbed the winding staircase to the first floor concourse.

From above, the Belfast Auditorium looks like a legless ladybird; a small dome for the stage and backstage area, attached to a much larger dome covering the audience. Inside, the floorspace was enclosed by a horseshoe of tiered seats, the entrance to which lay through small tunnels, officially called vomitories, running from the auditorium to the concourse outside.

I walked through the nearest vomitory and looked out over the auditorium. I was impressed not only by

10

its size – seven thousand people would be packed in here shortly – but by its grandeur. It had been built specifically for concerts. Its painted, plaster ceiling and wood-panelled walls were built for superior acoustics. It even had a thick carpet, hauled out for classical music.

I took in the staging for the gig. There were several different layers, a vast array of lighting rigs and one large central screen with two smaller screens off to either side. If there were live musicians, they weren't going to be seen.

'Boy bands,' I muttered to myself, 'Glorified karaoke.'

Exiting the vomitory, I made my way over to the group of stewards gathered on the concourse. I stood next to a female steward in her twenties, pony-tailed, and mumbled a hello.

'Hiya,' she chirped, before turning away to talk to someone else.

I suddenly became aware of a larger entity next to me and turned to find a much taller and broader young male Asian steward standing beside me.

'Hello,' I said.

'I hate tiered seating,' he responded gloomily, 'Why do they keep putting me on tiered seating?'

'Right.'

'I'm a big guy.' He spread his arms wide to demonstrate; an entirely unnecessary gesture. 'I am not made to get up and down stairs a hundred times. I am made for standing in front of the stage with my arms folded giving off a vibe that says *if you try to get past me, I will kill you.'*

'Yeah.'

'Not that I would kill anybody; it's against my religion.'

'Are you a Muslim?'

'No, no,' he replied, looking confused, 'I just don't believe you should kill people for trying to get on stage at a gig.'

'Oh, ok. I'm new to all this, so I don't know what tiered seating is going to be like. Er ... I'm Robbie.' I held out my hand.

'Sohail.' He took hold of my hand and enveloped it in his own.

'I get so sweaty,' he continued, 'It's not pretty, man. No one wants to be shown to their seat by a big guy with damp patches and sweat running into his crack.'

I forced myself to disengage from the mental picture.

The group of stewards was now about twenty in number. Some chatted quietly in twos or threes, others stood by themselves checking their phones before the shift officially started.

No phones out in work time had been hammered home at the training. There had been a lot of details to take in that night, but they largely fell into simple principles. Be helpful; know where people can pee and where the exits and smoking areas are. Be friendly; smile, chat and make the gig a happy experience. Be alert; assume emergencies will sometimes happen – so don't have your head stuck in your phone. There were a few other rules, such as not approaching celebrities if you ended up backstage, but for the most part being a good steward required a small amount of knowledge and a lot of common sense.

'Can I have everyone's attention please?' Tony began as he joined the group, 'First up, I'd like to welcome Robbie to the Belfast Auditorium and to working with Safe & Sound, this is his first night. Are there any other newbies?'

A relatively short steward, who must have been over eighteen, but looked twelve, put up his hand. After establishing his name was Ryan and assuring him he had no reason to be as petrified as he looked, Tony continued.

'Has everybody worked tiered seating before? Almost everyone. Tiered seating is pretty straightforward. Tickets are scanned at the front door, so all you have to do is read the row and the seat number and make sure people find the right seat. If you put them in the wrong seat, it buggers stuff up later on. Does everyone have a torch?'

I shook my head; it had never occurred to me to bring a torch.

'You can sign one out of the store in a minute,' the pony-tailed girl next to me said.

'Tonight's artists,' Tony continued, 'Are a bunch of tossers on a comeback tour because they snorted all the money they made up their noses. For anybody unfamiliar with their contribution to popular music, they are 'The Lads' who had a string of chart hits in the early nineties, including such classics as 'I Love your Hair' and 'You Make me Horny.' Bet you still have those seven-inch singles at home Ciaran?'

Ciaran, tall, mid-forties, but still with his twenties' waistline, smirked.

'I've been playing their greatest hits all week.'

'Capacity crowd tonight,' Tony went on, 'Three thousand seated, four thousand on the floor. Crowd profile will be largely female, in and around their forties, and some hassled-looking husbands dragged along. Toilets have been redesignated, there are male toilets at doors five and ten, everything else is female.'

'All the usual stuff applies. This will be a night of high heels and pink gin so please be mindful of people on the steps. Any slips, trips and falls, the first thing is always to offer medical assistance.'

Tony sighed heavily. 'It's going to be pretty wet out there tonight, guys. Good news is, it's Thursday, so it probably won't be as pissed as the weekend shows. Any questions?'

No one did, and so Tony allocated each steward to a vomitory. Coming to me last, he asked the two people on either side of me, Ciaran and the pony-tailed girl, whose name turned out to be Niamh, to keep me right until he had checked every post was covered.

Niamh was excited. While she wasn't old enough to have appreciated The Lads' music the first time around, her mum was a devotee.

'It's not the original band, of course, that's why Mum didn't come tonight,' she explained, 'Benny left after

14

the second album and became a fundamentalist, em ...'

'Christian?'

'Vegan. So the other four just carried on without him. But then Simon couldn't make it out of rehab in time for this tour, so they brought in Scooter instead.'

'Scooter?'

'He used to be a performance artist. He once covered himself in liquid marshmallow and stuck himself to the railings at Buckingham Palace.'

'Right.'

'In *London*.'

'Yeah.'

'And then he was on Big Brother and they had karaoke and everybody was really impressed with his singing voice and so when Simon couldn't make it, the other Lads asked him to stand in for this tour, because he was so well known after the marshmallow thing.'

'Right,' I replied, 'Just out of interest, why didn't they wait for Simon to finish rehab?'

'They planned the tour for when Bonzo finished rehab ...'

'Bonzo?'

'Yeah, his real name is Neville. So, when Bonzo dried out they started to practise for the tour, but that's when Simon started drinking again and he ended up back in.'

'Probably couldn't face another rehearsal of 'You Make me Horny'.'

'What?'

'Nothing.'

Niamh explained that the first task was always the seat check; any dirty or sticky seats, missed in the clean-up from the last gig, needed to be wiped down. After that, I needed to make myself familiar with the layout of that part of the Auditorium, noting the closest toilets, concession stand, and emergency exit.

'Doors open at six thirty,' Niamh reminded me on her way past. 'I always pee just before that, 'cause you might not get a break 'til late.' I nodded, and, for wont of anything better to do, wandered off to the gents.

I returned to the auditorium through Ciaran's vomitory.

'How's it going?' Ciaran asked.

'Er, good. Just remembered, I need to get a torch.'

'Oh yeah. C'mon, I'll take you down to the store.'

The Safe & Sound store was behind, and almost below, the stage. I followed Ciaran down a set of concrete steps and along an undecorated corridor. We passed a series of imposing double steel doors, all of which had been painted dark grey.

'Is this where they torture people?' I asked.

'No, no,' Ciaran replied with a straight face, 'They do that in the yard. Better drainage and more hygienic. Down here is storage for electrics, staging, spare seating, plumbing ...'

'Plumbing?'

'Thousands of people drinking run to the loo all night; you need a few plumbers on hand.'

'I've never really thought about it.'

'Further on down here,' he gestured towards a set of red steel doors blocking the corridor, 'You get to private catering and the green rooms, but don't even think about going for a wander.'

'The Lads wouldn't be high on the list of people I'd want to meet.'

'I mean in general,' Ciaran went on, with no hint of humour. 'Manys a bollockin' has been handed out to stewards walking through that area on the off chance of seeing someone famous.'

He stopped at a door marked with a spray painted '12.'

'This,' he announced, 'Is where you come for ... everything.' He pushed the doors wide to reveal a cavernous room with a dozen chairs at one end, circling two vending machines. Racks of coats and fleeces stood at the other end as well as a long table with several large flashlights sitting on it. He grinned.

'All the small torches have gone. I'm afraid you're left with one of the heavyweights. Grab one and sign it out with Stella.'

I picked up a working torch that was about the size and weight of a car battery, and brought it over to an elderly, plump lady with immaculately permed white hair, seated behind a small table near the door. She reminded me of a slightly younger version of my mother. She had clearly been eating something, as her mouth was full when she spoke.

'Mmf. Just write down you've taken a mnorch, sorry, torch, and the torch number – it's on the bottom.' She swallowed. 'This your first night?'

'Yeah.'

'Thought so. I saw Ciaran bringing you in. I'm Stella.'

'Nice to meet you, I'm Robbie.'

With a broad sweep of her arm, she gestured to the room at large. 'And this is my kingdom.' I again surveyed the concrete room; grey on all six surfaces.

'A wee drop of magnolia would have killed you?'

'Not in my command, I'm afraid, I only rule the clothing and the torches. Now, here.' Stella held out a single-finger Twix.

'Aw, thanks, but honestly, I'm grand.' Stella did not withdraw the chocolate.

'It'll be a long night and you'll need to keep your strength up,' she said seriously. I took the chocolate bar and slid it into my pocket.

'Thank you. You're very kind.'

'Now, have a good shift and remember to sign your torch back in at the end of the night. Don't be running off with it.'

'I'll not be running anywhere with this thing.'

Stella smiled.

Ciaran and I retraced our steps back to the concourse on the first floor.

'Is there anything else you need to know?' he asked.

'Em, I think I'm alright.'

'It's simple stuff. Show people down to their seats. Make sure they sit in the right places. Smoking is outside and they need to bring their tickets with them. That's pretty much it. Anything else, call one of us.'

We passed Safe & Sound's other new recruit, Ryan, standing at his position, still looking petrified.

'You alright?' Ciaran asked him. Ryan flinched.

'Yes, yes ... fine, yes,' he responded, hardly daring to make eye contact.

'Have you got a torch?'

'Yes.'

'Have you done your seat check?'

'Yes.'

'Have you looked at what type of sweeties they've got in the shop?'

'Em ... no.'

'Go and have a wee look.'

'Right.' Ryan looked, bug-eyed at Ciaran, before scuttling off.

'That's cruel,' I said, while grinning.

'Sure, it'll give him something to do. Better than standing here crapping himself.'

With the time almost at six thirty, I returned to my post. Tony was waiting for me.

'You got a torch?' I held it up.

'Slimline version.'

'Did Ciaran and Niamh explain the basics?' I nodded.

'Anything else you need to know?'

'Are we ever allowed to use tasers?'

'What?'

'Nothing. I think I've got it, thanks.'

'Anything you need to know, just ask. Don't bluff your way.'

'True.'

'Right, I'm off. Doors will be open in a minute,' Tony trotted away.

Niamh approached me from the next aisle.

'You got a wee torch?' she asked. I nodded. 'Great, then you're ready to go; doors'll be open in a minute.'

'Aye, Tony was just saying. Do people really rush in at six thirty? I mean, the seats are reserved.'

Niamh shrugged.

'There'll be a rush for the front downstairs, there'll be a few people come up for the seats, but most will come after seven.'

'What time do you think we'll be away?' I asked

'Usually we're wrapped up by eleven,' Niamh answered, 'You working in the morning?'

I shook my head.

'I don't work Fridays, so once this is over, it's the start of my weekend.'

'That's alright.' She seemed impressed. 'You any other shifts coming up?'

'No, not yet, but I've put down for a few things.' Niamh nodded sympathetically.

'It'll be slow at first, but the more regular you become, the more shifts you'll pick up. Depends how much you want to work.'

I shrugged.

'Three or four shifts a month would do,' I said, 'I'm just looking to top up my four days a week.'

'I'm getting married in the new year,' Niamh replied, 'I'm working full time, but I try to do another couple of shifts in the week to pay for things. Maybe after the wedding I'll not do so much, we'll see.'

'Right.'

'There's so much to pay for when you're getting married. Everything's money.' I knew immediately that Niamh wanted to tell me more than I wanted to hear, which, given that it was about weddings, was all of it, but I couldn't steer the conversation away.

'Take the reception,' Niamh said earnestly, 'There's obviously the meal itself, but the add-ons are endless. We could just have gone with the ordinary chairs, but they looked so plain, so we decided we should go for the chair coverings, but they didn't match the balloons, so we had to change them ...'

She was interrupted by several shrieks from the floor below us. The first fans had attempted to charge towards the stage, only to be obstructed by stewards politely, but firmly, asking them to not to run.

'Here we go,' Niamh said and went back to her position.

*

The next hour flew in as an increasing stream of excited female fans, occasionally with resentful male partners, and gay couples of both sexes passed through the vomitory. They displayed their tickets and I politely showed them to their seats. I became increasingly warm and sweaty from repeated trips up and down the stairs. I also resolved to buy a new pair of black trousers, ones with a little more room and less capacity to chafe.

The balance of the auditorium tipped from mostly empty to mostly full. The temperature increased, as did the noise of the crowd, emboldened by the first drinks of the night. By eight o'clock an almost-capacity hall greeted the support act, some wee fella too young for fully-established facial hair, playing a keyboard. His songs were completely unknown to the crowd, but he was warmly received with each one being applauded politely.

It was during the interval that I was first pinched.

With almost all of the seats filled and the majority of the audience having now firmly established the seat-bar-toilet triangle, I was staring into space across the auditorium and wondering how Sohail was getting on. Suddenly, I felt a sharp pull on my lower right butt cheek and took an involuntary step forward. A gaggle of five women, younger than me, though maybe not by much, continued walking towards the concourse giggling and laughing. None of them turned round.

It wasn't long after that until the lights went down. Switching on my torch I illuminated the stairway for those now hurrying back to their seats, eager not to miss The Lads' grand entrance.

I'm reliably told concerts are like a 'w.' They start on a high, the tempo is lowered, before building it up in the middle to keep everyone engaged, then there's another lull before the build-up to the big finish. I wondered if this one was going to be more like an 'L', starting at a peak, sinking quickly and never recovering.

I soaked up the building tension. I wasn't in any way excited to hear The Lads play, or rather sing, but being part of this mass of bodies was exciting; *this was fun.* My thoughts were soon interrupted.

'You've a gorgeous plump arse on you, big lad,' a slightly slurred voice whispered harshly in my right ear, before a hand grabbed my left buttock in what was a full-on grope.

'Ale!' was all I could muster in surprise as I stepped backwards. Two women, high-heeled, well-oiled, but nimble, moved past me on either side and on down the stairs, vanishing into their row. Slightly irritated now because, let's face it, my body is not a playground, I put my back safely against the wall of the vomitory.

At full volume, the intro to 'You Make me Horny' rang out across the auditorium. The Lads emerged onto the stage, cordless microphones in hand, and thousands of largely female voices sang along with every word. The first chorus was deafening. Momentarily forgetting about how my arse had become an object of desire, I was watching the rippling sea of bodies on the floor and the gentle surge towards the stage, when a hand pressed lightly on my lower back.

'Could you please keep your hands to yourself?' I blurted out, as I spun round to see a fellow steward stepping back, in surprise. A few inches shorter than me, she had long dark brown hair tied back neatly, and similarly dark eyes, now wide open in shock.

'Sorry ...' I began, 'Somebody just grabbed my arse a few minutes ago, and I'm a bit, er, jumpy.'

'I'm just here to cover your break,' she said, 'I don't do any sort of massage.'

'Right ... where do I go?'

'Do you know where the store is?'

'Yeah.'

'That's the break room. Ten minutes; don't be any longer, or other stewards won't get a break.'

'Right.'

Glad of the semi-darkness hiding my reddened face, I hurried away.

*

I lowered myself onto a chair in the semi-circle around the vending machines. It felt good to take the weight off my feet. Three other stewards were present; two were focussed on their phones. The third, hungrily consuming a sandwich, glanced up.

'Alright?'

'Aye.'

I fished the Mars bar out of my fleece pocket and demolished it in three bites. Both doors suddenly burst open, and the frame was filled by Sohail. He strode to a seat and sat down heavily. The steel legs of the plastic chair strained, but held. His hair was matted to his head, and he had three large sweat stains in his arm pits and chest.

'I fucking hate tiered seats!' he declared loudly, 'Look at me! No one wants to see this. *I* don't want to see this!' I couldn't think of any way to respond, so I simply nodded in agreement, before remembering my extra ration.

'Here,' I said, offering Sohail the Twix Stella had given me earlier, 'Keep your strength up.'

Sohail's despair gradually resolved itself into a grin before he accepted the gift and muttered, 'Cheers.'

'You want to make friends with Slopes,' the sandwich-eating steward said. 'He's always backstage or in the pit.'

'Slopes?' I asked.

'Yeah, big guy, been in security for years, knows his stuff. Doesn't like working with skinny fellas, says they're too easily pushed over.'

'No one's ever said that about me,' Sohail replied.

*

Back in the vomitory, I apologised to my break time cover again.

'I don't normally speak to people like that.' I was genuinely contrite and embarrassed, while at the same time taking in the fine features of her face and pinning her age as somewhere mid-forties. She laughed it off.

'Just keep your back to the wall for the rest of the night,' she advised. I watched her walk back down the vomitory to the concourse.

The rest of the gig was pretty much as Tony had described; alcohol-fuelled, but happy. The crowd were enjoying themselves, as were The Lads. I had to admit that what they lacked in musical ability, they made up for in charisma and effort; they knew how to work the crowd.

The music itself was tolerable; I even allowed myself to hum along to some of the songs I knew, including the inexplicable Elton John melody in the middle. 'I'm Still Standing' segued into 'Kiss the Bride' and then, bizarrely, 'Crocodile Rock.' But the audience loved it, danced, and no one complained about anything.

Only towards the end of the night a woman, late twenties, in a bright pink dress nursing a bottle of rosé with a straw in it, walked past me several times, looking increasingly agitated. Eventually, I intervened.

'Hi there,' I said, 'Are you ok? Have you lost someone?'

'Yes, I have,' she replied. She struggled not only to focus, but also to offer more information. There was a long pause.

'Who have you lost?'

'Him.' Long pause.

'Right.'

'Would that be your husband or a boyfriend?'

'Yes.' Long pause.

'Do you think he's lost?'

'No.' Long pause.

'Is there anything I can do to help?'

'Can you stop him being a fucking asshole?' she asked, looking at me directly in the face for the first time, albeit trying to focus on the side of my mouth.

'Er, no,' I replied, 'But I could keep an eye out for him?'

She jabbed me in the chest with an index finger.

'He will be,' she announced, 'Wherever he will be. That is all I have to say.' She walked unsteadily back to her seat.

After the final song, the vomitory seemed to fill up with people quickly, but it soon became obvious the crowd wasn't moving. I was initially uncertain why, until I established that a small group of men were gathered around a mobile phone at the concourse end.

'Gents!' I shouted, with all the stewardly authority I could muster, 'Can you move to the side, please?' The man holding the phone looked up and suddenly realised the logjam he had created.

'Sorry chief!' he yelled, 'Champions League semi – it's gone to penalties!' Suddenly reminded about the rest of the world, I tried to remember who was playing but my thoughts were interrupted.

'You fucker!' It was the woman in the pink dress, now without rosé. *'You abandoned me! You're never getting ...'*

I did not catch whatever was not being offered, however, as the crowd moved quickly out of the vomitory, into the concourse and eventually out into the night.

*

The building did not take long to clear. The Auditorium was cleverly designed to have one main entrance, but several exits. Everyone seemed cheerful

27

as they departed; even those still finishing their drinks in their seats that I had to politely move on. Only one woman gave me grief.

'*Do you know who I am?*' she asked me, unmoving and staring in my general direction with glazed eyes.

'Er, no ...'

'I used to be Benny's ma's hairdresser.'

'Right. Who's Benny?'

'Benny is one of The Lads.' She pointed at the ceiling in the manner of a street preacher. I thought back to what Niamh had told me earlier.

'I heard Benny left.'

'*What?*'

'I heard Benny left, after he became a vegan.' It was now the woman's turn to think.

'Well then,' she said, 'There's not much point me sitting here, is there?'

'No,' I said kindly. 'Have a good night now.'

'Yes, love, you too.' She pushed herself to her feet and gingerly made her way out of the row, stopping at the stairs to look back at me.

'Those trousers of yours are brave and tight.'

'*I know,*' I muttered.

*

Ciaran informed me, and a slightly less petrified looking Ryan, that a second seat check had to be done and the steward's report form filled in.

'Go through each row, note down any seats that are dirty, sticky or damaged.'

'Damaged?' I asked.

'Pretty unusual, but it does happen.'

'What about the bit here that says 'comments'?' Ryan asked.

'You need to give a wee review of the gig.'

'What?' Ryan looked petrified again.

'Just describe it a bit. You know, say you liked it; mention your favourite songs.'

Ryan's eyes grew wider.

'I don't know any of their songs.'

'That's all right,' Ciaran assured him, 'Just write about the staging, or the best costume change.' He walked away with a smirk on his lips. I rolled my eyes.

'Just skip that bit,' I told Ryan, quietly.

Proudly joining the ranks of my fellow stewards in yellow shirts, we carried out a 'sweep' from one end of the concourse to the other, checking our section of the building was entirely empty of punters. We gathered again, at the top of the stairs for the end of shift 'debrief' with Tony.

'Thank you everybody,' he began, 'That was a bit of a white-knuckle ride for a couple of you tonight, but I think it was ok for most. Anything else I should know about, especially slips, trips and falls?' There were no further incidents to report. One tall male steward at the back of the group said, 'I hate boke.' Other stewards laughed, but he didn't.

'Don't know what you're complaining about Jonny, you can hardly smell it up there!' a small woman with tightly permed hair said, 'I'm three feet closer to it.'

This produced a smile.

'Fair enough, Myrtle,' he replied.

Across the group I could see the steward who had covered my break. She was much prettier in proper lighting. Well defined cheek bones. I did not make eye contact.

With little traffic on the road, car park to home took ten minutes. After a box of microwave chips, a mug of tea and half an episode of 'Big Bang Theory,' I locked up and climbed the stairs for bed. Standing again in front of the mirror in the bathroom, I pulled the mustard shirt off over my head and regarded my reflection.

'Face might be bigger,' I said quietly, 'But your arse has still got it.'

I was tired, but not yet ready for sleep, as my mind played over the confetti shower of tiny incidences that night. And one in particular, that would, in time, change my life completely.

2. Tickets and a tiny trickle of blood

Despite applying for several other gigs, I heard nothing from Safe & Sound for a few weeks. Tony kept reminding me to apply in good time and be patient. Groping aside, I had enjoyed my first night and was keen to repeat the experience. It would never be a crucial source of income, but I hoped a few shifts each month might push the holiday boat out a little further. It also gave me more to do. Four days at work and three days off was pleasant in a way, but for a divorced fifty-something, it also had a certain monotony to it.

When I'd been a full-time employee, with a wife and two kids, the weekend never seemed long enough. Youth clubs, junior football matches, birthday parties, and nights out with friends left me exhausted by Sunday evening. Then the teenage years hit and I was running lifts at all hours. Sure, you can leave them to make their own way home, but then you don't sleep.

Back at the very beginning, my postman's round demanded early mornings but came with a mid-afternoon finish; lunch time if you had a light day and you walked fast. I was always home hours before Shirley. When I moved into the sorting office the hours became more regular, and, as I climbed the ladder to the heady heights of supervisor, overtime became more common. The arrival of two children meant there was no such thing as spare time.

That came to an abrupt end when Shirley and I separated. Aaron, my son, moved across the water to university. Paula, my daughter, was fifteen and became stubbornly independent. At that point an old school friend practically begged me to join him in a start-up printing firm. Something new seemed attractive and so, after the best part of twenty years at the Post Office, I jumped ship.

At first, it had all seemed so positive. I was working with a mate and involved in every aspect of the business. I managed a small team and developed a whole new set of skills. The late nights and early mornings helped fill the void left by the loss of the person at my side, the closeness of two children and a family home to return to at the end of the day.

Four years of chasing contacts, online marketing, networking, wafer-thin profit margins and unrelenting working hours were not enough to keep the small firm afloat, however, and the money finally ran out. I really don't think we could have given it anything more. All time became spare time for the three months it took me to pick up something else. Not a long stretch in the scheme of things, but long enough to be left with all the thoughts I'd been avoiding about my failures as a husband, father and manager.

There was no escape from a seemingly-endless ocean of time. The walls of my two-bedroomed end-terrace closed in. I don't remember much from that period, except a lot of sleeping late, mindless TV, crisps, and a numb feeling that left it hard to get anything done.

Application forms killed me, and I became rambling and incoherent at interviews. But suddenly, a really long shot came off and the offer of a job at Pathway changed things overnight.

While I was no expert on mental health, the interview panel considered me 'affable' and 'approachable,' and employed me to get alongside young people with mental health conditions and help them gain and sustain employment. It wasn't far removed from helping nervous young recruits in the sorting office find their feet. I got to know many of the clients well until they reached the point that they were ready to get on with life without my help.

The three-year contract went by in what felt like weeks, but I had also begun to deliver training to businesses about young people and mental health, and so I was offered a new, permanent contract; two days a week training, two days a week with young people and a three-day weekend.

I was in Starbucks, waiting for Paul to show up, when my phone rang. I saw the caller and braced myself.

'Hi Mum.'

'Hello Robert, I'll not keep you. I just found out the Mace are doing a four pack of kitchen rolls on offer this week. I've bought myself three packs, that's twelve rolls in total, and you can have four of them, so don't be buying in any for yourself.'

'Thanks Mum, that's great.'

'Just call round when you can.'

'I will, Mum, probably at the weekend.'

'Well, I'll be out at the WI coffee morning on Saturday, but I'll be back in after midday.'

'Grand, I'll leave it to the afternoon.'

'Ok, love, see you then, bye!' The line went dead before I could reply. The phone rang again.

'Was there cut-price loo roll as well?' I asked, without looking at the screen.

'I'm sorry?' said a much younger voice.

'Sorry, who is this?'

'Is that Robbie?'

'Yeah.'

'Robbie, it's Helen here from Safe & Sound.'

'Oh, grand,' I replied, screwing up my face. 'Sorry about that, I confused you with someone else.'

'No worries ... Are you doing anything this weekend?'

'You asking me out?'

'Yes. It'll be a cosy affair, just you, me, two hundred stewards and ten thousand screaming teenagers at Ormeau Park on Friday night.'

'How could I resist?'

'Well, the promoters now want everybody on site at 4:30, which means a lot of our guys aren't available. Does that work for you?'

'Fridays usually work well for me.'

In my rush to accept the shift, I hadn't even thought to ask who was playing. The app request arrived quickly however, informing me that the Electric Badgers were topping the bill. I'd seen the posters and thought it would be an interesting set. The Badgers had been around for a decade or so, initially as a thrashy, noisy rock group before becoming increasingly commercialised. In the last few years they had had a stream of danceable radio hits, hence

34

the mainly teenage fan base. An outdoor gig on a mid-Spring evening with a young audience; this had 'messy' written all over it.

*

The afternoon of the concert, I left my car a good ten-minute walk away from the park entrance, so as not to get snarled up in the post-gig traffic. In effect, this meant I had only driven five minutes from my house, but the thought of being on my feet all evening and then walking the whole cut home sometime near midnight wasn't a pleasant prospect.

A steady flow of yellow-shirted stewards, most of whom were carrying rucksacks, streamed in through the main entrance on the Lagan embankment. I wondered what people had brought with them, because I wasn't carrying anything. My hands were stuffed into the pockets of my newly-purchased black trousers – £19.99 from a Regatta store in the city centre. There was now adequate room for my car keys and loose change, and my mobile phone and a Boost bar were safely zipped into the two pockets of my yellow fleece.

The leisure centre and surrounding playing fields had been transformed into a concert venue with mobile catering, bars and a hundred portable toilets. Stewards stood around chatting or eating. Hassled-looking catering staff rushed about. There were also serious-looking people not in uniform, with large passes on lanyards round their necks.

Sign in was at a steel container behind some of the mobile catering units. I looked around for anyone I had met at the Auditorium, but there was no one I recognised. Feeling a little lost, I joined the queue leading up to a rickety wooden table underneath an industrial-strength gazebo.

'Name?' the woman at the desk asked sharply.

'Robbie McKittrick.'

'Grand. Number?'

'Em ... I don't think I have a number.'

'What's the number on your vest?'

'I don't have a vest.'

'Go and get a vest,' she said irritably, pointing off into the distance. 'Name?'

'Vests are in the container, round the end,' another steward said. I wandered back the way I had come.

The two heavy container doors were wide open, revealing half a dozen boxes of vests in various sizes. I picked up a large one and noted the four digit number on the back.

'Take some water,' a young woman instructed me, as she held out a bottle from the crates stacked up behind her. 'It'll be a warm night.'

I returned to the queue, which moved quickly until I reached the desk again.

'Name?' the woman asked again.

'Robbie McKittrick.'

'You're already signed in,' she said before looking up. 'Oh, it's you,' she added before rolling her eyes in a manner I didn't think was at all fair.

'Number?'

'S4507.'

'*Well done.* Name?' she asked the next person.

'Sorry, where do I go?'

'Outside,' she said in a manner that suggested she had said this many times already. She pointed vaguely beyond the container back to the road. I wanted to point out that, technically, it was all outside, but was nowhere near brave enough to say it.

'You wait on the road, young man' the steward behind me said, 'Supervisors just pick people as they need them. Come on.'

I followed the kindly gentleman, a good few years my senior, back along the line of stewards waiting at the desk. More stewards waited in clusters along the road at the entrance. My companion stopped beside another steward who was horsing his way through a large bag of Chilli Heat Wave Doritos.

'How's it going?' he greeted the Dorito-eater.

'Starving. I was on early shift and I ate my lunch at ten this morning. I haven't eaten since. Do you want one?' He held out the bag, but both of us declined.

'Thanks, but I couldn't deprive you of your dinner,' I said.

'Oh, this isn't dinner. Dinner's still in the bag!' he laughed.

'I'm Sam,' the older man introduced himself.

'I'm Johnny,' said the other man.

'I never knew that,' Sam replied. 'You've always been called Kettley.' I looked blankly at Sam. Johnny, or rather Kettley, sighed.

'I have been known, occasionally ...' he began.

'He is always talking about the weather,' Sam interrupted.

'Hang on,' Kettley responded in mock offence, 'Have I mentioned the weather once?'

'No, but you'll have checked it before you came out.'

'Anybody with any wit checks the weather before they do an outdoor gig in Belfast.'

'I confess I did,' I offered, 'And I'm Robbie.'

'Pleased to meet you, Robbie.' Kettley stuffed his empty Doritos bag into a side pocket of his voluminous rucksack. Sam had unzipped his and was rummaging through the contents.

'I have to ask,' I said, feeling a little under-equipped, 'What are you guys carrying in there?'

'Oh, you need to prepare for every eventuality,' Sam replied, 'I have some food, some water, sunglasses, a cap to keep the sun off, a hat to keep my head warm and my black waterproof coat, as approved by Safe & Sound for outdoor events.'

'I need to get one,' I said.

'You're going to need one tonight,' Kettley added, 'The sun's out now and we're all cosy, but once it drops down behind the mountain at about half eight, it's going to get very chilly. No cloud cover, you see.'

'Told you,' Sam replied. 'Here,' he held out a bag of Quavers, 'Hold on to that, I've got two bags in here.' I tried to refuse, but Sam insisted. Mildly embarrassed, I stuffed them into my fleece pocket as best I could.

By now, the road was starting to fill up with stewards, which seemed to be causing a problem for the other workers trying to move about.

'This looks like chaos,' I said.

'Sometimes it is,' Kettley replied, unwrapping a mint Club biscuit and biting it in two.

'True, but mostly it's organised confusion,' Sam explained. 'It looks mad now, but in fifteen minutes everyone will be on a team and heading out to their posts for the night. Anywhere you want to go?'

'How do you mean?' I asked.

'Some people have their favourite station,' Kettley explained, 'If you don't like the public, get backstage. If you like being busy, or you want to hear the gig, get on tickets.'

'Or toilets,' Sam added.

'Toilets?' I asked.

'Mostly just supervision,' Sam said.

'Supervision?' I had no idea what this meant.

'For this many people, there needs to be a one-way system round the portaloos. Sometimes you need to start a queueing system if too many people all want to piss at once.'

'Right. How do you pick a team?' I asked.

'Ah, you have to watch the supervisors,' Kettley said. 'After a while you get to know what position they cover, though sometimes that changes.'

'Oh yes,' Sam added, 'Many's a steward thought he was heading for a nice quiet street patrol, only to end up keeping order at a bar queue.'

'Well, I'm new to all of this, so I'll go where they send me.'

I really didn't mind; it was a whole new world and, at least for now, I was just happy to be part of what happened behind the scenes. A pick-up truck, stacked high with cases of water bottles and folding chairs rumbled past, causing the mingling stewards to move to the sides of the road. A small number of supervisors, distinctive in their luminous green vests had gathered at the sign-in container, deep in discussion.

'We'll be off in a minute,' Kettley commented.

Sure enough, it wasn't long before a dozen supervisors dispersed among the stewards. Sam, Kettley and I were approached by a burly supervisor, well in excess of six foot, packed into his green vest so tightly it must have restricted his breathing.

'You men,' the supervisor gesticulated towards the general area I was standing in, 'Come with me.' He ambled off with a rolling gait towards the entrance.

'Who's he?' I asked.

'That's Big Noel,' Kettley answered. 'He's usually backstage, but we're not walking that direction ...'

'We'll be on street patrol,' Sam said, 'Or maybe tickets.'

Big Noel stopped at the end of the driveway, counted up the stewards in the group and added a few more. One of whom, I immediately noticed, was the steward I had requested keep her hands to herself during my first shift at the Auditorium. Noel then set off down the embankment, stopping at a newly-created gap in the park railings.

'Gather in,' he commanded the following stewards, before addressing the group, a full head above anybody else. 'Who's worked Ormeau before?' Two thirds of the group put a hand in the air. 'There are several exits when the concert is over, but this is the only entrance. You'll be ticket scanning, but our first job is to set up the switchbacks on the way in. That'll slow the crowd down and get them in off the street. The switchbacks will then open out to ten aisles. At the front end, the SIA guys will be doing bag checks and body searches. At the far end you'll all be scanning tickets in pairs. The barriers are currently stacked on either side, so if you can divide yourselves into two groups and start bringing them over. Sam, Kettley, can you two give some direction?'

'I'd rather give direction than lift the bloody things,' Sam answered.

Setting up crowd barriers is not a difficult job, but it divides stewards neatly into two groups; those who can connect them by dropping two hooks simultaneously into two holes, and those who can't. The trick is to leave the 'holes' barrier on the ground, then lower the 'hooks' barrier down into it. Assuming, of course, that you've got the barrier the right way round to begin with.

The steward behind me was clearly not gifted in this department as I could hear her mutter 'frig sake', before she suddenly spun the barrier round in order to get the right coupling. Unaware I was standing behind her, she caught me broadside.

'*Shit,*' she said bluntly. I turned to see my break cover from the Auditorium, and grinned.

'You could kill somebody with one of those you know.'

'I'm so sorry,' she said, reddening, 'Are you alright?'

'I'm fine,' I assured her, though in truth she had cracked me pretty hard in the rib cage. To prove there was neither hard feelings nor physical damage, I picked up an end of the barrier and helped lower it into position.

'Well,' she screwed her face up, 'You told me to keep my hands to myself, but you never said anything about hitting you with a barrier.'

'Right,' I replied, 'To cover all eventualities, should I write you a list of stuff you're not allowed to hit me with?' She paused as if she was seriously thinking about it.

'That would be quite a long list,' she said.

'I imagine it would.'

'I'm Alison.'

'Robbie.'

I looked directly at her face. Some people's faces just radiate kindness, and hers was one of those. A little noise went off in my head, a happy noise, something akin to when Outlook successfully sends an email. It was accompanied by a small, but noticeable surge of attraction and the desire to give her my undivided attention for as long as she wanted it.

'We'd best lift some more barriers,' I said, and we moved away.

Despite the cack-handedness of some of the group, it didn't take long to arrange the barriers into a series of switchbacks and ten lanes. Big Noel gathered the team around for the briefing.

'Tonight will be a capacity crowd; ten thousand. The Electric Badgers have played Belfast several times before and have a strong following. There will be a fairly high teenage contingent tonight. Anyone under sixteen must be accompanied by someone over eighteen who'll be responsible for them. The SIA guys will be starting at five thirty, gates will open as soon as they are in position.'

'What's SIA again?' I asked Sam quietly.

'They have their Security Industry Accreditation. They've been trained how to search people.'

'And throw people out on their arses safely,' Kettley added.

'Why the early start?' one of the other stewards asked.

'The teenage element of the crowd,' Big Noel answered, 'They'll come with drink both in them and with them. If we get them inside, they're off the street and there's a limit to how much alcohol they can get in there.'

'Surely you can't get alcohol at all if you're under eighteen?' I asked quietly again.

'Fake ID,' said Kettley.

'Get your older mate to buy it for you,' said Sam.

'Right, it's all coming back to me now.'

'We'll have stewards monitoring the bars and the crowd to try to limit underage drinking,' Noel continued, 'Gates likely open around six, there'll be a DJ on from half past called Lord Anders. He specialises in hardstyle, which my notes inform me is a mixture of techno and hardcore. Whatever the hell they are.

The support act will be on at eight. Support tonight is Plastic Pregnant Dinosaur, an indietronica band from Norway. I'm just reading out words off this sheet, guys, I have no idea what they actually mean. Our job, for the next few hours at least, is scanning tickets. Has everyone used a scanner before?'

Several stewards' heads were shaking, mine included.

'It's not rocket science,' Big Noel went on, 'Point the wee light at the bar code or the QR code until it goes 'bing' and a smiley face shows up on the screen. Any problems; call me. What I need now is everyone to be in pairs and at the end of the lanes.'

The gaggle of stewards ambled into position. I found myself next to a serious-looking bloke with a long, pale face framed by flat lifeless hair. Early thirties, I guessed, but with an expression that said he had already seen enough of life.

'It's going to be a long night,' he said. *Longer now,* I thought.

'Ah, well,' I tried to cheer him up, 'It's warm and dry and we'll be busy soon. It'll fly in.' He stared off into the distance.

'The Electric Badgers are playing.'

'Er, yeah. Are you a fan?'

'No. I don't really listen to music.' I nodded in response, already knowing conversation was going to be impossible to sustain. Hearing someone say they don't listen to music sounds to me like someone saying 'I don't really like the taste of food' or 'I wish everything was grey because I don't like colour.' From

I was old enough to ask an adult to put on a record, I have loved and been surrounded by music. It's an essential part of my day; it lifts my mood and transports me to other times and places.

'Capacity crowd tonight,' my partner continued, stating the bleeding obvious again.

'Yes,' I agreed, 'So Big Noel was saying.'

'Ten thousand.'

'Yes, he mentioned that too.' *I'm dying here,* I thought.

'Gates will be open at about six.' *God almighty.*

Looking on down the line beyond Bleedin' Obvious, I could see both Sam and Kettley, each with other partners. Big Noel was working his way along the stewards with a large box of scanners, giving them out, checking they worked and demonstrating for anyone that hadn't used them before. Behind me, I could hear another steward holding forth about his time with Safe & Sound.

'I once had to carry Mariah Carey's slippers from the tour bus to her dressing room. They were in a box, so I didn't actually get to see them, but you know, it's nice to be able to say that you've held a box that contained Mariah Carey's slippers, and that you've stood outside a room that Mariah Carey might have been in.'

Glancing behind me briefly, I could see the shaved head of a short, squat steward. His pudgy arms folded, resting on the top of his stomach, he was leaning casually against a barrier.

'I once saw Gary Barlow from a distance, you know, he's not as tall as you would think, and his hair's thinner than it appears on the TV. And then, Christmas two years ago, I was in the pit directly underneath Ellie Goulding, and, you know, I never let my hair grow any length, so when she sprayed when she was singing, I could actually feel the tiny droplets of spit as they landed on my head. It was just amazing to think that I was standing in a steady flow of fluid from the mouth of the person who wrote 'Your Song'.'

'She covered 'Your Song,'' a female voice corrected him, 'She didn't actually write it.'

I quickly realised the other half of the conversation behind me, was Alison.

'No, no, she definitely sang 'Your Song',' the squat steward insisted.

'She did. But what I'm saying is that she didn't write it. Elton John wrote it,' Alison replied.

I couldn't help but weigh in.

'Technically, Bernie Taupin wrote it; Elton John set it to music.'

Alison turned to look directly at me.

'True, but I was trying to keep it simple.'

'I'm sure Ellie Goulding sang it,' said the squat steward, 'She did it that night of the gig. I was there.'

'Getting wet,' I added. Alison smiled.

'No, not at that point,' the squat steward explained, 'She had moved to another part of the stage for a slower part of the set. That's how they do it, it can't be all upbeat, there has to be time ...'

'To dry off,' I inserted.

'For the audience to calm down a bit, before they build up again for the big finish.'

'You done a lot of gigs, then?' I asked. Alison shot me a look.

'I have been there, done that, bought the t-shirt ...'

'That's half five now,' intoned Bleedin' Obvious.

'Is it? Right, I'm going to get a wee sneaky smoke break now,' the steward who had been there and done that declared, 'Big Noel will be alright with that, I've worked with him for years. I was once in his team for six consecutive sold out Daniel O'Donnell shows. Back in two minutes.' He hurried off down the lane and out of the entrance, removing his vest as he walked.

'Dying there, were you?' I asked Alison, who rolled her eyes and puffed out her cheeks.

'I've never met him before. He needed to tell me about pretty much every famous person he's ever met.'

'Met?'

'Well, I don't think he's actually *met* anyone famous, but maybe we haven't got to those stories yet.'

'There's plenty of time,' I commented. Alison glared at me.

'He's just been vaguely near famous people; but every near miss was special. Did you hear his story about standing at the back of Jon Bon Jovi's tour bus?'

'No, what happened?' I asked.

'He was standing at the back of Jon Bon Jovi's tour bus. *That's it*.'

I grinned. Alison, unable to help herself, also smiled. 'He once held a door open for Billy Connolly.'

'Well, that's kind of exciting.'

'No, wait, Billy Connolly's *nephew*.'

'Oh. Is he famous?'

'Not that I know of. Here we go again,' Alison nodded at her partner returning through the main gate, 'Take out your phone; pretend you're showing me something on it.'

'What?'

'*Phone. Now,*' Alison muttered urgently. I did as instructed and held out my phone. 'If I have to stand here, he has to stand there,' she said.

Sure enough, Been There returned to the end of the lane and stood where Alison had been standing. Noticing she was otherwise engaged, he immediately began talking to the steward on the next lane. Just as I was about to return my phone to my pocket, Big Noel arrived with a box of scanners.

'Big lad, I know you're new, but you're on duty now and we'll be opening the gates soon, so no phones out,' he said.

'Right, yes, absolutely,' I replied, 'Just checking the weather.'

'It's cloudy at the minute,' Bleedin' Obvious chipped in.

Big Noel explained the finer points of using a ticket scanner. Alison faithfully promised to keep me right, as did Bleedin' Obvious who proceeded to point out the laser, the handle and the scan button.

'There's other buttons too,' he said, 'But I don't know what they do.'

Big Noel moved on down the line of stewards.

'Sorry about that,' Alison apologised. 'Of all the moments he should be there.'

'Wouldn't worry,' I replied, playing with the scanner and shining the laser on my hand.

'So, you're an Elton fan then?' I asked, trying to open up conversation, 'You seemed to come to his defence pretty quick.'

'Well, yeah, actually,' Alison replied, 'But even if I hadn't been I still wouldn't have let someone attribute 'Your Song' to Ellie Goulding.'

'I feel the same way when people think 'Make you Feel my Love' is an Adele song,' I replied.

'Don't tell me you're a Dylan nut?'

'Pretty much. You're going to tell me you like his songs, but you don't like his voice, aren't you?'

'To be honest, I still wouldn't be a fan of the songs, even if Elton was singing them.'

'Aw, you're a Dylan hater?'

'No, too much effort. I'm Dylan-ambivalent,' Alison mused, 'Really couldn't care less.'

I sighed, recognising that finding a beautiful and interesting woman who also liked Dylan, was a gift life was never going to hand me. But in the words of Meatloaf, two out of three ain't bad.

'I'll settle for that,' I shrugged, 'Dylan isn't to most people's taste. My ex-wife and kids are a case in point. In fact, I think it might have contributed to our divorce.' I left my face in neutral.

'I can't tell if you're serious or joking,' Alison said.

'Serious about the divorce,' I answered, 'Joking about Dylan being the reason, although it probably didn't help. In fairness to Aaron, he could tolerate 'Blood on the Tracks' if I had it on in the car. Paula and Shirley on the other hand would rather have walked.'

'Aaron is your son?' Alison asked.

'Yep. Paula's my daughter. Shirley's my ex.'

We chatted aimlessly. Every so often Bleedin Obvious would alert us to something happening nearby. Slowly but surely, the atmosphere of the venue changed. Bar staff were busy filling plastic pint glasses, stewards were in position, their bright yellow vests clearly visible. The search people, with their blue SIA cards proudly displayed on their upper arms, were ready at the entrance. Supervisors in bright-green vests flitted in and out of view, every so often accompanied by someone of importance as denoted by the number of tags on their lanyards.

'Have you kids of your own?' I asked, before recognising the problems that could arise from this question.

'No, I haven't,' Alison answered brightly, 'One thing or another got in the road.'

I was uncertain about how to respond; it felt like I should, but for the life of me, I had no idea in what way. Alison may have sensed my confusion.

'I only moved in with my boyfriend, properly, just over a year ago. It's been a slow, em, thing.'

'Right.' Boyfriend. The word had the weight of a tombstone. I should have known. Oblivious to my sudden feeling of being buried alive, Alison moved on.

'What age are your kids?' she asked.

'Aaron is twenty-five,' I replied, 'Paula is twenty-three.'

'Are they away from home?'

'Aaron is, he lives in London. Paula's still with Shirley.'

'Too big to stay at yours at the weekend?' Alison joked.

'Yeah,' I said, 'Has been for quite a while,' I added, 'The separation with Shirley was hard on Paula, and it's never quite ...'

'Gates are opening!' Big Noel yelled from the entrance point, 'Stewards, make sure every lane is covered.'

'People will be coming in now,' said Bleedin Obvious.

*

Big Noel was right, ticket scanning is an easily picked-up art. Take ticket; scan ticket; listen for the happy little bleep of the scanner. For the first while, it felt like the happy little bleep was mocking me. The 'diddly dee' noise seemed to say 'never a chance' or 'you might've known' but a crowd of concert goers coming at you thick and fast offers little time for self-pity and I soon transferred my irritation to people who didn't have their ticket ready.

Here are some ways you can reduce a fast-moving concert queue to a stationary line of grumpy bastards.

One. If you're the ticket keeper for a group of five or six, don't give everyone their ticket until you are right at the steward with the scanner. Hand them out at your ease.

Two. Fold each ticket sheet in half as many times as you can.

Three. Don't offer your ticket to the steward, leave it in your pocket and make them ask for it.

Four. Don't make any effort to remember which of your many pockets you put it in. Take your time to search for it.

Five. If it's raining, make no attempt to keep your ticket dry. Let the ink run, or allow your ticket to become so wet the page separates.

To be fair, it's not always the people, sometimes it's the technology. Most scanners work most of the time, but they all have moments where they reject perfectly acceptable tickets. They do this deliberately, because scanners are independent-minded, devious little devils who like to piss you off.

After the initial influx of Electric Badger fans keen to reserve their space directly below the stage, the flow of ticket holders reduced to a trickle, allowing for some conversation between the stewards. Over my shoulder, I could hear Been There informing Alison of his experience.

'It's always like this. There's a rush at the start, then it slows down, then it builds up. We should be hitting peak traffic about seven. I've done gigs here for the last six years in a row.'

I could hear Alison murmuring 'Mm hm,' in a vacant manner, but it didn't stop him banging on about how the entrance gate used to be further down the park, or the size of the crowd, or the smell of the catering vans as they reached maximum frying capacity.

In fairness, he was right. Shortly after seven o'clock the audience was steadily moving into the park; the grass was covered in clusters of people sitting in groups, saving their legs for later.

I felt a little jealous that this had not been on offer to me in my teenage years. Concerts in Belfast were few and far between in the eighties. Always indoors, there were packed venues like the Ulster Hall or Kings Hall, even places like Maysfield Leisure Centre where I once listened to Dylan standing under a basketball net. Somehow my youth seemed a little worse off for not having had the opportunity to lie on damp grass drinking over-priced cold beer on a warm summer's evening with a bunch of mates.

As the number of entries increased, my scanner began to reject certain bar codes on home-printed tickets. Bleedin Obvious's scanner was rejecting certain professionally-printed tickets and so for a while we made do with swapping scanners in the hope that one of them would make the happy noise. This worked well, up until his scanner suddenly ran out of charge.

'I'll need to get another scanner,' he stated.

'I'll try to scan both lines,' I replied, realising as I spoke that scanning two lines of people coming into a gig, without letting anyone slip past was a tall order. *'But find Big Noel fast!'*

I began to scan two lanes in at once, as best I could, hoping frantically there wouldn't be a surge of people. Fortunately, just as Bleedin Obvious left, each line was held up. The first by a twenty-something man whose phone was having difficulty opening the app, and the other by a bleached-blonde teenage girl in dungarees giving out the tickets to her seven friends.

I scanned them all in, except for the seventh, rather inebriated friend whose ticket couldn't be read by the scanner.

'C'mon,' I encouraged it, 'Make the happy noise.' But to no avail. 'It's not scanning,' I began, but before I could add 'give me a minute' the teenage girl dissolved into tears.

'All my friends are inside,' she howled. I looked at her with more confusion than sympathy.

'Steady on there, we'll get it sorted.' I called for Alison on the next lane over. 'Can you scan that for me?'

'Sure.'

She scanned the ticket and it bleeped immediately. I smiled and returned the ticket. She brushed her hair out of her eyes and wiped the tears from her cheeks, leaving two long streaks of mascara across her face.

'There you go now. Have a good night – maybe take it easy on the gin.'

Next in line was a woman who had folded her ticket into the size of a fifty pence piece.

'Big fan of origami?' I asked cheerfully, but she didn't look amused. In the other line was a couple who couldn't remember who had the tickets and were busy sorting through his pockets and her bag. Neither of their tickets scanned.

'Alison!' I shouted in desperation. She turned around to scan all three tickets.

'You on your own?' she asked, startled.

'Yeah, the other guy's scanner died; he's away to get another one.'

'You can't really take two lanes at once,' she said, 'We need to get that lane closed down.' Before I could reply, however, Bleedin' Obvious returned.

'I've got a different scanner,' he explained, holding it up.

*

By eight o'clock the influx of ticket holders had slowed, and the monotonous drone of the DJ had ceased, replaced by the more enthusiastic beat of Plastic Pregnant Dinosaur. The crowd swelled to standing room only. Once again, there was time to chat.

'I was a bit panicked there, when you went off to change your scanner,' I said to Bleedin Obvious.

'It was really busy then.'

'Yeah,' I agreed, 'But hey, everyone in line was very patient ... and Alison here helped out when my scanner wasn't up to it.' Alison smiled. There were no more ticket holders in our lanes, so I kept talking.

'I wanted to ask earlier, when you said you were a bit of an Elton fan, what size of a bit are we talking about?'

'Every album, half a dozen books and seen him a few times too,' she replied.

'Posters on the wall?'

'No, but a couple of mounted tickets from shows in the nineties.'

'Ha!' I laughed.

'What's wrong with that?'

'Nothing. I have some of my Dylan tickets mounted. They're not up, still packed in a box somewhere, but someday they'll get pride of place.'

As the incoming crowd thinned, we removed the barriers to leave a single entry lane. Big Noel redeployed us in our pairs, and allocated break times.

'Support act will be finished by eight forty, main act on at nine. Position yourselves at the edges of the crowd. Look out for anybody needing assistance. Check the map on your briefing sheets and know where things are. Look out for other stewards needing assistance with crowd movement. Report back here at ten fifteen to staff the exit during egress.'

Alison and Been There were sent on a break first; me and my sidekick wandered off towards our allocated section of the crowd, closely followed by Sam, Kettley and a couple of SIA from searches.

'She was a big girl,' one of them was saying, 'I've never seen so much Buckfast under a bra strap.'

'Was there a lot of drink pulled?' Sam asked.

'Very little. Teenagers drink it fast; they don't keep it for smuggling in.'

For all the earlier concerns about drink-fuelled teenagers, from what I could see, the crowd seemed manageable. They were happy and responsive, singing along with the band at the start and end of the gig, with a lot of queuing at the bar and toilets in the middle. I noticed Sohail keeping order at a bar queue by doing little more than just being there with his arms folded across his expansive chest. Bleedin' Obvious and I watched as a team of four SIA stewards gently assisted a remonstrating punter towards the exit, the cause of eviction unknown. Beyond that, there was little of note.

One or two of the crowd ribbed us about being allowed to stand and watch the gig. The truth is, that while it's an enjoyable part of the job, it's nothing like the same experience as being there as a fan. When you're a punter, you meet your mates, buy a drink or two, find a nice spot in the crowd, enjoy the show and then think about a kebab. But when you're working, even if you get distracted by what's on stage, there's always a job to do. You become aware of the logistics and the safety concerns; you see behind the scenes. That can be fun, to be sure, but it's also like seeing Jim Henson's arm up the inside of Kermit. It's just not the same.

Late in the evening, as I was checking my watch and thinking about the end of the shift, out of the corner of my eye, I noticed a sudden movement in the crowd. A young woman, mid to late twenties, had fallen heavily. The crowd around her looked shocked and stepped back. I hurried over, closely followed by Bleedin' Obvious.

A second young woman stood over the woman on the ground, pulling on the sleeve of her t-shirt.

'C'mon Karen, you have to get up, you can't lie there,' she insisted.

Karen, however, was not responding. I introduced myself. The other woman told me her name was Meabh.

'Has she had a lot to drink, Meabh?' I asked.

'No, no, no,' she looked thoughtful, 'No more than usual.'

Meabh clearly had had a fair amount to drink herself.

'Karen? Can you hear me?' I said, inches from her face and loud enough to carry over the noise of the Electric Badgers. I thought I heard her groan in response but couldn't be sure.

'C'mon Karen. *Get up!'* Meabh tried again, pulling hard on Karen's arm, so much so that she dragged her a few inches along the ground.

'I'm not sure we should pull at her,' I said.

'She's not getting up,' Bleedin Obvious concluded.

'I've noticed.'

'Karen! C'mon now! *We'll get chicken nuggets!'* Meabh spoke loudly, bending over her prone friend in order to be closer to her head and almost collapsing on her. She leant on my shoulder for balance. 'She loves chicken nuggets. She'll be up in a minute.'

I wasn't convinced. I looked up at Bleedin' Obvious who nodded and looked away. I assumed he was looking for help.

'I wouldn't mind some chicken nuggets,' he said eventually.

'Go and get a paramedic!' I instructed, 'Or at least find a supervisor and they can radio one.'

'She doesn't need a paramelic!' Meabh shouted, shaking her head emphatically. 'She just needs chicken nuggets.' At this moment Karen sat up and looked around her blankly. 'See, I told you!' Meabh said triumphantly, hauling Karen to her feet. Instinctively, I put my arm on Karen's back and stood behind her, uncertain about whether she could sustain a vertical position. She couldn't. She collapsed backwards onto me.

I was able to stop myself falling flat like a domino, but unable to prevent myself from lowering heavily to the ground under Karen's dead weight. I momentarily panicked as an exploding noise came from my abdomen, until I realised it was the bag of Quavers Sam had given me earlier. Relieved I hadn't ruptured any internal organs, I tried to maintain a sitting position with Karen splayed on top of me.

'Now Karen, you're not allowed to sit on him!' Meabh admonished.

'You alright under there?' said a voice from behind me. It was Alison.

'Feeling a little awkward,' I admitted, trying to work out if my current predicament looked impressively gallant, or completely ridiculous. Alison bent down to Karen's face whose eyes remained closed. Been There stood behind Alison and looked at me blankly, seemingly confused as to why I was sitting on the cold ground with a young woman on top of me. He said nothing, however.

'Karen, can you hear me?' Alison said loudly. Karen seemed to speak. 'Can you say that again?' Again, Karen mumbled something.

'What's she saying?' I asked.

'I'm not sure,' Alison said, confused, 'It sounded very like, 'I don't want chicken nuggets.''

'But you *love* chicken nuggets,' Meabh insisted, 'Where's the nearest McDonald's to here?' she asked Alison.

'I think we need to get her help first,' Alison replied.

'I think I'd like to get up,' I said.

'Ah lad, you're doing a great job,' said a wag from the crowd nearby, many of whom had now begun to pay more attention to our sideshow than the Electric Badgers.

'I think, just for a moment or two, we should keep her there,' Alison said. I raised my eyebrows. 'She's sitting up, sort of. It's better than lying on the cold ground.' She adjusted some of Karen's clothing and closed her askew legs.

At that moment, the crowd parted further as two paramedics arrived, one pulling a wheelchair. Bleedin Obvious pointed out the woman in need.

'That's her there, lying on the ... lying on top of him,' he said.

'Alright, let's get you sorted,' said the first paramedic, an older man with bushy eyebrows, and shaved-down grey hair. The second paramedic, a slightly younger woman with short blonde hair in a bob, knelt down beside us.

'What's her name?' she asked.

'Karen,' I replied.

'Karen? Can you hear me?' the female paramedic asked loudly. Karen, for the first time, spoke loudly and clearly.

'I want chips,' she said, in a much deeper voice than I had been expecting.

'Where is the closest McDonald's?' Meabh asked again.

'Probably in the city centre,' Bleedin' Obvious replied.

'There's also one out towards Carryduff if you're driving home that way,' Been There added.

'Don't think she's driving anywhere tonight,' Alison commented.

'Alright, Karen,' said the first paramedic, 'We're going to try to lift you and get you onto this chair.' At this point, Karen opened both her eyes wide, saw the green uniforms of the paramedics and started yelling.

'Let me go! Let me go! Get away from me!'

She struggled to sit forward, flailing with both arms. An elbow hit me squarely in the nose causing me to see a few stars. The paramedics held down an arm each; the female one tried her best to calm the situation.

'It's alright, Karen, we're only trying to help you up.'
'I don't need any help!'

'Best you move away now,' the male paramedic told me. I wasn't going to disagree.

'Your nose is bleeding,' said Bleedin' Obvious.

I put my hand to my face and felt the wet blood trickling down my upper lip. Karen continued to struggle until both paramedics made the decision not to work against her. The male paramedic then instructed me to pinch my nose and hold my head down so the blood wouldn't run into my throat. He reckoned I only needed a paper towel to mop it up, but it's hard to see where you're going when you're leaning forward, so with one hand on my back Alison guided me to the First Aid tent.

'Now, that was new,' I could hear Been There saying as we left, 'I've never seen that happen before.'

*

The blood flow was merely a trickle, but it took a while to stop and so we only caught the tail end of the debrief.

'It's the walking wounded,' said Big Noel on our arrival, 'A couple of the guys here brought me up to speed. I was just saying it was a fairly quiet night – except for you, that is!' I grinned. 'If you can wait for a few minutes at the end, I'll get all of that written up.

After the debrief, Sam and Bleedin' Obvious came over.

'Ha! First outdoor gig and you end up needing medical attention,' Sam laughed, 'I take it you're alright?'

'I'm fine,' I replied, 'Bit tender round the nose, but fine.'

'She must have been swinging all round her to catch you up there.'

'Well, I was on the ground at the time.'

'What were you doing on the ground?' Sam asked.

'Long story. I wanted to get up, but Alison wouldn't let me.' Sam was confused but didn't ask anything further. Alison rolled her eyes.

'I take it you can get back to your car by yourself?' she asked, which may have been sarcasm, but I chose to take it as concern.

'I'm grand. I live in the east, short walk to the car, short drive home. Thanks for helping me out.'

'Least I could do.'

She touched me on the arm again before leaving. Sam bid me goodnight, just as Big Noel came over with his report sheet.

'I'm going to go and buy chicken nuggets,' Bleedin' Obvious announced before leaving also.

Big Noel looked at him blankly before turning to me.

'Ok, talk me through what happened with your woman,' he said.

Well, I thought, *she just touched me on the arm.*

3. Stand, and sent off

Not working every Friday means you can take on a shift at the drop of a hat. I seemed to become Helen in the Safe & Sound office's go-to steward for the Auditorium, filling in for people who dropped out at the last minute. The two Fridays after the Electric Badgers gig, I was back on tiered seating. Both times with quiet crowds at easy-listening events and nothing major to report.

Summer was fast approaching, and the football season was winding down. The last Irish League match is always the cup final. A show piece occasion played at the National Stadium in Belfast. Against all the odds, and with the benefit of some kindly draws, minnows East Side Rovers had made it through to the final against the mighty Linfield FC, the most decorated club in the country.

What might have been a relatively quiet affair took on a life of its own after an ill-judged tweet from Linfield's captain about the ease with which victory could be won. Yes, he actually used the word 'easy.' An arrangement then emerged, helped by social media, between the massed ranks of the supporters of all the other clubs who had nothing in common except their hatred of Linfield. Support transferred to East Side and what many had previously perceived would be a damp squib of a game, suddenly became the biggest-selling cup final in thirty years. Safe & Sound were asked to supply extra stewards to cover the stands for the East Side supporters.

Despite kick off being at 3pm, the shift began at midday so that everyone had time to become familiar with the North Stand, where the 'away' support would be. Built in two tiers, the North Stand had looked ultra-modern when it was built in the eighties. My Dad and I often wondered about the view from the more expensive seats in the upper tier, as we sat on the old wooden benches in the rickety Railway Stand. Not that we felt like we were missing out; the Railway Stand bounced when its supporters jumped up and down in a way the new stand never could, but one visit would have been nice. Now, however, the North Stand's youthful days were over, the rest of the stadium had caught up and it looked a little shabby by comparison.

I picked up another bright yellow Safe & Sound vest from a large white van in the car park and signed in at a folding table beside it. Underneath the stand, I caught up with Kettley and a group of several others gathered in a tight-knit group. There was suddenly an explosion of laughter, before one of the group asked, 'What do you search for?' I looked quizzically at Kettley.

'Have you seen the video of that big Asian steward?' he asked.

'No.'

'It's gone viral.'

He restarted the video on his phone and held it out to me.

It began with an enthusiastic late teen announcing to camera that he was going to demonstrate how to beat the bar queue at a gig. As he scuttled away across the grass it became obvious the scene was Ormeau. The camera zoomed in on a bar queue. Each bar queue had two lanes; the queue to the bar, and the exit from it – so that no one has to battle past a line of people with six pints in their hand. The young man attempted to sprint down the exit queue, and almost succeeded in getting to the bar, until a wide male steward suddenly stepped directly in front of him. Without time to turn or decelerate, the teenager smacked into the steward, who never so much as wobbled, and then fell flat on his back. At this point, the video became blurred as whoever was holding the phone collapsed into fits of laughter. I laughed too.

'That's Sohail,' I said.

'Never met him.'

'How many views has that had?'

'Just over four hundred thousand.'

'You're kidding,' I replied. Kettley shook his head.

Within a few minutes the supervisors split us up. I was in the group looking after the seated area in the stand, which suited me fine as I would get to see a bit of the game. Our supervisor, Leanne, was new to me. Of similar height, but definitely a lot younger than me, she was polite and direct, but not overly loud.

'Well, this is going to be an interesting one,' Leanne began, addressing our group, 'Irish Cup Finals are usually six or seven thousand fans in two groups and we're not normally here. Things have sparked into life this week, however. Ten thousand tickets have been sold and we're expecting more people to turn up at the gate. The weather is good and it's to get brighter this afternoon, isn't that right Kettley?' Kettley winked but said nothing.

'Ground capacity is eighteen thousand. The Football Association don't think we're going to be anywhere near that, but no one really knows. What we do know is that we're going to have an unusual mix of supporters in this stand. Supporters who wouldn't normally sit together but have united in their hatred of Linfield.'

She shuffled her briefing sheets and scanned through a couple of pages.

'There will be alcohol on sale and there may be some supporters with a skin full already in them, so be mindful of that. Seating wasn't allocated because there's usually plenty of room, but now that we're filling up we might need to encourage people to sit closer together and fill up the spaces. For now, though, people can sit where they want so you don't need to show them to their seats.'

I was sent, along with a ginger-haired young man, to a vomitory in the upper deck, almost at the halfway line.

I looked out over the pitch, resplendent in the May sunshine, and despite not having any knowledge about gardening, grass or ground, I recognised how beautifully prepared it was. It seemed a shame to let twenty-two sets of studs run all over it for ninety minutes.

'I hate football,' my fellow steward said, disrupting the moment.

'The view is wasted on you then,' I said. He shrugged.

'I really shouldn't be here,' he replied.

'You wouldn't be the first person caused by an accident,' I said, 'But sure, you're here now, don't let it worry you.' He looked at me blankly.

'I've had a headache all morning,' he said, placing one hand across his forehead. 'They usually develop into a migraine.'

'Right. Do you suffer from migraines a lot?'

'Yeah. Amongst other things.'

I immediately worried he was going to regale me with a long list of ailments. I was right.

'I have digestive conditions and I sprained my ankle last week, so those stairs are a killer. I also suffer from fatigue.' I stopped myself from saying 'don't we all' but held back in case he really was ill.

'If you have a migraine coming on, I'm not sure a football match is the best place for you,' I said, 'An hour or two from now, this is not going to be a peaceful environment.'

He shrugged again.

'We'll see how it goes,' he replied, 'I might be able to suffer it.'

Me too, I thought.

Across the stands stewards were fanning out. On the far side of the pitch I could see Alison talking to Niamh, who I'd seen every night I'd worked at the Auditorium. She seemed to be picking up every shift going, and I wondered how she managed to balance that with a full-time job and the wedding prep.

69

Despite how she chittered like a starling, I liked Niamh, and it worried me a little that she never seemed to take a break.

On either side of me stewards were leaning on the rails or sitting down talking to each other. Gates would open at half past one, and it wasn't even close to one o'clock yet. My fellow steward sat down, leant back, closed his eyes and groaned quietly, making Bleedin' Obvious look like the life and soul of the party.

At the end of the stand I suddenly caught sight of Been There talking animatedly with another steward I didn't recognise. At the next tunnel over I could see another steward I didn't know, with a completely shaved head and handlebar moustache, talking to an older woman who was sitting down. Then I realised she wasn't sitting down; it was the same woman I'd seen at The Lads' gig. Myrtle, I remembered, or more commonly, Wee Myrtle. I wondered how on earth she was going to keep order, if order needed to be kept.

Looking back at the pitch again, I was suddenly struck by how much I missed football. Not football on the TV, but physical, passionate, sweaty football right in front of you where you can see every touch and hear every swear word. Football matches had been central to my youth whether it was my Dad bringing me to my games with the local Boys' Brigade or to the occasional Northern Ireland game. Fast forward to Aaron's mini-soccer team with both Dad and I standing on the touch line trying our best to leave the instructions to his coach.

And then after Dad's passing, I was still there feeling the simultaneous joy of watching my then teenage son play a sport he loved and was good at, while also feeling the hole left by the man no longer at my side.

I don't think I ever got over it. When Aaron moved away, I lost my reason to be pitch-side, whether it was at a local park or a local stadium, and never went back. *But look at me now, Dad,* I thought to myself, *I've made it to the North Stand.*

My thoughts were interrupted by my fellow steward rubbing dramatically at the sides of his temples with his fingertips and moaning more loudly. I thought about pushing him over the edge of the rail to put him out of his misery, but decided that wasn't charitable. I wandered off to the loo instead.

Coming out of the Gents I saw Leanne making her way along the tunnel.

'Here,' I said, 'Just letting you know, the guy I'm on with, ginger hair, beard ...'

'Isn't well?' she asked, her face breaking into a smirk.

'No,' I replied, 'Says he has a migraine.'

'That'll be Mark,' she rolled her eyes, 'Finishes less than half the shifts he starts. No wonder they call him Sick Note.'

'Right,' I said, 'So I shouldn't be too worried then?'

'Oh, I'd be worried alright,' she said without any hint of a smile, 'You're stuck listening to him all afternoon.'

*

71

A few enthusiastic Linfield supporters entered the ground at the stroke of half one. After that there was almost nobody for another half an hour before it really started to get busy.

Football crowds, in my experience, are friendly. There's a lot of casual conversation and easy banter between the fans. I greeted one elderly gentleman struggling to make it up the steps to the second level.

'Afternoon, how's it going?'

'Well, young fella,' he paused to catch his breath, 'I'm still above ground.'

'Ah now, you've years to go yet.'

'Not if there's any more of these feckin' stairs.'

He made it to the end of the tunnel and leant on the rail overlooking the pitch.

'The aul place is looking well these days,' he commented.

'Is this the first time you've been here since it's been done up?'

'First time I've been here since I saw Best play in the seventies.'

'That must have been amazing.'

'Naw, he was fat and shite by that stage.'

Summoning up the blood, he began to climb further into the stand.

It wasn't all affable, however. A few minutes before kick off a group of about a dozen young lads came through the tunnel. They could be heard long before they could be seen. Rocket-fuelled, they were unabashed and, much as I love a bit of atmosphere at a game, intimidating. *Please don't give me any aggro,*

I thought, as they filed past me each waving East Side Rovers flags.

The away support made its voice heard; the massed ranks of non-Linfield support were doing their best to make sure East Side didn't concede early on. Every tackle, throw in and clearance was cheered, and it was beginning to have an effect as the Linfield players found it hard to get rhythm into their game.

Ten minutes in, my little group unrolled a banner. It looked like a double bed sheet had been ripped in two and then safety-pinned together lengthways. The writing was not of a professional standard, nevertheless the spray-painted text 'FUCK OFF LINFIELD!' was clearly legible.

Leanne hadn't said much about flags or banners at the briefing. They're a part of football matches and the professionally-printed banners that hang over the edge of the stands had already been cleared by each club. SIA should have picked up anything more offensive at the gate, but this could easily have been sneaked inside in a jacket. I nudged Sick Note to look up.

'I don't think that's going to be ok,' he said.

'Me neither,' I replied and set off up the steps, deciding on a bold, direct approach.

'Sorry guys,' I began assertively, 'You can't have that up here. I'm going to have to take that off you.'

The first bloke on the row, who was not holding any part of the banner, turned to stand opposite me. He was not overtly aggressive and he was a few inches shorter, and skinnier, so I wasn't feeling intimidated, but he was very deliberately blocking the row.

'It's just a banner,' he said, 'You're allowed banners.'

'It's a free country,' the next guy along chirped up.

'It's an offensive banner and you know it,' I replied.

'It's communicating our true feelings about Linfield,' the first bloke said, smiling happily at me with glazed eyes, 'If you don't like it, tough shit.'

'Whether I like it or not isn't the point,' I replied. Opting for a firmer tone, I added, 'But it's an offensive banner and I'm going to take it off you.'

This was greeted by a chorus of 'Oooohs' from the whole group, and I immediately noticed my mistake.

Glancing behind me to check on Sick Note, I suddenly realised he hadn't followed me up the stairs. He was back down at the end of the vomitory, picking his nose thoughtfully. Not that having the back up of a pasty-faced bloke on the edge of a migraine was going to increase my level of authority, but I was now on my own and had just upped the ante with no immediate way to enforce the banner's removal.

'Lads,' I said, smiling, 'I'm just doing my job. I'm asking for your help here. You have to take it down.'

But it was too late. You can start friendly and then get tough, but you can't start tough and then try friendly. I was weak and they knew it. I had lost the first round, I needed to accept defeat gracefully and go get reinforcements. I walked back down the steps while they cheered.

I had intended to go and find Leanne, but she was already coming out of the vomitory, tucking her walkie talkie back into her belt. I began to tell her what had happened, but she didn't stop.

'I know, I'm on it,' she said on her way past. Uncertain about what to do, I followed her at a polite distance. She stopped at the end of the row where the offending article was still being displayed.

'Fellas,' she began, 'You can't hold up that banner, you need to give it to me now please.' Once again, the young man on the end of the row blocked the way, although this time, he didn't seem just as confident. I didn't hear what he said, but Leanne's response was clear enough.

'You can give it to me now and stay, or you can keep it and my security guys are going to remove you from the stadium.' There was minimal discussion as the ex-bed sheet was rolled into a ball and handed to her.

I followed Leanne back to where Sick Note was standing at the mouth of the tunnel.

'I did try to get it off them,' I explained, anxious that she wouldn't think I had just stood there looking at it, 'But they weren't having any of it.'

'It's alright,' she replied, 'Sometimes it just needs a direct threat. The BBC nearly broadcast it though, the IFA were going ballistic.' She nodded back up the stand, 'Just keep an eye on them.'

Thankfully the game came to life with East Side going toe-to-toe with Linfield; an absorbing encounter that kept my little group out of any mischief for the next while. Just as the favourites looked as though they were gaining the upper hand however, a mistake at the back let an East Side forward clean through on goal. A Linfield centre back took him out with a clear foul and was sent off.

This sent the noise level through the roof as the Linfield fans howled in protest and the East Side fans now knew they really had a chance of winning. Their advantage increased when, ten minutes before half time, East Side's striker headed his team in front. The North Stand erupted. My group celebrated by running up and down the stairs of the stand waving their club flags.

I let it go for a moment or two, figuring they would tire themselves out. They didn't. They added to their repertoire by running up and down some of the largely vacant rows in the stand, irritating other spectators in the process. With half time approaching, people were beginning to exit the stand by the stairway to get to the bar or the hot food stands, so there was also a risk to safety. Telling them to stop however, was going to cause its own problems.

As they were coming down the stairway in a row, I attempted to block their passage with both hands spread wide.

'Lads, I need you to sit down,' I said, trying to sound as reasonable as I could, 'There's other people on the stairs and I don't want an accident.'

Directly in front of me, nose-to-nose because he was on the step above, was the same young man that had been at the end of the row earlier. He had an East Side flag in either hand. He turned to the group behind him and, without moving, began a chant of 'East Side! East Side!'

I waited for this to die down and, when there was a gap, I politely asked again that they sit down for everyone's safety. The East Side chant was then replaced by the well-known footballing classic, 'Let's all do the bouncy!' The entire group began to bounce up and down, singing and flag waving. I decided not to give ground. At the very least if they were here annoying me, they weren't bothering other people. Trouble was, they were blocking the stair way.

The 'bouncy' came to an end and was replaced by a rousing chorus of 'We hate you Linfield!' At the end of which, I became aware of another luminous yellow vest at my elbow.

At first, I assumed it was Sick Note, but it turned out to be Wee Myrtle from the next block. Mid-fifties, tight-permed hair and well shy of five foot, she used a tone that could weld steel.

'Right, you lot, wise up! Sit the fuck down and get out of people's road!'

Flags were instantly lowered as the group looked at her, then at each other, then finally at the ground as they shuffled back up the stairs to their row. Wee Myrtle and I descended the stairs to where Sick Note was standing, surreptitiously checking his phone.

'Put that away,' she said, 'How many times do you need to be told?'

'I was just ...' Sick Note began.

'Checking the NHS web site to see what you're dying of,' she finished, before turning to me, 'Leanne wants you to give Sam a hand down in the tunnel during half time.' I nodded and made my way down the stairs.

Leanne wasn't far away.

'What's your name again?' she asked.

'Robbie.'

'Ok, Robbie, don't take this the wrong way, but I'm going to let Myrtle look after that bunch up there because she's been doing this for years and she doesn't take any shit. I need more cover down here during the break because it's not technically outdoors and nobody's allowed to smoke or vape. They have to go to the designated smoking section at either end. Work with Sam, and politely ask people to move on down if they light up. Thanks.'

I nodded as Leanne set off down the tunnel, feeling slightly crestfallen that curtailing the antics of a few inebriated young fellas appeared to have been beyond me. Sam ambled over.

'How's things young man?' he asked.

'Things are fine, Sam,' I replied, adding, 'Although I think I might have just been sent off for incompetency.'

I explained what had happened. Sam breathed deeply and sighed.

'I wouldn't give it too much thought,' he said, 'You get moments like that. Most shifts are quiet, but there's always one out there that comes with a bit of aggro. That's why I always opt for the quiet life. Something simple, without any hassle, that'll do me rightly.'

I looked around me at the tunnel we were standing in; a damp breeze-block wall on one side, the back end of the stand on the other, and a network of steel frames above us.

'Not the most interesting place to be for six hours, though,' I said.

'Ah now,' he replied, 'In my youth, I'd have been itching to be in the crowd and see a bit of the game. But these days, I'm happy wandering about out here. Most of the time you're doing very little, but if somebody wants to pay me for standing around doing nothing, that's fine by me.'

'I take it you're retired now,' I said.

'You think I'm old?' he asked pointedly. I tried to roll it back, but he interrupted. 'Of course, I'm old, I'm into my seventies, retired nearly ten years now.'

'What did you do?'

'I was a security guard in civil service buildings. Mainly at Stormont, but they moved me around every so often.'

'Were you there long?' I asked. Sam chuckled.

'Almost all my life,' he answered, 'I started out as a joiner, but I got sick of building sites, so I made the move in my late twenties, and then stayed there 'til I retired.'

'You must have seen a few things around Stormont in your time.'

'Happy to say I saw frig all,' he replied, 'There were a few near misses and lots that I heard about from others, but I've had a pretty quiet life. Some of the guys liked to be busy; they liked people coming and going, the rumours and scandal. Me? I liked the paper in the morning, tea breaks and a wee nap in the car at lunch time. I like a bit of chat and craic too, but I don't get too involved. Do the job, but don't overdo it, if you know what I mean?'

I nodded. I knew exactly what he meant; I knew his type well. I'd worked with guys like him for years; dependable, unflappable and entirely predictable. They'd clock in two minutes before a shift started; they'd take their tea break at the same time every day with the same newspaper, tell the same kind of joke, clock out at the same time and drive home in the same make of car they always drove.

I also knew it wasn't for me. Don't get me wrong, I've been a man of routine for most of my life, but there has to be some variation. Staring into space for hours on end was my idea of hell.

'What stage are you at, youngster?' Sam asked.

'Well,' I replied, 'I'm a fifty-two-year-old youngster.'

'Still a pup ...'

'A divorced pup. Ex-husband and sort of ex-father.' Sam raised his eyebrows. 'One son in London who works twenty-four seven; one daughter here who's always busy.' I shrugged, 'They have their own lives now; that's how it's supposed to be.'

'I know what you mean,' he replied. 'I had three of my own. We didn't have a big house and for a few years we lived on top of each other, but then they moved out and things moved on. There are grandchildren now and they take a lot of running after.'

I wasn't exactly sure what Sam meant, his life didn't sound in the least bit similar to mine, but the half-time whistle blew and the tunnel quickly filled up with supporters. Together we patrolled the length of the North Stand answering questions about the nearest bar or burger stand. The occasional smoker lit up, but no one resisted our requests to move down to the smoking section. It's funny; growing up it felt like half the crowd at a match was smoking and we watched the game through a grey haze, but now there was a new norm.

The second half got under way promptly; Linfield still a goal down, though Sam and I were reliably informed that East Side had been hanging on at times. The tunnel largely emptied, but small clusters of men remained, pints and burgers in hand, sharing stories, laughing loudly. I grinned. *This is how men meet,* I thought. The match is just the venue, the real event is the banter and the connection.

Sam and I continued to pace up and down as if we were out for a stroll in the park.

'How many grandchildren have you?' I asked.

'Eight altogether,' he answered. 'Two groups of three and a pair. Though the pair belong to my youngest daughter, so she might catch up yet.'

'That must make for a houseful. Are they all local?'

'They are. They all live in Belfast. Get-togethers don't happen in our house, though,' he shook his head, 'We just don't have the room for them, most times we go to theirs. Eight kids in one place, it's noisy.'

'I can imagine.'

'I take it there are no grandchildren yet?'

'Not yet,' I said, 'But Aaron's been going steady for a couple of years now, so maybe in the next while. Who knows?'

'Do young people still 'go steady' these days?' he asked.

'To be honest, Sam, I wouldn't know,' I replied, 'It was a long time long ago when Shirley and I went steady. I don't think my kids can imagine the world we grew up in.' I struggled to remember it myself; dating Shirley now seemed like someone else's life.

'What about your daughter?' he asked. I shrugged.

'I'd be surprised if there hadn't been a boyfriend or two; she's outgoing, chatty. But that information has been kept well away from me.'

'Not chatty with you then?'

'No,' I said, pausing to choose my words carefully, 'She's twenty-three now, and it's not cool to hang around with your old man ...' I tailed off, as my head flooded with memories. I used to be the sun in Paula's universe; somehow, I had been downgraded to a passing comet.

My thoughts were interrupted by a roar thundering down the vomitories emitting from the South Stand opposite. Linfield had equalised. I had to admit, with the game now balanced at one all and with the underdogs having a one-man advantage, I really wanted to see what happened next. If East Side got back into the game, or even took Linfield to extra time or penalties, this would be remembered for years to come and I didn't want to miss it. I looked at my watch.

'Twenty minutes to go,' I said to Sam, 'Don't you want to see what happens?'

'A little bit,' he admitted.

We continued to patrol the length of the tunnel, stopping longer at each end of the stand where we could see some of the game. There was almost no one in the tunnel now; every small group had returned to their seats. As the final whistle approached, both teams looked exhausted and were making mistakes.

With the ninety minutes up, a misplaced pass along the East Side back line allowed a Linfield player to intercept. He rounded the keeper and slotted home. With little time to restart the game and the East Side spirit well and truly broken, Linfield won the cup.

The fans in the North Stand stayed long enough to applaud the East Side Rovers players off the pitch, and then began to stream through the vomitories, along the tunnel and out the gates. By the time the trophy was presented, we had the North Stand swept and clear and were ambling round the ground to steward the Linfield fans when they eventually left the stadium.

I was standing at one of the main gates when Alison walked past me and said hi.

'Here,' she said, doubling back, 'You live in east Belfast, don't you?'

'Cregagh Road,' I said.

'It's just ... Niamh was saying ... Do you know Niamh?' I nodded. 'Niamh was saying her boyfriend was meant to pick her up, but something's happened and he can't get here, so she was looking for a lift. I think she lives somewhere around Castlereagh.'

'If she needs a lift, I can take her,' I said.

'Are you sure?'

'No bother.'

'Great, I'll go and see if I can find her. I'll see you where we signed in.'

She hurried off back the way she came.

Our vests were quickly returned and with no lengthy debrief the shift was at an end. Niamh hurried over to me, checking a lift was ok.

'Are you sure you don't mind?' she said.

'It's no problem. I'm going that way.'

'I really appreciate it,' she continued, 'Damian was to come and get me but he's got held up and he wouldn't be able to get here for at least an hour so I'd have to think about getting a bus into town and out again which I could do, you know, it wouldn't be that bad, but you know, it's the end of the shift and, you know what it's like, you just want to get home and sit down for a while.'

'No worries,' I assured her.

Her stream of constant chatter continued all the way to the car. Mostly she talked about what the shift had been like, even though not much had happened. She was always chatty, but her manner struck me as very different to before; she seemed on edge.

Inside the car, the stereo came to life on ignition, and blasted out the country rhythms of 'Working on the Highway.' Niamh shot me a split-second look,

84

which I figured meant 'I don't know why people your age listen to this.' I hastily turned it off.

We drove slowly across Belfast, catching the tail end of the traffic leaving the streets around the stadium. Rarely getting beyond second gear I quietly drummed my fingers on the steering wheel while Niamh continued to talk, repeatedly clicking and pulling open a popper on her coat pocket.

'I mean, I love that we have our space now, but I never thought there'd be so much to do having your own house. I mean, there's your usual housework, the dishes never stop, washing, ironing ...' I grinned; I gave up ironing years ago. 'But then, you want to make the space yours, you know? So even when you're just sitting watching TV, you're thinking, we could repaint that room, or we could add in a set of shelves in that corner, that would give us somewhere to tidy away all our stuff. You just seem to gather stuff up so easily, don't you?'

She left no space for an answer and carried on talking. It struck me, that she wasn't really talking to *me*, she was just talking. I began to pay less attention to what she was saying and more attention to what she was doing. The popper on her coat clicked for the thousandth time. She was leaning forward in her seat, hardly taking a breath between sentences. Her face was so tense she was frowning.

We crossed the Lagan and stopped at some lights. I was beginning to think that perhaps being in the car with me, a bloke twice her age who she hardly knew, was freaking her out a little, when suddenly she breathed out heavily. Her whole body seemed to sag. Her hands became still, and she sat back in her seat.

'I think my fiancé is cheating on me,' she said simply.

I looked directly at her for a few seconds, until the lights changed, and I had to look ahead again. I was a little startled, but not shocked. Affairs happen. I said nothing and waited.

When nothing came, I felt I should ask.

'What makes you think that?'

She looked out of the passenger window.

'This happens all the time,' she said, 'He's late. Other things come up. Things take longer than they should. He doesn't answer his phone. There are times I just don't know where he is.'

She sat quietly for a moment and then added,

'That makes me sound like a controlling bitch.'

'That's not what I'm thinking now, if that helps,' I said.

She continued looking away from me.

'When I ask him where he's been, or why something took so long, it always seems to end up as an argument,' she said, 'And that's what he calls me.'

The traffic freed up and I needed to ask Niamh her address. I decided not to ask anything else, leaving it up to her to offer more information; there's no escape when you're stuck inside someone else's car. She sat quietly for the few minutes it took to get to the end of her street where she insisted I drop her off.

When I pulled over, she had the door open before the car came to a complete stop. 'I'm sorry,' she said,

'I shouldn't have said any of that. Thanks for the lift, I really, really appreciate it.'

Before I had time to reply, she exited the car and made her way swiftly down the street without looking back.

4. Tickets, and totally taken

It was certainly the hairiest queue I had ever seen. Most men my age opt for the short trim on top and clippers up the side, largely because we can't be arsed with paying our hair any attention. This bunch of twenty or thirty early birds, however, had enough hair to tie down a cruise ship.

They had come to the Auditorium to worship at the feet of Fret Boy, a grizzled ex-roadie who had worked with Iron Maiden and Ozzy Osbourne and was now enjoying his fifteen minutes of fame after coming third on 'Britain's Got Talent,' playing a Gibson 'Flying V' guitar with his teeth. Without penning a single original song, Fret Boy had subsequently topped the charts on several occasions by raiding the back catalogue of seventies hard rock bands, supported for the most part, by teenage boys who loved classic guitar riffs. His fame had peaked at Christmas, securing the number one spot with a thrash metal recital of 'Ding Dong Merrily'; a version so utterly unlistenable virtually every major radio station left it off their play list. Fret Boy's devoted fan base screamed 'censorship' and downloaded it in droves.

I walked past the line of leather-jacketed acolytes and into the Auditorium to sign in and buy my one shot car parking ticket. The lads must have been melting as the first days of June had brought a mini heat wave, and the early evening sunshine was strong.

On tickets this time, I made my way over to the group of stewards forming at the side of the foyer. I could see Ryan hovering nervously at its edge, busily poking at his mobile while glancing up every so often, presumably to ensure he wasn't under imminent attack. There were one or two other faces I recognised, but the rest seemed new to me. I was about to join one of the clusters when a hand was placed gently on my back.

'Hello!' Alison chirped with a broad smile across her face. Same pulled-back brown hair; same russet-brown eyes.

'How's it going?' I returned the smile.

'Same old,' she replied, 'Another day's work serving customers and then here, to be nice to people some more.'

'Where do you work?' I asked.

'Marks and Spencer's. Customer services, at the minute.'

'Was it a bit of a sprint to get here?'

'Yep, but I work in town, so it isn't so bad. Knock off one job at five thirty and here for six. No time to eat though.'

There was no time for further conversation either as Tony began to address the group while handing out briefing sheets and ear plugs. I went to put my mobile on silent, but realising it was low on battery, switched it off instead.

'Right,' Tony began, 'I want to welcome Kate, she's just starting with Safe & Sound tonight, be nice to her.

Make sure she doesn't get attacked by the hairy hordes coming in.'

Kate, blonde-haired, slight, and probably early twenties smiled uncertainly. Alison, only a couple of stewards away, leant towards her and gave her a thumbs up. Kate nodded and her smile became more convincing.

'Tonight's headliner is Fret Boy,' Tony continued, 'Who needs no introduction since he's been friggin' everywhere in the last year. He is wildly popular with his fans, but nobody else really gives a shit. Only two thousand tickets were sold for this event until the promoters added Therapy? and Stiff Little Fingers to the line-up, which has bumped the numbers up. We're not at capacity tonight, but there'll be about three thousand on the floor and we're nearly full upstairs.'

'For reasons best known to himself, Fret Boy, despite being in his early fifties, likes to fling himself off the stage into the crowd and 'surf.' This inevitably causes others to try it, so it's likely to be a bit of a rough night down at the front, but that's not our problem. Any questions?'

'Any chance of getting in later?' A young, male steward with collar-length hair asked. Tony regarded him with suspicion; the young man looked at the ground.

'Are you a Fret Boy fan in disguise?' he asked. The steward shrugged and mumbled something.

'We'll be sending at least half of you off to cover breaks in other parts of the auditorium, so I daresay you'll get to see some of it,' Tony added. 'Can everybody pick up a scanner?'

We did our usual self-sort into pairs at each entrance point and adjusted the barriers and turnstiles. When you attend a gig, it looks like you gain entry through a wall of steel. When you're a steward, you realise how flimsy the entry point is. The barriers are lightweight, and although the turnstiles are heavier, they have wheels on the side so even the smallest steward can tip them over and take them away. When a gig is winding down, the entrance barrier is dismantled in about ninety seconds.

I was hoping that Alison would pair up with me at a nearby set of turnstiles so I could avoid striking up conversation with another new steward. I like meeting people, but I'd spent a week taking on several new clients and to be honest, I wasn't up for another introduction. Also, it was Alison; easy to talk to, easy to look at and all round pleasant. Alright, I know that's not exactly a description worthy of Shakespeare, but even if she was off limits, I was still interested. 'Sniffing' we used to call it when I was a teenager.

Alison spoke briefly to Kate, who Tony paired her up with the Fret Boy fan steward and to my delight, Alison walked back over to me.

'I'm starving,' she said. I glanced at my watch; it was now six thirty, doors would likely open soon, and a break would be at least a couple of hours away.

'I have a Kit Kat in my pocket,' I volunteered, and then added hurriedly, 'My fleece pocket ... I wouldn't offer anybody chocolate that had been down ...'

'Stop talking,' Alison interrupted, as I reddened, 'I'll be fine, thank you. I can manage until later.'

She was immediately let down by a loud squeaking and rumbling.

'Is that your stomach?' I asked. Now she reddened. I whipped the Kit Kat from my fleece with a flourish. She took it gratefully.

Like checking your mobile, eating on duty is also prohibited, however the general rule is that it's not a problem if no one sees you doing it. Alison, clearly practiced in the dark arts of surreptitious consumption, had half the Kit Kat out of the wrapper and into her mouth in one fluid motion.

'So,' I began, scrabbling for conversation, 'How long have you worked at Marks and Spencer's?'

'Just over a year now,' she replied through a full mouth.

'What's it like?' I asked, shuddering at the inanity of my questions, but it was all I could think of.

'S'alright,' she answered, swallowing, 'Customer Services, so you're always dealing with exchanges, refunds, complaints. It's not really what I want, but it'll do for now.'

'What type of thing are you looking for?'

'I used to work in an outdoor clothing shop; I was there about fifteen years. I like the outdoors. I get excited about outdoor gear; I don't get that excited about refunds.'

She tossed the other half of the Kit Kat into her mouth.

'So are you looking for a move?' I asked.

'Hm, half-heartedly,' she mumbled, 'I keep an eye on the job ads, but it feels like I've just started at this job, and I only moved to Belfast about a year ago, so there's been a lot of change recently. M&S isn't long term, but maybe I'll stick it for a little while longer.'

'Where were you before you moved?' I asked, aware that I seemed to be carrying out some kind of background check, but Alison didn't seem to be bothered.

'Coleraine.'

'Coleraine?'

An hour or so outside Belfast, but if you live in the capital, where most things are within easy reach, then Coleraine is a day trip. Call me a nut job, but in that moment, Alison became very slightly exotic.

'Yes,' she replied, 'All the way from Coleraine. Why is it Belfast people are amazed by someone moving to Belfast from Coleraine?'

'Just seems like a long way.'

'It's a full sixty minutes away; more in heavy traffic. Sometimes people starve to death in transit.'

Her face remained entirely straight.

'Alright, alright,' I replied, 'I'm from Belfast. Coleraine's where you go for your holidays.'

'Near where you go for your holidays,' she corrected.

'That too. But why did you come *all the way* from Coleraine?'

'That would be the boyfriend,' she said, and that feeling of being buried alive returned. 'And a bit of a story.'

I shrugged.

'I'm not going anywhere.'

'He's originally from Belfast but moved up to the north coast a while back. We got together about ten years ago, or so. It's been a bit of an on and off thing. His Mum hasn't had the best of health over the last while, so he made the decision to move back down, and I came with him.'

I really only heard the on and off bit properly.

'That explains the new job.'

'New job, new house, new city, new relationship with my boyfriend's mother,' Alison raised her eyebrows, 'New relationship with my boyfriend because we hadn't properly lived together before.'

I found a green shoot of hope springing from this last disclosure, closely followed by a pang of shame that I was wishing a relationship break-up on someone.

'I can see why you're not rushing to change jobs then.'

'Yeah, it can wait,' she replied, 'Besides, what I've got really isn't that bad. I don't mind M&S and I quite like this.'

Alison gestured to the Auditorium foyer, which was now bustling with the usual last-minute preparations before the doors opened. Tony was animatedly talking to someone through his radio, catering staff were wheeling trolleys of food and bar staff were ferrying crates full of plastic beer bottles. Behind the merchandise stand ridiculously priced Fret Boy t-shirts were being pinned to the wall.

'Would you ever wear one of those?' Alison asked.

'Not even if you paid me,' I said, looking at the designs, 'I think there comes a time in a man's life when he can't get away with wearing a t-shirt showing a cartoon of a fifty-something bloke playing an electric guitar with his teeth.'

'Was there ever a time?' she asked.

'Not really.'

'I'll stick to Elton, thank you,' she said.

'Alright, I never got asking you the last time, but what is it about Elton?'

Alison shrugged. I found myself liking how she did that, and realised I was turning into a besotted idiot.

'I think you never really grow out of the music of your youth.'

'You still listening to Culture Club?' I interrupted.

'Maybe not *all* the music of your youth,' she admitted, 'But someone bought me the 'Too Low for Zero' album for my tenth birthday, and I played it to death.'

'Vinyl or cassette?' I asked.

'Cassette,' she said, 'The stylus on our record player was knackered; if you wanted to listen to something properly, you had to play it on cassette.'

'First album?' I asked.

'Think so, yeah,' she said, 'There was a Shakin' Stevens album I used to play a lot at that time, even though it was shit, but I really fell in love with Elton. I used to play 'I Guess that's why they Call it the Blues' over and over again. Which, if you think about it, is a curious choice for a ten-year-old.'

She laughed. I liked her laugh even more than her shrug, and no longer cared what that said about me.

'Rolling like thunder ...' I began.

'Don't go there,' she interrupted. 'So, that was it. I began asking for Elton John albums when they came out, and since Mum liked him too, she was happy to supply them. But I still think that if I was to hear him now, for the first time, I'd still like the music.'

I grinned.

'What's that face for?' she demanded, 'I bet you got into Dylan in exactly the same way.'

I grinned more.

'I admit it,' I said, 'It was a mid-teen thing; someone gave me a compilation – on a C60 cassette tape – and I was hooked.'

'And then you explored his back catalogue ...'

'Took me about ten years, but yeah, as soon as I had the money, I made sure I had every album he ever made.'

'Same for me,' she said, 'I started with the eighties albums, which even I will admit are not the best, but they're attached to a time. 'Reg Strikes Back' ...' she tailed off and looked away momentarily.

'What about it?' I asked.

'It's a synth-driven album, I'm pretty sure if I played you it, you'd hate it, but I was fourteen when it came out. It takes me back. But in my late teens and twenties, like you say, once I had the extra cash and I could buy the early stuff, then I really became a fan.'

"Crocodile Rock'?'

'Not 'Crocodile Rock.' Have you got Spotify?' I nodded. 'Go and listen to some of his early albums the whole way through, like 'Tumbleweed Connection,' 'Honky Chateau,' 'Goodbye Yellow Brick Road.' Songs like 'Take Me to the Pilot,' 'Elderberry Wine,' 'Mona Lisas and Mad Hatters,' you'd be amazed at what hidden gems are in there.'

'Wait a minute,' I said, "Mona Lisas and Mad Hatters' is one of my all-time favourite songs.'

'Stop taking the piss.'

'I know that song inside out!' I protested.

'Sing me the opening lines,' she demanded.

'I don't do singing. Not before the fourth pint anyway.'

'You don't know it.'

'It's on 'Honky Chateau.' Em ...' I began to hear the intro playing in my head, 'And now I know, Spanish Harlem are not just pretty words to say ... I thought I knew, but now I know that rose trees never grow in New York City. *There!*' I added for good measure. She seemed both shocked and impressed, both of which delighted me.

'Alright, you win,' she said. I tried not to look smug. 'Favourite song ever,' she added. I filed that away for future reference.

'Doors opening in two minutes folk!' Tony called along the row of turnstiles. The line of excessively hairy people had grown since I had walked past them earlier. Almost every fanboy – and as far as I could see this section of the crowd was exclusively male – was wearing a black t-shirt. The front of the building was still catching intense sunlight and the black leather jackets had now been removed to avoid heat exhaustion.

I checked the scanner light against my hand just as the doors opened and the front of the line streamed in. First through the door was a tall, gangly teen with light brown hair that fell to the middle of his back. I had to give him credit, it must have been washed that afternoon because it was completely devoid of any greasiness and streamed out on either side of him catching the light from behind. Momentarily, he was angelic. He held one arm in the air in the time-honoured rock salute.

'Dude!' he yelled loudly enough that several of the stewards flinched. Ryan jumped so much he very slightly threw his scanner in the air but managed to catch it again.

Dude Boy marched straight towards me and, having retrieved his home-printed ticket from the hip pocket of his ripped jeans, thrust it towards me and yelled, 'Rock n roll!'

I scanned his ticket and as he clunked through the turnstile, I glanced up at the next teen punter coming through. He looked me in the eye and with a totally straight face said,

'Ignore him, he's a dick.'

'Aw, let him be,' I said, trying to humour him, 'He's just excited.'

I didn't exactly catch what he said on his way past me, but it was something like 'you don't have to stand beside him for the next four hours.'

The initial flurry did not last long. Less than a hundred early birds all hurried to the barrier directly below the stage to secure their spot in the front rows and the foyer quietened down again.

'So how have you found life in Belfast?' I asked. Alison shrugged, beguiling me even more.

'You've got an Ikea and a better choice of restaurants, but your river is piss-poor to be honest,' she said.

I grinned, but while I was trying to find a way to slag off the Bann, she turned serious.

'Can't say it's been easy, but ...' she hesitated. 'I'm trying to avoid saying 'it is what it is' because that seems to be what everyone says these days, but in this case, it really is what it is. You have a choice, and you pick what you think is best and go with it.'

There was silence for a few seconds. I was a little shocked. I'd meant it as a light-hearted question, but suddenly she was baring her soul to answer it. I'm ok with serious, in-depth conversation, but I cursed the fact we were in the foyer of a concert hall about to fill up with hairy metal fans. Not an ideal setting to go deeper.

'That's the short answer to your question,' she said, with a smile, which was right up there with the shrug and the laugh.

'Yeah, turned out it was a bigger question than I intended it to be,' I replied.

'It's a good question though, and I've maybe avoided answering it because when things don't go as smoothly as I thought they would, my solution is to get busy doing something.'

'That's one way of dealing with it,' I said.

'Yeah, but it's a short-term solution ...' she tailed off. 'So, what else is on your Spotify play list right now?'

This panicked me. I like to think I have fairly wide listening tastes, but memory is my problem, and with new-fangled listening methods like Spotify, you can flick from artist to artist without really paying attention to names and album titles. Ask me what I'm listening to and the only thing I can recall is Dylan, the Beatles and Springsteen. That's when people glaze over, thinking they have discovered a boring old fart who hasn't listened to anything new in the last couple of decades.

'Gaslight Anthem,' I said. Alison nodded.

'Springsteen soundalikes?' she asked.

'Kind of, yeah, maybe a little rougher around the edges.'

'David Gray,' I added.

'The man they used to call the new Dylan,' she replied.

'He wasn't the only one.'

'True. He's not bad. I have a copy of 'White Ladder."

'Doesn't everybody?'

She laughed, and I swear the foyer got brighter.

'Yeah, it was one of those albums,' she said.

'I had a Chesterfield Kings album on this morning.' She looked at me blankly and shook her head. 'Kind of like the Stones,' I explained.

'God,' she said, 'You don't like to push the boat out too far, do you?'

'What do you mean?'

'Sticking to classic rock. I bet you have a subscription to *Mojo* magazine,' she accused.

'I do not have a subscription to *Mojo*,' I stated bluntly and tried to look her in the eye, but couldn't.

'No, you just buy it in the newsagent's every month. Because you've never got around to filling out the form on the web site.' This was in fact completely true, but I wasn't going to admit it.

'I don't buy it *every* month,' I mumbled, but again, couldn't make eye contact because I knew rightly I *did* buy it every month, read it cover to cover every month and noted any interesting new albums from the review section with a yellow highlighter. *Every month.*

The stream of fans coming in through the door now became more pressing and there was no opportunity to redress the balance of classic rock artists. Not that I could think of too many others off the top of my head anyway, though I knew that if I went through my playlists I'd find quite a few female vocalists from the Americana/new country genre.

Bizarrely, the only artist I could think of who was even vaguely alternative, was Glen Hansard. In between scanning tickets and greeting excited teens, I found myself debating whether this would improve my standing with Alison or diminish it. I had a bit of a soft spot for the songs he wrote for the film 'Once' and there were a couple of other albums I had pretty much played to death. However, he was yet another bloke on an acoustic guitar and therefore had to have been influenced by Dylan in some way.

I resolved the issue by deciding that when I got home that night, I would sit down at the kitchen table and write out a list of ten artists I frequently listened to that could not be directly linked to classic rock. I would then learn off this list so as I was fully prepared for any similar situation, should it arise, in the wild hope that it might be a contributing factor to me being a suitable replacement should things go pear-shaped with Alison's boyfriend. Quite a tangent, I know, but your mind goes to strange places when you're repeatedly scanning tickets.

I was distracted from this chain of thought by a couple of outliers in the queue. The line, stretching from me to the door, went black t-shirt, black t-shirt, grey shirt with chains attached to it, brown jacket with white shirt and striped tie. The latter was worn by a grey-haired man, who was definitely of retirement age. As he came closer, I realised he was holding the hand of a woman, presumably his wife. She was much shorter, hair set in a perm, and wearing a fur coat.

Looking around him nervously, the man approached me, eyes wide. He held out their box office-printed tickets.

'Good evening folks!' I greeted them cheerily. Both of them nodded in return. I scanned the bar codes on the end of their tickets. The scanner made the unhappy noise. I tried again, with the same result. I tried the QR code to see if that made any difference. It didn't.

'I'm not sure what the problem is,' I said, holding the tickets up to take a closer look. Then it became obvious.

'Ah,' I said, 'You're going to see Andre Rieu.'

'That's right,' the man replied. 'Is there something wrong with our tickets?'

'No. There's nothing wrong with your tickets, but you're in the wrong place.'

'What?' said the woman sharply.

'Andre Rieu is playing in the Waterfront tonight. This is the Belfast Auditorium.'

'This isn't the Waterfront?' the man said.

'No.'

'Right. Where is the Waterfront?'

'It's down by the river, in front of the ...' I couldn't bring myself to finish the sentence.

'Oh,' the woman suddenly understood, 'I know the one you mean now. That was where we saw The Krankies one Christmas.'

I thought about this.

'Are they still touring?' I couldn't help but ask.

'No, not any more,' the woman explained, 'She has osteoporosis and her back just can't take performing, but they were still going up until a few years back.'

There was a disgruntled, forced sigh from a black t-shirted ticket holder directly behind the couple.

'Well, I have to say,' the man said, completely oblivious to the rest of the queue, 'This is a bit of a relief, I really wasn't sure what I was coming to.' He looked around at the array of long hair and increasingly irritated-looking faces behind him.

'We don't really know much about Andre Rieu,' she said, 'Our son bought us the tickets to try to get us to go out more.'

'After Little and Large stopped touring, and Rod Hull died, we sort of lost interest,' he explained.

I nodded, as if I was genuinely sympathetic to the crushing blow of no longer being able to see Emu live.

'Of course, Rod's son, Toby, tried to carry on, but it was never the same,' she said wistfully.

'Never the same,' the man echoed sadly.

The bodies in the queue behind were now audibly restless.

'Well, I'm sure it'll be a great gig,' I said, 'If you hurry now, you'll only miss the start.'

'We'll do our best,' he promised.

She waved and shouted 'Cheerio' over her shoulder. The next pair of Fret Boy fans stepped forward.

'*Wankers,*' one of them said to the other.

*

The queue surged to peak influx, which lasted for about fifteen to twenty minutes before dying back to a trickle. Inside the hall, Therapy? opened proceedings and the crowd responded enthusiastically. Tony closed down some of the entry points and began to reallocate the team. Ryan and three of the others were sent on a break, and four of us stayed put. Alison and I remained on the entry; another pair scanned punters out for a smoke break.

I caught myself just smiling at her and tried to stop it.

'One of the things I like about Belfast,' Alison said, out of nowhere, 'Is that you can be anonymous. I could walk around Belfast all day and no one will notice me. It's also one of the things I most dislike about Belfast. I really haven't made up my mind about it.'

I thought for a moment before replying.

'You like the space, but it seems like there's too much of it?'

'Something like that,' she said. 'Everybody knows everybody in a small town. And if they don't, they won't be long in finding out. It's what makes it home. It's also what makes it ...'

'Like prison?'

'No, I'd never say that. I don't know, sometimes you just want a break; a breath of fresh air.'

'Not sure I've ever described Belfast as a breath of fresh air,' I laughed.

'No, not literally.'

'Sounds like you think you'll go back to Coleraine at some point?' I ventured.

She shrugged. God, she was Olympic standard at it.

'Maybe. Who knows? But it feels like I only just got here. You've got to give these things time.'

A group of several concert goers charged through the front doors, which was impressive given they looked like they were all in their sixties.

'Sorry we're late!' the first one said panting and fishing his folded ticket out of the inside of his denim jacket.

'It's alright,' I said, 'We don't take a roll call.'

'Have the Stiffs been on yet?' another one asked.

'Not yet,' I replied, 'Therapy? are mid-set, you're in good time.'

There was a collective sigh of relief. Each ticket scanned through easily and they disappeared into the hall.

'Have you always lived in Belfast?' Alison asked.

'All my life,' I replied. 'Can't imagine living anywhere else, although I understand what you mean about space. I do like to escape every so often.'

'Where to?'

'A forest, the coast, or a small mountain. Anything with a trail and no concrete.'

'Yeah,' she replied, 'I think everybody needs a bit of that. That's one of the things I miss in Belfast, you have to drive for a while before you find enough space. In Coleraine, the beach is just down the road. My Dad walks along the shore almost every morning; it takes really gruesome weather to keep him indoors.'

'I can see why you'd miss that,' I said, 'And I can see why, if I had that option every day, I might be willing to trade Belfast for it.'

Ryan and the others returned from their break and Tony instructed us to go on ours. He asked me if I wanted to see any of the gig; I shook my head. Alison also declined the offer. As we left, he turned to Ryan and another fairly tall steward and sent them down to the front, below the stage. He'd been told the team there could do with some extra staff as there had been more crowd surfing than expected. Ryan's eyes widened in fear. As he set off for the front of the hall, he looked back over his shoulder, almost pleading for someone to save him.

'He looks petrified,' Alison said.

'He is,' I replied. 'Still, it'll be character building.'

Back stage in the break room we met a few others, Stella among them, who was making short work of a Picnic.

'Do you not want to be in there tonight?' I asked her, tongue in cheek.

'My days of loud music are over,' she said. 'But I had my time.'

'Any interesting gigs?'

'I saw the Stones in the Ulster Hall in sixty-four,' she said, crumpling up the Picnic wrapper and pulling out a mint Aero from her handbag.

'Seriously?' I was impressed. 'What was that like?'

'I can't remember much of it. Me and my friend fought our way to the front, and there was this one bit, when Mick came near the edge of the stage. My friend Jean grabbed him by the ankle and yelled, 'Say something to me, Mick, say something!''

'And what did he say?' Alison asked.

'Fuck off,' Stella said, popping a piece of Aero into her mouth.

On the return journey, I couldn't help but stop to stick my head into the gig from the door at the side of the stage. I couldn't really see the band, but Stiff Little Fingers were assaulting the ears with 'Barbed Wire Love.' Momentarily, I wished I had opted for going in. The front of the crowd was lapping it up, pogoing and climbing all over each other. I couldn't help but wonder if Fret Boy was going to be a bit of an anti-climax.

In profile, I could see Sohail facing the audience below the stage; a one-man barrier to anyone who would even think about trying to get near the band. Beside him I could see the newly-positioned Ryan, looking like he had been thrown to the lions. Completely sucked in, I lost track of time until Alison tugged at my sleeve.

Back on the entrance barrier, everything was quiet again.

'Have you ever heard the Stiffs before?' I asked Alison.

'I've been listening to the Stiffs all my life,' she replied, 'My Dad is a big fan, he has most of their albums, and he doesn't believe in playing them quietly. In fact, he doesn't really believe in doing anything quietly; I kind of miss that.'

'Did you live with him?'

'Yeah,' she replied, 'Most of the time. I never really left home, but I split my time between there and Andy's house.'

'Andy is your boyfriend?' *The competition,* a part of my brain added. Another part added, *stop being a twat.*

'Yeah. Kind of the other half of my life. He and Dad have never seen eye to eye, so for a quiet life I try to keep them apart.'

'And your Mum?' I asked.

'Never really been a problem,' she said. She took a long pause. 'Mum died when I was fourteen.'

'Oh, ok. I'm sorry.' What else can be said in those moments?

'That's alright,' she smiled, 'It's a long time ago now … I'm still here.'

I nodded.

'How has your Dad taken the move to Belfast?' I asked, before adding, 'If that's not too personal a question ..? I feel like this has got very deep for a barrier outside a Fret Boy gig.'

She laughed again, and I had to physically stop myself from joining in.

'It's fine. Dad isn't wild about it, but we're still talking. He just doesn't like Andy; never has, and unless Andy changes radically, I don't think he ever will.'

'Personalities?'

'Sort of,' she began, 'Actually, no. It's actions. Dad is constant, reliable, thorough; if he says he's going to do something, he'll do it. Never late, never forgets, always there.' She paused.

'And Andy is the anti-Dad?'

She laughed again, and this time I allowed myself to smile.

'Pretty much. Scatty, messy, disorganised, forgetful; in ten years I think he's remembered my birthday about twice. He's constantly organising to go places and do things with his mates. On the upside, he's curious and spontaneous and adventurous, but ... he's never really in the room.'

'So it's taken a while for you two to actually live together?' Alison looked away for a moment and I wondered if I'd overstepped the mark. When she turned back, the look on her face told me I had. *Shit.*

'Yeah,' she said, 'Something like that.'

Dead air hung between us, until it was filled by the roar of the crowd as Fret Boy emerged on stage and the first few chords of 'Highway to Hell' rang out across the auditorium. I had to admit, it was loud rock played well.

'I've heard worse,' I said.

'Andy's not that bad,' she said.

'No, I meant Fret Boy.'

'Oh. Right.' She smiled, 'Still, Andy's not that bad. It's just that being attentive isn't his strong point.'

Something inside me wanted to argue the point. There's something wrong if the person you're with isn't good at paying you attention. I, by contrast, *was* good at paying attention. I was paying *very close* attention.

'So what about you?' Alison neatly switched topics. 'I know there's an ex and I know there are kids ...'

I shrugged. I doubted if this had any comparable effect on her. I made a mental note to develop a more adorable shrug.

'Little to tell. I'm just ambling along on my own.'

I felt like I wasn't giving much away, but it was hard to know where to start. The surroundings didn't seem to lend themselves to exploring the collapse of your marriage and its long-lasting consequences.

'Intentionally?' she asked.

'Am I intending to be on my own? No, that was definitely plan B!'

Even as I said it, I knew it wasn't true. There was no plan B. I had never dreamt there would be anything other than staying married and living together as a family. Alison didn't respond and I took that as an invite to carry on talking.

'I suppose you could say that neither Shirley or I were fully paying attention and it all kind of collapsed slowly, like bits falling off ...' I really wasn't sure what analogy I was going for, '... like bits falling off something that bits fall off, until there was ... no actual, assembled structure.'

A butchering of language, I know, but still better than trying to explain how we'd stumbled along in a rut until Shirley found someone else and then it all came apart with the force of a landmine, and the pieces were never going to be put back together.

Alison furrowed her eyebrows.

111

'Think of all the amazing lyrics you've listened to over the years. That's the best you've got?'

'Alright,' I said, trying harder, 'Like snow, gently sliding off an Alp in spring.'

'Very nice,' she replied, and I couldn't tell if she was being sarcastic or not, 'And the snow has never come back to the Alps?' I looked blankly at her.

'Not the original snow, no,' I answered, uncertainly, 'But maybe someday there'll be a fresh, seasonal coating ... to be honest, I think I've lost the run of this metaphor.'

'I was trying to ask if there had been anybody since your ex, but I can see where you were having difficulty.'

I laughed.

'No there hasn't been anybody else. Not yet.'

I have always wondered where the conversation would have gone next if it hadn't been so bluntly interrupted by Tony yelling as he ran past.

'Robbie! Inside now!'

He charged off into the concert hall and I followed him as quickly as I could. He was legging it down the pathway at the side of the crowd, and then, three quarters of the way along, he suddenly disappeared into the mass of bodies. I did my best to stay with him, unsure of where we were going or what we were getting ourselves into. I assumed it was a fight, that's the most likely incident when people are soaked in alcohol and crammed into a small space. I knew it couldn't be medical because I'd be the last person needed.

Tony was several bodies ahead of me and it took a few moments to catch up, trying to squeeze through spaces that weren't there. Some people got out of our road as best they could, other people just made us go round them. At last, I got a hand on Tony's shoulder.

'What's up?' I yelled over the noise of Motley Crue's 'Kick Start My Heart.'

Tony pointed towards the stage.

Not far from us, a body was being carried above the heads of the audience, in the traditional crowd surfing manner. Usually, the surfer is spread out like a starfish, allowing as many people as possible to push them upwards, but this body was waving its arms and legs in all directions. It was also wearing a yellow shirt and black trousers and, although it was hard to hear properly, appeared to be screaming.

It was Ryan.

As best we could, Tony and I attempted to squeeze our way through the crowd towards him, but we were beaten to it by other stewards, arriving from different directions. They managed to grab him by the legs and pull him down, until eventually his feet touched the floor. Tony, the closest supervisor on hand, took charge and led him to the side, out the door and into the corridor near the break room.

Another supervisor, female, slender and smaller in height than Ryan joined the group.

'Sorry kiddo,' she said, 'I really wasn't much use to you there. Are you alright?'

Wild-eyed, Ryan looked around him as if he had no idea where he was. Tony put his hand on his shoulder and Ryan flinched.

'It's ok, son,' Tony said, 'You're back on planet earth now.'

'I lost my shoes,' Ryan said suddenly. All of us looked down.

'No, you're fine,' Tony said, 'Both your shoes are still on your feet.'

Ryan looked down and studied them hard.

'Yes, they are,' he said, and then added, *'Is it nearly over?'*

'It is for you son,' said the female supervisor. Tony asked me to take Ryan and get him sorted with a cup of tea. I led him away while the others dispersed.

There were only a handful of people present in the break room, Stella was one of them. She had a cup of tea in one of Ryan's hands in no time, closely followed by a Double Decker in the other.

'What *exactly* happened?' Stella asked him, as the three of us sat together near the vending machine. Ryan didn't answer.

'He was crowd surfing, sort of,' I said. Ryan made a low moaning noise. 'But against his will it would seem.'

'Right,' Stella said, still perplexed, 'Never heard of that happening before.'

We sat together for a while, not really saying much. Slowly, Ryan came around.

'It was awful,' he said eventually, 'There were people coming out of the crowd and into the pit and we were helping them down. And there was this one guy coming, and I was holding out my arms to catch him, and then, suddenly, I was being pulled forward and I was away ...' he tailed off as his eyes widened.

'Yes,' Stella said, 'Definitely a new one.'

Other stewards came and went, and with Ryan talking again, and nibbling on his chocolate bar, I felt I could leave him in the capable hands of Stella. I headed back down the corridor towards the entrance and met Sohail coming the other way.

'Hi there!' he said loudly, patting me so hard on the shoulder I nearly fell over.

'Did you see what happened to Ryan?' I asked.

'Who's that?' he asked.

'The steward that got dragged into the crowd.'

'Oh, he's called Ryan,' Sohail said, 'Didn't know that. Yeah, I was standing beside him when it happened. *It was hilarious.* Two or three guys in the crowd just grabbed him and passed him back. And then everyone else joined in. They didn't put him down for ages!'

'They didn't put him down at all,' I said, 'We had to go in after him!'

'Oh ...' Sohail looked thoughtful, 'Is he alright?'

'Think so. Bit traumatised. He's in the break room now.'

'I'll see him in a minute then,' Sohail replied and wandered off down the corridor.

Back at the entrance the barriers and turnstiles had been removed for egress. Stewards were dotted about the entrance, generally trying to stand as far from the door as possible to avoid the draught. Alison was chatting to the female steward who had just started that night and I chose not to join them. *Best not to overdo it,* I thought. Instead, I hung around as close to the entrance to the hall as I could so I could hear the final strains of classic metal hits being sung passably by a bloke my age.

I was staring into space when my thoughts were suddenly interrupted by Niamh stopping right in front of me.

'Robbie,' she began earnestly, and in a low voice, 'Hi. Em ... I just wanted to say, look, I hope you don't mind me saying this, but, if you could just not tell anybody else about, you know, what I said to you in the car the other week?'

'Of course not,' I answered, completely truthfully, because it had never entered my mind to tell anybody. 'I haven't told anyone – and I wouldn't.'

'Ok,' she said, 'That's good. It's just, you know what the rumour mill is like round here, everybody knows everything, and anyway,' she took a deep breath, 'I've decided I was just being stupid. We're getting married and it'll all be fine.'

'Ok,' I said, 'If you're fine, then that's ok.'

She looked at me with a face so full of confusion it was clear she was anything but.

'Yes,' she said, 'I'm fine. *I'm totally fine.*'

She scuttled off into the throng of people who were starting to drift towards the exit as the concert came to a close.

The hall cleared quickly, the building was swept and there were no slips, trips or falls to report at the debrief. Walking out of the building, I waved goodnight to Alison at a distance and switched on my mobile phone. There were five missed calls and three text messages from Shirley asking me to call her, before a final one that said Paula was in hospital and I needed to phone her back.

5. Ward and worry

The Royal Victoria Hospital, Belfast, is where both my children were born, but it's also been the scene of visits to see older relatives coming to terms with the damage of a heart attack or stroke, as well as the overwhelming sadness that descended like a thick fog when Dad 's life ended. What had been, many years ago, a cosy family of four, became three, and every happy memory of growing up suddenly became tinged with loss. The hospital, for me, is primarily a place where things are never going to be the same again.

I found Shirley in the waiting room at the end of the ward. She exhaled forcefully when she saw me, and her shoulders lowered visibly, releasing the tension. She stood up and moved towards me, leaning over the low coffee table in the middle of the room with an outstretched arm. I leant over it also, not entirely sure what I was leaning into. She placed a hand on my shoulder, I placed a hand on her elbow and our heads moved past each other briefly before we parted again. If there is a check list for a hug, I'm not sure we ticked enough boxes.

'It's good you're here', Shirley said simply, sighing loudly again and sitting back down. I sat opposite her.

'What's the news?' I asked.

'Nothing yet,' Shirley replied, 'That's starting to worry me, I think they should have said something by now.'

I had phoned Shirley as I left the Auditorium. Paula had been complaining of a sore stomach for the last couple of days, but assumed it was indigestion or a cramp. By teatime the pain was worse and had moved from her stomach to her lower right abdomen. She had been unable to walk, and then unable to move and then she started vomiting. Shirley had phoned the local GPs' surgery and the doctor returned the call within minutes, advising to get Paula to A&E as soon as possible as she thought it sounded like an inflamed appendix. The doctors at A&E concluded that not only was it inflamed, it may have burst, requiring immediate surgery. By nine o'clock in the evening, she was heading into theatre.

I glanced at my watch, it was now twenty minutes to twelve, so I guessed there had been a couple of hours of surgery.

'Did they give any indication how long the operation would take?' I asked. Shirley shook her head.

'But I've been looking at a few sites on Google.'

I wasn't sure how helpful that was but I managed to keep my face in neutral and said nothing.

'A routine appendectomy can be quite quick, if they're doing a keyhole thing, but it takes longer if the appendix has actually burst,' Shirley informed me. 'Although that was on an American web site, so things might be different here.'

'I'm sure European appendectomies are much the same,' I suggested. She shot me a look. 'I'm just saying that's probably right, I can't imagine it's any different.'

She seemed to accept that I wasn't looking for a punchline. And I wasn't. I was fighting down a rising sense of panic. I had struggled to keep the car on the road to get there; thankfully it was only a ten-minute drive.

I don't think I've been a 'helicopter parent.' For the most part I've tried to let my kids find their own way in the world and be available when they needed me. But in moments of crisis, I want to fix things. I want to make things right. I want control, and I don't do so well when I can't have it.

'Should I go and find someone and ask?' I said. Shirley nodded, but as I stood up, she changed her mind.

'Wait,' she glanced at her watch, 'Let's leave it to midnight. They've been so nice ... I don't want to bother them.'

I settled into my seat again.

We sat in silence for a while. I would have fiddled with my phone, but the battery was all but done and I left it alone in case I needed it later. I tried not to stare at Shirley. Bleached blonde long hair, immaculate make up (as ever), still slim, but not as slim as she would have liked. Never ever as slim as she would have liked. New glasses, I noticed.

Shirley. My teenage crush, my youthful bride, my closest friend for the longest time, the mother of my children and, in some other universe, the partner I would grow old with. Yet here we were, connected in memory and family, and separated by our inability to heal what had fractured us.

The significance of our circumstances suddenly occurred to me. This was the first time we had been in a room alone together since just before we separated. The dark days of long, drawn-out arguments that petered out into weary discussions, then reignited into debates and became arguments again. After that, we communicated via phone, text, or email, and when we had to meet, there were other members of the family present. Or solicitors.

Shirley began to talk about the last couple of days. The first signs of pain, how it had spread, what the doctors had said. I asked a few questions, but for the most part I listened, grateful to be brought into the story. Paula had been in a lot of pain by the time they arrived at the hospital. Shirley described the moment when she had kissed Paula's forehead and watched as she was wheeled off to surgery.

'I've never felt so helpless,' she said simply, as two plump tears flowed down either side of her face. I stared at the coffee table, a lump in my throat.

At five minutes to midnight, a female doctor, dressed in blue scrubs and much younger than both of us, entered the room and sat two seats away from Shirley. I'm sure she introduced herself and I know she gave us some details of the operation, but beyond the phrases 'burst appendix' and 'open appendectomy' I can remember nothing else before the words, 'she's in recovery now and she'll be awake in a few hours.'

Relief flooded over me to the point that the room became blurry. Shirley asked a few questions and there were some details about Paula having stitches, needing antibiotics and remaining in hospital for a few days.

The doctor stood up to leave.

'Is she going to be ok?' I asked.

'Yes,' she said, 'There is a very, very high recovery rate for this type of procedure and she has youth on her side too. But it'll take a few weeks before she's back to the way she was.'

I nodded and thanked her.

The doctor asked us to let Paula sleep for a few hours before we saw her. We agreed to remain where we were and stay out of the way.

We each expressed our relief and, in various ways, repeated to each other what the doctor had said. Then we ran out of words and sat in silence. Not directly opposite each other, we both stared straight ahead, unable to connect. Perhaps unwilling to connect, and yet there we were, each of us with the only other person in the world who was feeling exactly the same way.

I left to get coffee. Shirley requested a packet of crisps and a muffin. I walked down the corridor smiling; comfort eating would be Shirley's way of getting through the next few hours. The muffins in the hospital shop were enormous and enticing so I also bought one for myself, along with a four pack of Twirls to keep our strength up.

I hovered over the magazines for a moment; it would help put the time in, but would it appear rude to read when the other person wasn't? I considered buying something for Shirley too, but balked at this because it might seem like I was making sure we didn't have to talk to each other.

This is how complicated it gets.

I returned to the waiting room with no reading material in hand. Shirley thanked me for the supplies and together we dissected our muffins on the coffee table.

'So,' I said, 'How have you been?' She shrugged, and I tried to remember a time when I loved every mannerism.

'I'm fine. Nothing new; still working away.'

Shirley had joined a solicitor's firm as a junior administrator not long after we were married. After several changes in partnerships later, she was now practice manager.

'Patterson and Mateer?'

'Patterson, Mateer and McMurray. Slightly less property these days, slightly more family. What about you?' I also shrugged.

'Still at Pathway, doing a bit more training and a bit less meeting anxious young people; it's all good.'

'And a wee bit of time in yellow?' she asked, nodding down at my unavoidable uniform. I grinned.

'Yeah, I'm still on four days a week, which I don't mind, but this gives a wee bit of extra money – and a bit of music and craic.'

She smiled. There were still echoes of the high energy, fast-talking teen from my youth, but she was older now and some of the intensity had drained away. Or maybe it was because it was after one in the morning and the adrenaline of the last few hours was being replaced with relief and exhaustion. We sat in silence for a few minutes, sipping coffee and spilling muffin crumbs.

'I've joined a gym,' she said suddenly. I raised an eyebrow involuntarily. 'Don't look at me like that! I have a personal training programme; I'm doing really well.'

I couldn't help but laugh.

'What's so funny?' she demanded, on the edge of taking offence. I shrugged.

'It's the thought of you lifting weights,' I said. *Covered in fluorescent lycra,* I thought, but I kept that to myself.

'I *can* lift weights!'

'I'm sure you can,' I assured her, 'It's really good you've joined a gym; I just never thought of you as a gym person.'

She sighed.

'No, me neither, I suppose. But needs must, and some of the girls from work are mad keen. They dragged me along to a free trial night and it wasn't so bad.' She stuffed the end of the mountainous muffin into her mouth. 'I'm not a big fan of lifting weights. Or the running machines either to be honest, but if you go with a group you do get some chat. It fills up an evening or two in the week.'

Shirley absently put her hand up to cover her mouth, as if she had said too much.

An emptiness hung in the air. Mary, Shirley's mother had died just over a year before, after a long period with cancer. Mary had needed a lot of care, especially at the end. I imagined this loss, and the time and space created by her absence, had not been easy. I didn't mention it, however. There was already enough emotion in the air and besides, this was an area of our lives we no longer shared.

I wanted to ask if she was seeing anyone else, but I didn't. That felt completely off limits. The gym story made me think there probably wasn't, and I began to wonder whether I preferred there to be someone or not. I didn't have any strong feelings about it, but I think I leant towards hoping there was, or that there would be. What was done was done; we were running on separate rails now, so why not wish Shirley some happiness?

'How's your Mum?' Shirley asked. I smiled.

'Same as always. Obsessed with 'Coronation Street,' what the neighbours are up to and forever in pursuit of a bargain.'

'Is she well?'

'She is. Still out doing the messages every day, still gets a bus everywhere. She never stops.'

We sat in silence again, while I felt bad for not mentioning Mary. She had always been very kind to me, and I'd stood beside Aaron at her graveside to pay my respects, but somehow she remained in my thoughts, and I didn't express them in words.

Eventually Shirley cleared the table of muffin cases, crumbs and empty coffee cups and put them in the bin in the corner of the room. She dusted down the front of her clothes and picked up her handbag.

'I'm going to go to the loo,' she said, 'I might pick up a magazine on the way back, is there anything you want?'

'See if they have a copy of *Q*,' I said.

*

We read for a while and slept for a while, though it was hard to call it sleep as waiting room chairs are not made to allow your body to relax without cutting off some of its circulation. At four o'clock, another older couple joined us. Their son had been in a motorbike accident and was now in for what seemed like fairly complicated surgery. They were upset and didn't offer details. We didn't ask.

Just after five, a nurse in a red uniform put her head round the door, checked who we were, and asked us both to step out into the corridor.

'How is she?' Shirley asked.

'Paula is fine,' she answered, 'She's awake, but remember she's coming round from a general anaesthetic, so she's groggy and a bit disorientated. You can go and see her, but I would ask that you only stay for a few moments because she needs to rest; that's the best thing for her.'

We readily agreed and followed the nurse to recovery.

I'm not sure what I had expected, but aside from Paula being a little paler, she looked exactly as she always did; dark brown hair, Shirley's wide eyes, my hooked nose, and high cheek bones that may have come from her granny Mary. Her eyes were closed. The nurse touched her lightly on the arm and she opened them slowly.

'You've got some visitors,' the nurse said.

Paula nodded and the nurse stepped away, allowing Shirley to sit down on the bench at the top of the bed. I hesitated, and then sat next to her.

'Hi, love,' Shirley said, 'How are you?'

'I'm fine,' Paula replied looking directly at her mother. Her eyes closed again. 'I'm just really tired.'

'I know, you've been through a lot,' Shirley said, 'Are you feeling alright? Are you in any pain?' Paula shook her head.

'What time is it?' she mumbled, eyes half-open.

'Just after five in the morning,' I said. Paula's eyes blinked fully open and she seemed surprised.

'Oh. Dad. Hey,' she said, 'You're here.' She closed her eyes again.

'Yeah, I'm here,' I said, which was all I could say because there was suddenly a lump in my throat. *Of course I'm here.*

'I'm sorry,' Paula said.

'What are you sorry for?' Shirley asked.

'I can't stay awake.'

'Go back to sleep,' Shirley said firmly, not that Paula had any option. 'It's what you need. I'll come back later with all your stuff.'

Paula mumbled something neither of us could make out, and then both Shirley and I stepped away from the bed. I wiped both my eyes. Shirley touched me lightly on the elbow as we made our way out of the room, glancing over our shoulders as we left.

The nurse was waiting for us outside.

'How long will she need to sleep for?' Shirley asked.

'She'll be sleeping a lot for the next couple of days,' the nurse replied, 'But she'll be in better shape in another few hours. By mid-morning she'll likely be a bit more with it. We'll take good care of her; get yourselves some rest and don't be hurrying back. She's not going anywhere for a while yet.'

I nodded, as did Shirley, though I knew she'd be back within the hour if she could.

We walked in silence into the car park, where the early morning summer light was already bright and strong. We stopped at the pay point.

'Are you alright?' Shirley asked quietly. I nodded. 'You?'

'I'll be happier when I see her up and about,' she said, 'But it'll come. Not fast enough, but it'll come.'

Our cars were in the same direction, so we walked on together in silence until Shirley spoke, just as we were parting.

'There's a chance here, you know,' she said.

'A chance for ..?'

'For you and Paula.'

I nodded. Another lump formed in my throat.

'There never seems to be the time to ...' I started to say, but I couldn't finish.

'Yeah,' Shirley sighed. 'But there's an opening now.'

'I know,' I agreed. The surprise in Paula's voice echoed in my head. 'It can't be like this ...'

'Get some rest,' Shirley said, 'You were working tonight. Last night. Whenever that was. Come back later in the day.'

I nodded again, I seemed to be doing a lot of that.

We parted, each going to our separate cars. Tears streamed down my face as I pulled away.

*

Saturday went by in a sleep-deprived blur. By mid-afternoon, Paula was awake and talking; sleepy, but making sense. Shirley and I left late afternoon but came back in the evening. We kept our visit short, however, as Paula was tired.

By Sunday I was properly awake and alert again. Visiting time, both afternoon and evening were packed with family and a couple of Paula's friends too. There was much banter, both inside the ward and outside in the corridor as numbers were restricted.

On Monday I was back at work and with appointments that couldn't be moved around, I could only visit in the evening. I brought my mother along, who gave Paula a bottle of Lucozade and three bags of Quavers, because when Paula was five she'd said those were her favourite crisps and her granny had never forgotten. Shirley, her sister and a couple of Paula's cousins also visited, and the bedside was noisy.

I had spoken to Paula, albeit in a small group, for three days straight; something which hadn't happened since before Shirley and I separated.

On Tuesday morning, I was just leaving a coffee shop after meeting with a young person, when I picked up a voicemail to say my lunch time appointment was going to be postponed. An emergency root canal treatment, which was described in considerably more detail than was necessary, meant they couldn't meet with me. With a gap in my day, I decided to chance my arm with an out-of-visiting-hours call at Paula's ward. Visiting wasn't supposed to start until two, but I hoped there wouldn't be too much fuss if I called in a little bit earlier.

I rang the buzzer at ward entrance, fully expecting to be given the Spanish Inquisition about why I was there early and having fully prepared a whole sob story about busy working hours and this was the only time when I could get to see my only daughter. I needn't have bothered; I was buzzed in, and no one asked me anything.

Paula was sitting up in bed reading a magazine with her earphones in. She didn't notice me until I was right at the end of the bed.

'Dad!' she said, more loudly than was necessary, before pulling the earphones from her ears.

'Hi, love,' I replied, leaning forward again, wanting to kiss her on the head, but chickening out and patting her hair instead. Her eyebrows furrowed in confusion, but she quickly recovered a more neutral expression. I sat down on the edge of the thin bench at the side of her bed and leant one arm gently on the rail.

'So, how are you today?'

'Pretty good,' she replied, 'All things considered. I'm not feeling as tired, I'm not feeling as sore, and I've more of an appetite.'

'All good signs. Any word of when you'll get out?' She shook her head.

'I normally see a doctor late morning, at least I did yesterday and today. She just checked my charts earlier and asked me how I was feeling, but she didn't say anything more.'

'Are you fed up yet?'

'Not yet,' she said, 'At the start I was sleeping so much, but now that I've a bit more energy I don't think it'll be too long in coming.' She smiled. I remembered again how much I missed that. 'I'm already missing Netflix.'

'Can you not get it on your phone?' She pulled a face.

'I can, but the wi-fi is patchy. Lots of usage I suppose. Maybe I'll be home for the weekend.'

I looked around at the room. There were three other beds, two of which were occupied by women closer to my age than Paula's, both of whom had earphones in and were busy tapping at their mobiles. Staff came and went in the corridor, but the room was quiet.

'What are the others like?' I asked quietly.

'I don't really know them,' Paula said. She nodded at the woman in the opposite corner of the room. 'She doesn't talk to anybody and has her headphones in all the time. This one,' she nodded at the bed next to hers, hidden by a partly-pulled curtain, 'Was in surgery yesterday morning so she's been asleep most of the time, but we moaned about the food together last night.'

'Was it bad?'

'It was probably ok if you like Spaghetti Bolognese, but ...'

She tailed off. She didn't need to finish the story. Spaghetti Bolognese used to be Paula's favourite meal until, one night when she was eleven, a viral stomach bug caused her to projectile across the kitchen floor. The sight of spaghetti sliding across ceramic tiles, which offered little by way of traction, was enough to stop her eating it forever.

'What about the staff?' I asked, changing the subject.

'Staff are all fine. The doctor is really nice, but she's here for, like, three minutes. The blue nurses never stop, the other ones in pink ...'

'Auxiliary nurses,' I added.

'Yeah, they're more chatty. The cleaner never stops talking, she's good craic.'

'That's good,' I said, and then realised I was running out of things to talk about.

'What are you reading about?' I asked, and then looked at the magazine on her lap. It was upside down, but the headline was clear enough; 'Five things every girl should know about the female orgasm.'

'Never mind,' I said hurriedly.

Paula reddened, as did I. Both of us looked away.

'Are you off work this morning?' she asked. I explained what had happened but skipped the root canal details.

'I was kind of hoping I'd get a little bit of time to talk to you,' I began, deciding that it was now or never, 'On your own.'

She gave me eye contact for a split second and then looked down.

'Yeah?' she said.

I took a deep breath and made my request.

'I would like a bit of time with you. Just you and me. We haven't done that in a while.'

She shook her head.

'No,' she said quietly. There was a long pause, and then she added, 'You haven't been around much.'

I took another deep breath and moved out of the shallows.

'I've wanted to be,' I said.

She looked up quickly.

'Well, there was nothing stopping you,' she said, tension in her voice.

'I know that,' I said, 'But it's been hard to know where to begin, we've been ...' I chose my words carefully, '... we haven't been doing things together for so long.'

She nodded and seemed to relax a little.

'I think I'm too old to be taken to the zoo and McDonald's.'

'You'll never be too old to be taken for a milk shake,' I said.

She smoothed the bed covers and turned over the page in her magazine, which I was grateful for, because the orgasm-related headline was still catching my eye.

Paula looked straight at me.

'Maybe we could stay in touch a little bit better when I get out of here,' she said. I nodded, but that's not what I was asking for.

'I was hoping for a little bit more than that,' I said, and then I pushed the envelope, 'I'm your Dad, I want to have more than an occasional text.'

'This isn't the time,' she said.

I looked around the room. The other two patients still had their headphones on. The woman to Paula's side appeared to have fallen asleep, either that or she consciously had her mouth open and was drooling.

'When is the time?' I asked, 'I know this is awkward, but I feel like I miss a lot. I've missed you a lot.'

'I don't want to do this now,' she said quietly, but firmly.

I chose to keep going.

'I don't want it to be the way it has been.'

'Well that's how you made it,' she snapped.

Her voice didn't rise in volume, but her words had the ferocity of gunfire. 'You left, and you didn't look back.'

There it was. Everything Paula had wanted to say for years.

I took both my arms off the rail and leant away from the bed. Both of us stared down at the covers. She rolled the flex of her earphones back and forth between the index finger and thumb of her right hand. Resisting the urge to respond, I chose not to speak for a minute.

Life happens. Minute by minute. Shirley and I slowly did less together and we didn't notice how far we had navigated away from each other, until there was someone else. Shirley gets no credit for bringing them into it, but at least she told me herself. Instantaneously, the ground shifted. I couldn't regain the balance I had always taken for granted and we fell headlong into questions and unwelcome answers, and disbelief and damage and blame.

They say there's a law of diminishing returns. In our case increasing amounts of information and discussion led to a decreasing capacity to maintain constructive conversation and give ourselves a chance to get out of the hole we were in. She didn't know what she wanted, which was at least honest, and I didn't want to hang around waiting to see.

And so we had a choice. We could have carried on what seemed like endless discussion and hurt-soaked argument, but it left us worn out and weary and no closer to fixing the damage. It seemed to me like the relationship was beyond repair and the best way forward was to accept it and try to make the best of it. I left, and yeah, in some ways, I didn't look back.

'I didn't want to leave,' I said, 'But I couldn't stay.'

'Couldn't? You didn't try too hard.'

Every syllable was an accusation. I didn't want to argue. I didn't want to bring Paula into the pain of the time. The hurt of betrayal. The bite and tear of unwanted reality. The helplessness of knowing the options were limited and none of them looked any good. Besides, I didn't think Paula knew anything about what had really happened, I certainly had never told her, and I wasn't going to bring it up now.

'There wasn't any other way,' I said again, softly, 'Things changed, there wasn't a way to go back. It was …'

'Don't you dare say it was complicated,' she hissed, 'I'm not stupid, I know it was complicated. Life's always complicated.'

And then her tone changed. In one breath her anger dissipated and her sadness leaked out.

'But life was good. We had a good life. Aaron and I had happy childhoods, and then it stopped, suddenly. It was over in a weekend.'

'It took a lot longer than a weekend.'

'Not much longer. All of a sudden you were packing your bags and driving off down the road.'

'I moved round the corner.'

'That doesn't matter,' her eyes began to fill up, and her voice tightened, 'I don't care where you were, you weren't home anymore.'

Two large tears rolled down her face. I lifted a tissue from the box on the set of drawers at her bedside and handed it to her.

'You could have stayed,' she said flatly, 'It could have been different.'

I had never come closer to telling Paula about Brendan. It was the perfect card to play. I would be the victim and Paula might like me more. Shirley would be the villain and I might wreck the relationship Paula had with her. I sat quietly, however, until Paula broke the silence.

'It didn't last long with Brendan,' she said.

'What?' the shock was like being drenched in ice-cold water.

Paula shrugged.

'I don't think it lasted very long,' she said again. 'He called at the house a couple of times in the weeks after you left. Mum just said he was a friend, she never said he was ...'

'We'd split up ...' I began to say, uncertain of what she knew. Paula stared at me.

'I was the third person to know,' she said.

'What ..? How did you know?'

She took a deep breath.

'Friday afternoons, we had this stupid personal development session. Half the class used to beak off and the teachers never really cared. I didn't skip it every Friday, but sometimes Claire and I would get out of school at lunch time and jump on the first bus that came along and go and find a chippy and a park.'

'You got a *bus?*'

It was a stupid thing to say, but I was reeling.

'Well we weren't going to hang around anywhere near school.'

Fair point.

'We were in this park one Friday, just finished our chips, when Claire said, 'Is that your Mum over there?' And it was. We could see her on a bench at the other side of the park, sitting on her own.'

Paula's earphone flex was now being twiddled into a blur.

'We were just sitting on our blazers on the grass and we moved away behind some bushes so that we couldn't be seen, but we kept watching her. And then Brendan turned up.'

She stopped talking and stared out the window at the grey sky hanging over the red brick buildings below us.

'I knew who Brendan was because he'd been in Mum's work for years. Any time I had to meet her there, he'd say hello. He sat down next to Mum. And then they kissed.' She took a deep breath. 'And that's when it all fell apart.'

Another tear ran down her face. I lifted the box of tissues over to her. Neither of us spoke for a long time.

'So, you know how complicated it was?' I said eventually. She nodded.

'Does Mum know you know this?' She shook her head.

'I don't want her to,' she said.

'I'm not going to tell her,' I replied, 'But I'm sorry you've had to carry that all this time.'

For the first time for many years, I picked up her hand and held it in mine.

'Were you not hurt by it?' she said.

'By Mum and ...'

'Yeah.'

'Of course, I was hurt by it. I was crushed ... devastated.'

I tried not to let any irritation creep into my tone, but how could she think anything otherwise?

'It didn't seem that way,' Paula said simply.

I forced myself not to talk for a moment.

'Why did it not seem that way?'

She shrugged.

'You seemed sad. Flat. Like you had given up. You did give up.'

There was an element of truth in everything she said.

'One person can't save a relationship; it's a two-person thing,' I said. 'We talked and talked and then some. But in the end, it seemed like the best way forward was to go our separate ways.'

'I lost Aaron too,' she said, 'He went to university at the end of that summer.'

'I know,' I said, 'I lost him through distance, and I lost you even though you were just round the corner.'

'You never bothered.' She took her hand away.

'You were never available.'

'I was angry. I wanted it to go back to being the way it was.'

'And what was I meant to do?' I could feel a level of anger rising in me and I couldn't help it. 'Follow you around until you talked to me? You were sixteen, seventeen, life was opening up, you were making your own plans and I wasn't in them.'

Both of us looked away, tears in our eyes, lumps in our throats, hurt in our very bones. We had spent a long time avoiding the things that needed to be said, and now they had caught up with us.

'You let go,' she said quietly, 'I didn't want you to let go.'

And suddenly I saw what I had been missing all along. She didn't want to avoid me; she wanted to be found. My head and heart went back to when she was three or four years old; big smile and pig-tails. We played hide and seek around the house. She was small enough to fit in the most curious of spaces, and she would always giggle to give herself away. Because what's the point of playing hide and seek, if you're not going to be found? She always wanted to be found. The guilt from not having tried hard enough to find her was overwhelming.

'Alright?' A skinny figure in a black leather jacket appeared at the end of the bed and threw a Fry's Chocolate Cream bar towards Paula. It landed next to her magazine. 'That'll keep you going,' he said, sitting down on a chair opposite me.

'How you doing?'

He reached out his hand to me, across the bed. Dazed, I shook it without much energy.

'Dad,' Paula said, 'This is Deano.'

'Hiya,' Deano said brightly, 'You're her Dad, then?'

'Yes,' I said, taking in his face properly for the first time. If ever there was a moment to *not* do this introduction, it was now.

'Jeez, it's warm in here,' he said, standing up again and removing his leather jacket, which he then hung over the rail at the foot of the bed. His face seemed familiar, but I couldn't place it.

'You don't really see her much though, do you?' he asked.

'Deano ...' Paula said, widening her eyes at him. Deano looked back blankly.

'What?'

Paula simply sighed and changed the subject.

'You on your lunch break?' she asked.

'Aye. Well, sort of.'

'He's a rep for Doritos,' Paula explained, 'So he's always out and about in the wee van.'

'Deano from Doritos?' I asked.

'That's what they call me,' Deano said proudly, a smile spreading across his face. Once again, I tried to place him; he seemed so familiar.

'I had a couple of deliveries out in Holywood, so I thought I'd stop in on my way,' he said.

'But your office is in east Belfast,' Paula said.

'Aye,' Deano agreed.

'So it's not on your way,' Paula said.

'It is if you drive this way first,' Deano replied, without a hint of humour. He turned to me. 'Do you like Doritos?' he asked.

'Eh ... yeah,' I said, 'They're alright.'

And then it hit me. Deano had been the ringleader of the group of East Side supporters who had given me such a hard time at the FA Cup Final.

'So,' I turned to Paula, 'You and Deano here are ... an item?'

'I'm not really sure what an item is,' Paula replied, 'But if you're asking if we're going out together, then yeah we are.'

141

'About six months,' said Deano.

'Over a year now,' Paula corrected him.

The nervous tension of the previous conversation had left me ragged. The adrenaline was still coursing and I couldn't keep the edge out of my voice.

'Right.'

There was a short pause before Deano spoke.

'Chilli Heatwave are flying off the shelves at the moment, I don't know what's going on.'

'Wait,' Paula's tone cracked like a whip. She glared at me. 'What do you mean, *'right'*?'

On a different day, and a different time, I might have made light of it, shrugged it off and said, 'oh, nothing.' But on that day, at that time, I chose to steamroller on in.

'Deano and I have already met,' I said heavily.

'Have we?' he asked, 'Do you run a sweetie shop?'

'No, I was a steward at the FA Cup Final.'

'I was at the FA Cup Final.'

'I know,' I replied, 'You were the wee bollocks that had a banner that said, 'Fuck off Linfield'.'

'Aye! That's right,' Deano, missing my tone entirely, eagerly confirmed the story. 'I remember making that. Me and Shitepants in his dad's garage, we found all this old bicycle paint 'cause his Da used to have a shop where ...'

'And then I couldn't get the bloody thing off you.'

'Did you take it off me?'

'I did. Well, I tried to, it was actually another steward who managed to get it off you ...'

'Right, right,' Deano interrupted, 'I wondered what happened to that banner. I don't remember any of it, to be honest, I was so *totally blocked* that day. I'd been drinking Smirnoff Ice from lunchtime, and then we kept drinking after the game. But – and here's the funny thing – when I woke up the next morning I was in this house, face down at the kitchen table on top of a Monopoly board. When I sat up, I had a property card stuck to my face!' Deano started to laugh uncontrollably.

'Where was that?' Paula asked.

'Pentonville Road, I think. One of them blue ones, anyway.'

'Not the card, *the house,*' Paula continued, 'Where was it?'

'Absolutely no idea,' Deano said, 'But it was near a wee bakery 'cause we all got sausage rolls. Very good for hangovers you know.'

I had heard enough. I stood up and said something about needing to get back to the office. I'm sure Paula could see the contempt on my face.

In an alternative universe, I hugged Paula at the end of the most honest conversation we'd ever had, and we promised everything would be different. Instead, I said I would text her later on, mumbled something to Deano, stuffed my hands into my pockets and ambled off out of the room and down the corridor.

I was heading for the exit, when I almost bumped into an older man in a tartan dressing gown and slippers who had just walked out of another room.

'Sam!' I said, recognising him instantly. For a split second, he looked blankly at me, then his face seemed to register something close to shock, before he recovered his composure.

'It's eh ...'

'Robbie,' I helped him out, 'From Safe & Sound.'

'I know that,' Sam said, 'I just can't do names. I never forget a face. Names I can never remember. How are you?'

'I'm grand, but how are you? You're the one in here.'

'Ach now,' he replied, and seemed to search for an answer, 'I've had a few aches and pains. Stomach issues mainly. They think it might be an ulcer, but nobody's quite sure.'

'Flip. Have you been in long?'

'A couple of days. But I should be home soon.'

'That's good.'

Sam looked away, eyes darting in all directions. I see that look all the time, from young people looking out of the conversation.

'I was just in seeing my daughter there – burst appendix. Gotta rush back to the office now. Hope everything is ok with you.'

I clapped my hand on his shoulder.

'I'll be grand,' Sam replied.

I made my way to the exit.

6. Back gate and bad temper

Some people stay home for the Twelfth of July celebrations and scarper afterwards; others go away before it begins. Either way, the net effect on the stewarding industry is that July becomes downtime as outdoor gigs tend to wind up in June and don't kick off again until August.

It was a surprise, therefore, when Helen from Safe & Sound phoned me near the end of July to ask if I was free to work the following Saturday in Ballyclare.

'I need a few staff to do all day, from nine in the morning through to ten at night.'

I had nothing planned, and to be honest I'd been a bit bored. Work was slow and I hadn't had a stewarding shift from the end of June. I had decided to try to book a week away somewhere warm in the autumn, so I only took a few days and spent them painting the kitchen. White and 'Putting Green' if you're interested.

Once again, I made the mistake of agreeing to the shift without asking what it was. I checked the app on my phone; an event called 'Big Boots in Ballyclare.' Google told me it was a line dancing and country music festival, kicking off in the afternoon and running through into the evening. Not having had any previous experience of line dancing, or much interest in the kind of music people in a line dance to, I had no idea what to expect, but I was concerned about what several hours of cheesy country music might do to my mental health.

145

Saturday came and, an experienced steward now, I loaded up the car boot with my dedicated Safe & Sound backpack, complete with lunch, water and snacks, cap, raincoat, extra fleece, waterproof trousers, sunglasses and sun cream. Welcome to the north of Ireland; any weather eventuality can happen. I drove across Belfast and north to Ballyclare on the newly-widened A8. Not a long drive; I was there long before 'Born in the USA' had completed its first play through.

Smooth tarmac and empty roads give a man space to think. I wondered if I'd remembered to lock the back door again after I had put last night's empty pizza box into the blue bin. I wondered if pizza boxes could go in the blue bin. I wondered if I was eating too much fast food. I wondered if I'd spend the rest of my life living on my own.

I'm not looking for sympathy, but up until Shirley and I split, I'd never lived on my own. I don't like it. Sure, I get to play Dylan whenever I want. The TV remote is always mine. The bathroom is always free and long hair never clogs up the sink. But these things mean little when set against leaving the house and not saying goodbye to anyone. Or wishing yourself goodnight. Or cooking meals for one.

My Ford Focus ate up the miles on what was a bright morning with all the signs of a warm day to come. Not for the first time a stray thought wandered into my head asking if things could have worked out differently with Shirley. Not for the first time I let it pass with little interrogation. We did what we did, and it was done. Anyway, life wasn't so bad, we were all still alive and still talking. I had my own space, good work and a mother who had just left me a twelve pack of chocolate mini rolls that were on offer in Tesco's. I was happy.

I turned off the motorway for Ballyclare while I continued my life assessment. Aaron was in London and always busy, and Paula was round the corner and hard to reach. The acrimony had dissipated with Shirley, but it's hard to count that as a positive. Meaningful work was a definite plus point, and you couldn't put a value on a supply of cut-price supermarket products, but God the positives list seemed short.

So was I happy? I thought I was when I left the house, but now I wasn't so sure. Evidence of happiness was sorely lacking.

As I turned into the car park at Six Mile Water park, another stray thought entered my head. *What about getting a tortoise? You've always wanted a tortoise.* I like dogs, but dogs are a commitment. A tortoise, however, was more self-sufficient.

This was immediately countered by another thought. *The gateway to happiness is not getting a tortoise; get a grip.* I turned off the engine, physically shook my head and got out of the car.

Six Mile Water Park is a green strip either side of the river of the same name, almost running into Ballyclare's town centre. Our instructions were to park with the organisers and providers' vehicles at the southern end of the venue. The festival marquees had

147

been placed centrally at the widest part of the park. Parking there was limited, so supply vehicles would come and go via this remote entrance.

A handful of other stewards were gathered around an open boot in the makeshift car park putting on fluorescent yellow vests, but there was no sign of a supervisor yet. I immediately spotted Sick Note, Bleedin' Obvious and Been There. Choosing the lesser of three evils I wandered over to Sick Note.

'How's it going? Not many of us here, is there?' I said, looking around me.

'It doesn't open until midday, so most staff are coming in later. They need people to do the gates.'

Never having 'done' a gate before, I wasn't sure what this would entail.

'Who's in charge?'

'Leanne. She was here earlier giving out the vests,' he said, 'But then she cleared off.'

A long pause followed. I was about to fill it by asking him how he had been, but I caught myself in time.

The group stood around chatting about the weather and the lack of gigs at this time of year. We tried to compare notes about line dancing, but nobody knew anything. Leanne returned eventually and called order.

'Well, I thought today was going to be pretty straightforward, but we've already had our first curve ball,' she began.

Apparently, a group of Independent Free Presbyterians, a fundamentalist breakaway from the Free Presbyterians, had turned up to protest at the park gates. This was owing to an unfortunate typo in the local newspaper, which had advertised the event as 'Big Boobs in Ballyclare.'

'What type of event did they think it was going to be?' someone asked.

'I don't know,' Leanne answered, 'And I was too scared to ask.'

'Is nine o'clock not a bit early for a protest?' I asked.

'The minister still has his sermon to finish off so they're only going to stay until one.'

'Why are they still protesting, if there's no, eh ... boobs?'

'They thought about it,' Leanne explained, 'But since they're also opposed to line dancing, they decided to stay. One of them is away to Woolworth's now to get a big marker to change some of their signs.'

'How many of them are there?' someone else asked.

'Four,' Leanne said, 'The minister, another older man, a younger man with an accordion and a young woman, probably in her late teens. Whoever is on the front gate needs to keep an eye. We've agreed they can protest outside the gate as long as they don't block the entrance.' She took a deep breath. 'We're running a little late here, so let's crack on.'

We were each put into groups and sent to different entrances into the park. Sick Note and I were asked to remain at the back gate in order to control whatever traffic was coming and going. Our orders were simple, anyone organising or contributing to the festival had already been given a bright green badge to display on their dashboard. They *and only they* had permission to park in the grounds.

'No badge, no entry,' Leanne said.

Sick Note and I nodded in agreement. Leanne went off to check on the other positions.

The entrance ticked over with a steady flow of contributors eager to get set up for what they hoped would be a busy afternoon. I had no sense of the number of line dancing and country music fans who would be descending on Ballyclare, but the amount of activity seemed to suggest there would be plenty.

The first few vehicles were straightforward; a pick-up truck stacked high with PA gear, a tractor and trailer stacked high with straw bales and a large white van with 'Magherafelt Line Dancing Supplies' emblazoned across the back. All had the required green badge and were admitted without question. The trouble began with the red-haired woman in the Range Rover who did not have one.

'Tommy told me to swing the Rover in here,' she insisted.

'I'm really sorry,' I said as apologetically as I could, 'I don't know who Tommy is and our instructions are to make sure nobody parks without a green badge.'

She didn't attempt to argue the point and, with a dramatic roll of the eyes, drove off. The two cars behind her both had badges, and we were back on track. Five minutes later, however, Leanne returned.

'Did a woman come to this gate in a red Range Rover?' she asked.

'A few minutes ago, yeah,' Sick Note said. 'But she didn't have a green badge, so we didn't let her in,' he added proudly.

'That was the organiser's wife,' Leanne replied, 'And now he's pissed off about it.'

'Where is she now?' I asked.

'On her way back. Let her in.'

Tommy's wife duly arrived and both Sick Note and I waved her into the park. She did not make eye contact with either of us.

'How were we supposed to know?' Sick Note asked, sounding slightly hurt.

'Wouldn't worry about it.'

By mid-morning the coming and going of vehicles had almost stopped. Sick Note and I relaxed in the sunshine of what was building towards a hot afternoon. The Six Mile Water gently flowed past and we agreed there were worse places to earn a few quid. Sick Note seemed in remarkably good health. He did regale me with a story of how he had had his tonsils out the previous year after an abscess in his throat, and in turn I shared some of the gory details of Paula's burst appendix, but aside from that he was much brighter than he had been at the FA Cup Final.

Our relaxed state was interrupted by the horn of a blue Corsa and an agitated young woman behind the wheel.

'Can I park here?' she asked, hanging out of the window.

'Do you have a green badge?' I asked.

'What's that?'

'You have to have a green badge to park here, otherwise you follow the signs for car parking nearer the town centre and walk in.'

'This is an emergency,' she said, 'Nuala McNaney forgot her make-up bag and I'm delivering it.'

'Who's Nuala McNaney?' Sick Note asked.

The woman in the car stared at him in a hostile manner.

'She's a country singer, and she's the first act on, so she needs this *now*.'

'Is she on at one?' I asked. The woman nodded.

'I need to get this to her as fast as I can.'

Sick Note, however, was doing the math.

'It's half eleven now,' he said, 'So she's got ninety minutes yet. You'd have plenty of time to park ...'

The woman's withering stare stopped him in mid-sentence.

I looked around me, there were still a few spaces left for cars and so I took an executive decision.

'Look, we're not supposed to let you park here, but since this is an emergency,' in the broadest sense of the word, 'You could park here briefly, leave off the make-up, and then come back and take your car to the main car park. Would that be alright?'

The young woman readily agreed this would be acceptable and a catastrophic episode in Nuala McNaney's career was averted.

The rest of the morning ticked by without incident. Sick Note and I covered each other for breaks. He sat in his car for ten minutes playing with his phone, and later I took a wander out to the main entrance to see what was happening.

With an hour to go until opening finishing touches were being applied to some impressive mountains of hay bales and there were lots of people in Stetsons hurrying about. The smell of ten types of fried food – the onions especially – made me hungry.

The four-person protest at the front gate was still going. The minister, clad all in black, held an open bible, and was attempting to preach to anyone who would stop long enough to listen. At that point, it was only me. Behind him stood an older man with a large sign in either hand. One had the biblical text, 'I have come that you may have life and have it to the full,' and the other that had previously said, 'No Boobs in Ballyclare', but now had the word 'boobs' scored out and the words 'line dancing' untidily squeezed in. Beside him the younger-looking man was playing his accordion gently in the background. Even though he was only meandering his way through a hymn tune, he was working in harmonies and variations that I had to admit were pretty easy on the ear.

I was approached by the fourth member of the protest, a young woman in a plain grey dress and black beret. She smiled and held out a small leaflet. I didn't really want it, but I didn't want to refuse her, so I took it. The title was 'That was your life' and it told a short cartoon story that began cheerfully enough but ended up with the central character being led off by the Devil to burn in hell for eternity.

I listened to the accordion playing for another minute or two, before nodding my appreciation and heading back to the far end of the park to check for green badges and watch the river flow.

The festival kicked off at one. Right on cue we could hear the dulcet tones of Nuala McNaney and her three-chord brand of country music drifting across the park. Leanne appeared just as a battered Volkswagen Tiguan pulled into the entrance and a hassled looking thirty-something bloke in a checked shirt, shoestring necktie and immaculately manicured beard leant out of the window.

'I need to drop off two jugs!' he announced.

'I'm sorry?' Leanne asked.

'I need to drop off these jugs,' he said, gesturing behind him to the back of the car. 'They're not wee, you know.'

'Ok?' Leanne seemed confused.

'They're musical instruments; I'm talking *great big jugs here*!'

'Don't tell the protestors,' I chipped in.

'*What?*' Leanne and the driver said together.

'Nothing.'

'This car park is reserved. To park here you have to have a green badge from the organiser,' Leanne insisted, 'You'll have to park nearer the town and walk back.'

The driver looked concerned.

'They're heavy yokes, you know,' he said, 'Both of thems is bass jugs, and they didn't have room for them with the rest of the band's gear, that's why I had to bring them on late, only I had to finish up the milking first.'

I could see Leanne still wasn't quite understanding.

'Right ... so ...' she began uncertainly, 'You have two jugs that belong to a band?'

'Gareth McGurnaghan's Big Jug Posse.'

'Is posse the collective noun for big jugs?' I asked.

Both of them ignored me.

Realising there was enough space for a few more cars, Leanne decided the easiest way out of this conversation was to let him park. The man with the immaculate beard thanked her profusely and then asked if it would be possible to borrow one of 'yer strappin' lads' to carry the other jug. Leanne hid the disbelief on her face and instructed Sick Note to carry a jug, then take his half-hour lunch break, before coming back to cover mine.

Together, Sick Note and the jug enthusiast lifted two large ceramic jugs out of the Tiguan and staggered off in the direction of the marquees.

'You couldn't make this shit up,' Leanne said under her breath.

*

Half an hour came and went. Nuala McNaney's songs of love gone wrong were replaced by a more upbeat electric combo, whose lead guitarist seemed to be able to play every note on the fret, but whose lead vocalist had a voice like a variable speed angle grinder. Their set finished just after half two, and there was still no sign of Sick Note. I wondered if he had been sent to cover another station, but I also knew that Leanne would have told me. I was beginning to wonder if he had lived up to his name and been struck down with something, when, to my delight, I saw Alison walking towards me across the park.

'They were having a welly throwing competition,' she informed me, 'Except not a welly, a cowboy boot, you know, with a big heel on it. And that eejit ...' I presumed she meant Sick Note, '... wandered into the middle of the area where the boots were landing.'

I started to laugh.

'It's not funny,' she said seriously, before she too began to giggle, 'One of them hit him square on the back of the head and knocked him out cold. He was just lying there, face down on the grass.'

'Did you see it?' I asked.

'No,' she said, 'Not live,' she added, a little shamefacedly.

'What?'

'I saw it on YouTube.'

'It's on YouTube already?!'

'Ballyclare has excellent connectivity, who knew?'

Sick Note had been out cold for almost a minute. When he came to, the paramedics carried him away on a stretcher, put a cold compress on the back of his head and made arrangements to get him to Antrim hospital to be fully checked over.

'That's why I'm covering your lunch,' Alison concluded.

'I hope he's alright,' I said.

'Yeah, I think he will be,' Alison replied, 'He was talking before he left, but it was a heck of a whack he took; those heels are not to be messed with.'

'I'm just wondering ... Did the boot throw still count?'

'Robbie!'

'Seriously, though, if you had a really good throw and then it was disqualified because of some dozy steward, you'd be rightly ticked off.'

Alison rolled her eyes.

'Are you going on your lunch or not?'

I was torn between wanting to stay and chat to Alison and a change of scenery from standing at a gate with almost no traffic. The need to stretch my legs won out. Leaving my yellow vest in the car and slapping some sun cream across my forehead, I grabbed a sandwich from my bag and headed off towards the marquees.

The festival was now buzzing. The good weather had brought people out in droves – and judging by the variations in dress code, not everyone was a line dancing or country fan. I watched a group of three goth teenagers, replete with thick black woolly hats, strolling through the crowd munching their way through a bag of mini doughnuts. I wondered if the good people of Ballyclare had simply come out to support a local event or to stare at the country enthusiasts; it was hard to know.

The line dancing was in full swing. The marquee now had all its sides rolled up and the wooden dance floor was covered with checked shirt wearing dancers of all ages shuffling, tapping and sliding in unison. The latest live band actually sounded good and covered a range of country classics from 'Jolene' to a couple of Steve Earle tunes I rather enjoyed.

I didn't see Gareth McGurnaghan's big jugs anywhere.

Wandering to the periphery of the event, where the fast-food wagons had circled, I spotted the accordion player from the protest deep in animated conversation with another accordionist. They appeared to have swapped instruments and each was pointing out various features to the other. I wondered briefly if this would count as apostasy. Was a fundamentalist Christian risking eternal damnation with such an association? Selling your soul for rock and roll was one thing, but selling it for accordion music ...

With a few minutes to spare, I hurried back to my lonely outpost, hoping to chat to Alison for a few minutes before she left, and wondering if I was going to be left on my own until the end of the day.

It was not Alison I returned to, however. Been There was now manning the gate.

'How's it going?' he greeted me brightly as I slipped back into my yellow vest.

'Not bad. Fed, watered, ready for action.'

'I'm the replacement for Sick Note,' he said, enthusiastically. 'Did you hear what happened?' He fished his mobile phone out of his pocket.

'Heard about it and saw it on YouTube.'

Been There looked crestfallen.

'Oh. I was there, you know. Thirty feet away from him.'

'It might have been you.' If only wishing made it so.

'Not a chance,' Been There replied confidently, 'Vigilance,' he tapped a finger to his forehead, 'Constant vigilance. One of the things you learn in this job is always to be aware of your surroundings.'

A bright orange Skoda Fabia pulled into the open gate behind him. The driver nudged the horn gently, but the beep was enough to jolt Been There a few inches off the ground.

'Mind your back, Batman,' I said, noting the green badge on the dashboard and waving the driver on.

'It was a nasty accident,' Been There continued as we watched the driver park, lift a pair of cowboy boots from the back seat and change out of his Nikes.

'Were you first on the scene?' I asked.

'You kidding?' he answered, 'You wouldn't catch me near anything like that. I don't do blood.'

'There was blood?'

'Well, no,' he admitted, 'But there was a lump. At least, that's what they tell me.' He thought for a moment. 'I remember being told of a roadie falling twenty feet from the top of Debbie Harry's staging. Few years back. I wasn't there myself, but I have it on good authority that when he landed he was straddling a piece of scaffolding.' He nodded seriously. 'Ruptured testicle,' he added with a widening of the eyes.

'Just a ruptured testicle?' I asked, not really wanting to open up a genitalia-related discussion but finding it hard to believe someone could fall twenty feet open-legged onto a thick metal bar and only have a ruptured testicle.

'A ruptured testicle can be a nasty business,' he replied.

'I wouldn't doubt it.'

'There was another time I saw this steward get their tackle trapped in the doors of an overly crowded lift …' he began, but I had already drifted off to watch the rippling river water as it reflected the cobalt blue of the south Antrim sky. My thoughts were with Alison, and if there might be a chance to catch up with her later.

Been There droned on with story after story. He didn't need me to speak at all and I wondered how anyone could lack such a basic level of self-awareness. The highlight, or indeed lowlight, was a long and involved tale about having once seen Nathan Carter's accordion being taken out of a box and polished. That sentence covers the salient details, but he was able to string it out to the same length as a 'Lord of the Rings' film. By four o'clock, I could take no more and decided it was time for an afternoon break.

I had no real desire to return to the festival, figuring I'd had my quota of country music, however, if I'd stayed at the car, there was always the chance Been There would have followed me over. I sought out a food van and bought a cup of tea. On my return journey past the main stage, I saw Alison hovering round the back and made my way over.

'This your post?'

'Yep,' she answered, 'Keeping backstage clear of anybody that isn't a musician or sound guy.'

The strains of a prolonged violin solo filled the pause. Alison winced.

'Not a fan of country then?' I asked.

'Don't mind new country,' she said, 'But this stuff,' she stopped to allow a succession of whining guitar notes to serve as an example, 'It's hard to listen to after,' she glanced at her watch, '*Three hours?* I can't believe it's only three hours; we're not even halfway through yet.' I grinned. 'Easy for you to laugh.'

'Not in the slightest,' I argued, 'I am stuck in the back of beyond with Been There.'

'Been There?' she queried. I forgot that was only his name in my head.

'You know, short hair, squat, always been there and done that – a story for every occasion.'

'And not one of them interesting,' she added.

'I am alone with him until ten o'clock tonight. Genuinely, no amount of money is worth that.'

Alison laughed.

'We might get a chance to move around later,' she said, 'Leanne's good like that.'

'I don't mind staying out there,' I said, sounding grumpier than I meant to, 'I just want rid of him.'

I glanced at my watch. Sadly, my break time was over.

*

Time dragged. There was so much of the day left not even Been There could fill it with his stories. He finished up with how he thought he had once seen Garth Brooks eating a gravy ring, and then silence descended on us. I felt the kind of relief you have when the road works gang outside your house packs up and goes home for the day.

By teatime, the sun was still beating down and the evening was pleasantly warm and sleepy. The Six Mile Water beside us continued to move, almost imperceptibly; small clouds of flies hovered over its banks. The strains of yet more country music drifted across the park from the festival. A new band had taken the main stage. Three or four female voices sang in close harmony, lightly backed by acoustic guitars, and for the first time I wanted to hear more. There was a party in full swing, and I was right at the fringes of it.

Just after seven o'clock, Alison joined us, interrupting Been There's story of his recent prostate examination.

'Leanne's letting some of us change position,' she said. 'I'm happy to come out here for a while.' She turned to Been There. 'I thought you might like to take my position?' My heart leapt.

'What, stuck listening to all that *country shite*?' he replied. My heart sank.

'It's backstage,' she added, 'You need to check who the artists are ...' She didn't need to finish, Been

There grabbed his backpack and headed over to the marquee.

'Played like a bluegrass fiddle,' she said.

I grinned.

'You had enough country then?'

She nodded.

'Although, that last group, the girls with the harmonies, I wish I'd stayed for them. They were amazing.'

'Little bit like early Larkin Poe,' I said.

Alison's eyes widened and I enjoyed being able to put some points on the board.

'*Get you!* Something that isn't classic rock.' I let it be. 'Touch of The Staves in there too,' she added. This was lost on me. 'Girl band, close harmonies, but more folk than country.'

Alison looked around.

'You got a cushy wee shift out here,' she said. 'Quiet, nothing to do, nice river to look at.'

'Yeah,' I agreed, 'I've had worse.' Although I'd pretty much forgotten about the river.

'It's busy over there,' she nodded back towards the festival, 'A lot more people came than the organisers were expecting. Backstage was ok, but it was a bit mad in other places.'

'Helps the day go quickly.'

'Yeah, but Niamh and Jonny were having a total 'mare with the line dancers.'

I wasn't sure what kind of catastrophe could be caused by line dancing.

'How so?'

163

'The dance floor can hold about a hundred at a time,' Alison said, 'But by mid-afternoon it was packed, so they had to start queues. Turns out line dancers are impatient queuers. Niamh just looked totally hassled.' She looked back at the festival. 'Niamh always looks hassled these days.' She paused. 'She used to talk a lot – she'd put your head away if you were with her for a long shift – but ... She parked at mine this morning and we travelled out together. She was really quiet in the car ... didn't seem to be herself at all.'

I shrugged.

'I've only worked with her on one shift,' I said. Which was true.

We both stared at the river for a moment.

'So,' she said, 'What have you been up to lately?'

I shrugged again.

'Little to report. Work is always slower in the summer; shifts are harder to come by. I've started to paint the kitchen.'

'Rock n roll.'

I had little else to say.

'I've been thinking about getting a tortoise.' I could see Alison had no way of responding to that, so I added, 'My daughter Paula was in hospital for a while, but she's on the mend now.'

Alison looked shocked and I explained about the operation and her recovery.

'So have you been seeing a bit more of her?' she asked.

'Yeah, sort of.'

'Sort of?'

'Well,' I kicked at the gravel of the car park with the toe of my boot, 'She's pretty much back on her feet now. Normal service has resumed.'

'And what is normal service?'

'I call in every so often,' I said, realising how feeble it sounded. 'We went out for coffee once,' I added, hoping to beef up the evidence for a semi-healthy relationship with my daughter.

'Coffee. Once.' Alison repeated.

'It's a big step forward from coffee, never.' I replied getting slightly defensive.

'Fair enough, but it doesn't sound like you're happy with it.'

I shrugged again, noticing how much I was doing that and made a mental note to stop. I stared away to the river, but I knew Alison was looking at me.

'Daddies and their daughters,' I said, 'We all just want to return to when they were five and we were king of their world.'

Alison let a full minute go by before she spoke.

'Yeah, but you can't have that. It's not on offer.'

'You could let me dream,' I said, trying to make light of things.

'I could,' she said, 'But that won't do you any good. You can't go back to the way things were. No one gets to go back. No one ever steps into the same river twice.'

'Apt,' I said, 'And very profound.'

'Some dead Greek bloke said it first, I can't take the credit. But it's true. The good news is, while you can't

165

go back, you can go forward. It'll be different, but different can be good. Different might even be better.'

I could feel the tension gathering in my chest. Numbers rose unbidden in my head. Eight years since Paula and I disconnected. Sixty-one, the age my own father died at. Nine years until I reached that age. Not that I expected to go at sixty-one, I had high hopes of being around a good deal longer, but funny things happen in your head when you realise you're living through what were your old man's last years.

'What's the biggest obstacle to something different happening?' Alison asked quietly.

I reached for the joke answer.

'Her boyfriend is a brainless twat,' I said.

Alison laughed but challenged me.

'That's a cop-out.'

'Yeah, I know. But I was just thinking about when I met him. Deano. Deano who sells Doritos. And has about as much intelligence as one.'

'Ah Robbie,' she said, 'You don't want to be that kind of daddy.'

'I can't help it. You get introduced to him and your heart just sinks.'

'Get over it,' she said, bluntly, 'Take it from me.'

'But ...'

'No buts.'

'She's a bright girl, I just don't understand what she's doing with him.'

'And if she wasn't going out with him, you'd have a better relationship?' she asked.

I sighed.

'Course not. I'm just looking for someone to blame because it's easier than figuring out what to do next. And Deano makes for a pretty easy target.'

Alison reached into her backpack and lifted out a four-finger KitKat. She broke it in half and offered me two of the fingers. I politely declined, but she insisted. I took a bite of the two fingers without breaking them apart.

'These are two separate things,' she said.

I looked down at the fingers of KitKat.

'There's no rule that says you can't eat it this way.'

'No, dipshit, Paula's relationship with you and Paula's relationship with her boyfriend. You've got to figure out how to build a relationship with her no matter who she's with. That's none of your business.'

'Easy for you to say.'

'Yes it is,' she replied, with a little more heat than I'd expected, 'I've lived with that tension for ten years.'

'Fair enough,' I conceded, 'I know you're right.'

We both watched the river again.

'Everything runs its own course,' Alison said quietly.

'You can't resist a river metaphor, can you?'

'Shut up and eat the rest of your KitKat.'

I did as I was told.

'How are things with the old man, these days?' I asked, rolling the foil up into a ball and putting it in my pocket. It was her turn to shrug.

'Being down here helps,' she said.

'The distance has improved the relationship?'

'No,' she replied, 'I'm just further away.'

'Oh.'

'Yeah, *oh*,' she looked at me hard, 'That's why I'm telling you not to start something now that might still be in motion in ten years' time.'

She lifted a water bottle out of her rucksack and drank from it.

'Tell me the last three albums you listened to on Spotify,' she said. I struggled to remember.

'Jason Isbell, live album.' She nodded appreciatively, more points on the board.

'And the Beatles' 'Rubber Soul' and 'Revolver', back-to-back.'

'God, Robbie, you really are classic rock boy.'

'*I love those albums!*'

'I know, that's my point!'

'I do branch out a bit,' I tried to defend myself, 'It's not the only thing I listen to.'

'Get out your phone,' she ordered.

'We're not supposed to …'

'We're miles away from anyone,' she insisted, 'Let's look at your 'recently played' list.'

I'll admit it, I felt a little bit violated. It wasn't quite the same as being asked to take my penis out in public, but having someone critically examine what music I'd been listening to did make me feel naked. Thankfully my play list of mainly sixties and seventies albums did have two or three new bands Alison approved of, and even one she didn't know. All in all, I came out of it ok.

After we'd looked at mine, she showed me hers. Most of the artists I hadn't heard of; lots of new country, lots of piano-based light rock, some acoustic guitar-based singer-song writers.

Nine o'clock wasn't long in rolling around.

The last country chord rang out across the park and right on cue, country fans, line dancers and the vaguely-interested of Ballyclare began to head home. Most exited through the front gate, leaving us well alone, but as the evening wore on, contributors began to amble to their cars, usually carrying large bags or wheeling trolleys laden with whatever gear they had. With a busy road not far away, the flow of traffic needed a measure of control. Suddenly we had a job on our hands.

Alison and I stood on either side of the gate. A stream of vehicles exited, at the rear a packed Renault Scenic. I was screwing my face up at how heavily it was sitting over the axle, when she said,

'Andy and I aren't living together anymore.'

Gravity pulled hard at my jaw bone.

'Really? When did that happen?'

'A couple of weeks ago ...' I waved out a white Volkswagen Polo and didn't catch the rest of what she said. Out of all the time we'd had, I couldn't believe this was the moment we were discussing her and Andy.

'I'm sorry,' I said.

'Well,' she replied, 'It's just that ...' But again, the next part was cut off by the exit of a large pink van with 'Line dancers do it in formation' written on it.

'I didn't mean, I'm sorry, like, I'm sorry to hear that,' I tried to explain, 'I meant I'm sorry, as in I didn't hear the end of your sentence.'

'Which sentence?'

'When you said it was a couple of weeks ago.'

'Oh right,' she said. 'Yeah, it was a couple of weeks ago.'

'Ok. Well ...' I tried to find words. Alison waited.

'Ok. Well. *What?*' she said eventually.

'I just ...' I began, 'You know ...' I really didn't have much, aside from generally welcoming the fact that she wasn't with Andy anymore, but I knew not to say that out loud.

'I know *what?*' she asked.

With the benefit of hindsight, there was a definite edge to her voice, but I didn't pick up on it at the time.

'Maybe it's for the best,' I said simply.

'That we don't live together?' she asked.

I nodded, while noticing how she had stopped blinking.

'How the hell would you know?' she asked.

'Well ...' I was hoping for a long line of cars to crawl through the gate, giving me time to think of how best to get out of this, but there was literally nothing but Alison staring at me with flushed cheeks.

'I meant that, from what you've told me before,' I tried to shift the focus back to her, 'It seems like it's been a difficult relationship, and maybe now that it's over ...'

'It isn't over,' she interrupted, 'I said we're not living together anymore. Andy's mum has been ill, and he's moved in to look after her.'

'Oh,' I said, wishing desperately that I'd asked for some clarification first, 'Right, I thought that you'd spilt up.'

'No, we haven't. But it's good to know you have an opinion on that.'

A series of cars began to exit the car park. Alison remained on the gate while I stood on the road and waved vehicles out.

'Look,' I began, a few minutes later, 'I didn't mean to ...' but I was interrupted by a tall young man, presumably a farmer, judging by his t-shirt that had a picture of a tractor and 'if she's not blue, she'll not do' written on it. He began by asking if we had seen his identical twin brother, and, after establishing that we hadn't, went on to tell us about everything that had happened during the day. He seemed to have enjoyed himself immensely.

When he finally left us, I began to speak, but Alison interrupted me.

'Just leave it.'

We spent the next fifteen minutes either waving traffic out of the car park or standing in awkward silence. Feeling like I had fallen off a cliff, I distracted myself by playing with my water bottle; drinking, rolling it around in my hands. At one point I tried a bottle flip, but it landed on its side. It seemed childish to try again.

A few minutes before ten, the light now fading, I watched Leanne followed by a gaggle of other stewards making their way from the festival towards us. I knew there was only a tiny window in which to try to make amends.

'Look, Alison,' I said, not giving her time to interrupt, 'I said something I shouldn't have. I spoke out of turn. I'm sorry.'

'It's fine,' she said, not looking at me. And then she sighed. 'It might be over,' she added.

I didn't respond, I'd learned my lesson.

'We haven't split up, but we're not in much contact right now, so ...' she tailed off. She looked at me. 'Maybe it is for the best.'

'I don't know what to say,' I replied, 'I think I've said too much already.'

'Tell me what you think,' she said quietly.

That caught me off guard, and so I did.

'I think he's a prick and you deserve somebody much better,' I said.

'For fuck sake Robbie!' she exploded.

'What?'

'You can't say that!'

I was confused.

'But you asked me what I was thinking.'

'But you can't think *that!*'

'Oh. Right. I wasn't sure what the rules were.'

'I've spent ten years of my life with Andy.' Alison's voice was rising and she couldn't see that behind her Niamh and Bleedin' Obvious were the first stewards to arrive back in the car park. 'If you think he's a prick,

172

what does that say about me for staying with him all that time?'

'Well, I don't think *you're* a prick,' I began, but got no further.

'Well thanks for that, Robbie, that's *really* good to know!'

'All I meant was,' I stopped to take a deep breath because I could feel the heat rising, 'That, fun as Andy is, there might just be someone else who could treat you a bit better. It's not exactly been the most stable of relationships, has it?'

I instantly regretted the last sentence. It was the stab of a finger into the centre of a large bruise.

'It's been ten years!' she said, loudly enough for the other stewards now gathered at Leanne's car to look over. 'Ten years of my life! Yeah, it's had its ups and downs, but it's been a ...' she paused.

'Decade?' I said, attempting sarcasm, but accidentally getting it right.

'Yes!' she yelled.

Bleedin' Obvious, the closest steward to us, was now staring at Alison's back with his mouth wide open.

'You can walk away from a relationship – you know this as well as I do – you can give it all up in one sentence, pack your bags and get out. But you leave something behind and there's nothing to walk into.'

She had a point, but I wasn't prepared to give ground.

'There might be,' I argued, 'You can go forward, that's what you said!' I couldn't help myself, even

173

though I was also very aware I needed to shut this down.

'But you don't know that at the time! You can't be sure about anything. I'm not sixteen anymore; this might be the only relationship open to me. Unless you're about to ask me out?' she challenged.

She had both hands on her hips and her face was red. Behind her, a dozen stewards looked on, without making any pretence that they weren't totally absorbed. It wasn't how I had imagined it, and I confess I *had* imagined it, but the adrenaline was high and it seemed like now or never.

'Yeah. Alright,' I said loudly, 'I'm asking you out.'

There was a long silence, broken by one of the organisers slamming a van door in the farthest corner of the car park, and shouting, 'That's her now, fella! Ready to rock n roll!'

I looked away towards the river. Alison initially looked down at the ground, until Leanne coughed pointedly, causing her to turn around. She covered her eyes with one hand.

'Busy day folks,' Leanne said, 'I don't want to keep yous much longer, but I need to know if there has been anything unusual to report.' And then she added, 'Aside from...' and nodded in our direction.

Nobody said anything so Leanne thanked us for our time, and we dispersed.

Alison hurried away and I decided not to give chase with an audience watching. Avoiding eye contact with anyone, I got into the car as fast as I could and pulled away quickly, heart beating wildly.

Needing to pee before the drive back to Belfast, I drove round to the main entrance, and used one of the Portaloos.

The two big marquees and the gigantic stacks of hay bales remained, but the festival was over, and the park was almost completely abandoned.

Returning to the car I felt both dejected and stupid. I sank into the driver's seat heavily and tilted my head back onto the head rest.

Sitting up again, I saw the girl in the long grey dress who had been one quarter of the anti-line dancing protest, emerge from behind a stack of hay bales, pulling another girl in a checked shirt and skinny black jeans along by the hand. The first pulled the other towards her, kissing her briefly but firmly on the lips, before they dropped hands and walked together out of the park gates, oblivious to my observation. As much as I could tell, they both seemed happy; content in one another's company. I let them walk past the car before I turned the key in the ignition and headed back to Belfast.

7. Auditorium and acclaim

For the most part, the Belfast Auditorium lies empty over the summer months, resting up before another run of concerts kicks off at the end of August and doesn't stop until the middle of June the following year. Promoters focus on filling bigger outdoor spaces, for four or five nights in a row if they can, with crowd-pleasing bands who play songs well-oiled audiences can sing along to.

'Summer' can be a misleading word to use about Belfast in August. On the whole, the best weather occurs in May and June; July and August tend to be greyer, damper and chillier, but this doesn't stop crowds of young people dressing like they're in Ibiza and drinking like Prohibition might be on the cards.

The BBC had planned a series of outdoor concerts over the first weekend in August. I can only suppose there was a feverish planning session in a board room somewhere and too much attention was paid to the suggestion 'pop hits of the eighties played by orchestras.' Maybe it was the only post-it on the 'fresh ideas' flip chart.

To be fair, some of the line-ups looked good; Glasgow's Hue & Cry and Deacon Blue would have been a great gig, as would Bonnie Tyler and The Alarm appearing in Cardiff. Manchester, playing host to Rick Astley and Sinitta, sounded like hell on earth, while Belfast's line up was a curious combination of Feargal Sharkey and Kylie Minogue. Feargal Sharkey, once the lead singer of the Derry band The Undertones, was a draw to those of us keen to relive our youth. A classical version of 'A Good Heart' would have appeal, but I was less convinced that what we really needed was a woodwind arrangement for 'I Should Be So Lucky.' Ulster has suffered enough.

Plan A was for two sets, backed by the Ulster Orchestra, outdoors on the Titanic slipway at Belfast Harbour. The normally dismal August forecast took a turn for the worse, however, with Belfast set to catch the end of a huge storm from the mid-Atlantic with not only heavy rain forecast, but potentially fork lightning too. The BBC decided that while fifty-somethings on foldable chairs being fried to a classical version of 'The Locomotion' might be entertaining to some, it was probably more of a 'when pop concerts go wrong' late-night Channel 5 kind of thing. A hasty decision was made a few days beforehand to bring the concert indoors to the Auditorium. Grateful for a night out, some craic and extra cash, I signed up for the shift.

I arrived ten minutes early, which gave me sufficient time to get signed in, buy my one shot and then assume a position in the foyer where I could watch the door but not be seen. I needed to know if Alison was going to be on the shift. A week had passed since our performance in the car park. A week spent in cringing embarrassment and cursing the fact that I had said what I thought. Also, a week spent languishing in the knowledge that, just as the possibility of developing some kind of relationship with Alison outside of work had been born, I had killed it stone dead.

Part of me wanted her to be on the shift so there would be a chance to speak to her again and move on from our last exchange. Part of me wanted to hide under a very large duvet and never speak of it again. It would have been bad enough if the embarrassment had been limited to ourselves, but to have created a scene for at least a dozen other stewards in the giant rumour mill that is Safe & Sound, I assumed the story was out there somewhere.

I was back on tickets again, in a group where I didn't think I knew anyone else's first name. I opted for keeping a low profile, pretending I was looking at my phone, while all the time watching the door for Alison. She hadn't made an appearance by the time the briefing started so I assumed she wasn't going to be there.

Brian, the supervisor, was new to me. He was probably a little younger than me, with a smaller waistline and less grey hair. Looking at him, I promised myself that no matter how late the gig was, I would *definitely* do Park Run in the morning. Brian seemed bored and ran through the briefing sheet without enthusiasm.

'Seats have all been allocated, but they were free, so some people might not turn up and we'll be under capacity. This should be a fairly calm event; it's people who like orchestras, so I can't see it getting rowdy. Alcohol shouldn't be a huge issue either. After ingress, I'll be splitting the team as usual; some of you will cover breaks, some of you will stay put. If you end up inside, please be aware this is being filmed. I doubt the cameras will be focussing on the stewards too much, but 'upstairs' is a bit paranoid about it. If Control see someone on their mobile or standing with their hands in their pockets or picking their nose, they'll be letting supervisors know sharpish.'

With little else to say we each picked up a scanner and assembled ourselves into pairs at the turnstiles. I stood next to a younger bloke who, I immediately recognised.

'Alright? How's it going?' Paul said, holding out his hand. 'I didn't expect to see you here.'

Surprised, indeed amazed, I shook his hand and laughed.

'Or you.'

I had been meeting with Paul for the best part of a year to talk about his ever-changing employment. A year ago, he could barely look me in the eye, and he wasn't keen on being in crowds. He had improved, but we had been sticking to jobs that kept him away from dealing with the public, so this was a major turn of events.

'You never said you worked in yellow,' he commented.

'Not long started,' I replied, 'I only picked this up a few months ago. What about you?'

'This is my third shift. I did a couple of the outdoor ones at Ormeau in June and then I haven't had anything since.'

I didn't know what to say, but Paul said it for me.

'I know what you're thinking. 'Paul can't cope with people, so what's he doing here?''

'Well, I wouldn't say ...' I began.

'It's alright,' he assured me, 'I'd be thinking that too, I mean, every job I get is hiding in a storeroom somewhere.' I tried to keep my face in neutral. 'Until this one,' he added.

'What changed?'

'A mate suggested it, and of course I told him to piss off, but he kept nagging me and eventually I thought, alright, I'll give it a go.'

'And ..?'

'Starting the first two shifts were fuckin' terrifying, I won't lie to you. I mean, thousands of people all over the shop, but, by the end of the night, it was alright, I kind of got used to it. Maybe sometimes you just need to do something completely different.'

I nodded. 'I think you might be onto something there, Paul.'

'So, are you a big fan of Kylie then? She's got to be your era.'

I initially assumed he was joking, but he said it with such a straight face I couldn't be sure.

'Not a huge Kylie fan, no. And not really my era either, I'm a sixties and seventies man.'

'Oh,' Paul looked thoughtful, 'I didn't think you were that old.'

'I was a child in the seventies, but I like a lot of sixties and seventies music. It's what I grew up listening to.'

Paul turned to look at a nearby Kylie poster.

'Still, she's alright looking, for her age.'

I hadn't really thought about it, but yeah, as people in their fifties go, the years had been kinder to Kylie than most.

'I could definitely fancy Kylie,' Paul said, with sincerity. 'You know, if she asked me out, I wouldn't say no. And it wouldn't be because she's rich and famous,' he added swiftly, 'I'd go out with her because she's a decent-looking woman.'

If only Kylie could be here right now, I thought. To hear Paul describe her as 'decent-looking' would do her esteem a power of good.

'The age difference wouldn't be an issue, like,' Paul continued.

'It's good that you've thought it through, so, you know, if the opportunity ever arises and Kylie Minogue asks you out, you won't be thinking on your feet.'

We stood quietly for a moment, before Paul spoke again.

'What's the oldest bird you'd go out with?' he said.

I laughed. *Bird,* I thought, there's a phrase I didn't expect to hear from someone so young. Maybe it was making its way back into the vernacular.

'Haven't really given it any thought.'

'How old are you?'

'Fifty-two.'

'Ah right,' he said, nodding, 'You maybe don't have an upper limit then.'

'What?'

'You know,' he said, completely straight-faced, 'You're getting on a bit now, so the gap between you

181

and the old bird wouldn't be that big, so you probably don't have a limit.'

'*I have a limit,*' I said tetchily.

Of course, I didn't have a limit because it had never been a relevant question. It's like asking which offshore island you'd store your excess millions on. Now that Paul was making the assumption that I was old enough to date someone in their eighties and the age gap wouldn't really matter, I needed to find a limit fast.

'*Well?*'

'Well what?'

'What is it?'

I panicked.

'S-Sixty-two,' I said, 'Ten years older.'

It sounded reasonable enough, although I was also silently apologising to my first crush, Lesley Judd, the ex-Blue Peter presenter who was now in her seventies. I suddenly realised that, while any chance of a relationship was indeed remote, I had just ruled it out.

Paul looked thoughtful.

'Don't really see the point,' he said.

'Of what?'

'Of your limit. I mean, I couldn't tell the difference between a woman in her sixties and a woman in her seventies. They're all just Nana to me.'

I took a moment to take in Paul's view of the world. There was young, not quite as young, and old. I was old. It really didn't matter what age I considered myself, someone who had only lived for a couple of decades saw me as having one foot in the grave.

'How young would you go?' Paul asked.

'Doors are opening,' I said, 'The ticket holders will be coming in.'

*

Brian was right, it wasn't a capacity crowd; ingress was steady and stress-free. As Fergal Sharkey came on stage at seven, Brian split up the team. Paul and I were asked to take our breaks first and then head up to tiered seating to cover the stewards on the vomitories. We set off for the break room backstage.

'That'll increase your chances,' I said to Paul as we walked.

'Chances?'

'Of Kylie asking you out.'

'Eh?'

'Well,' I explained seriously, 'At one of those moments during the gig when the concert hall is lit up, she might see your youthful physique back lit in the vomitory and think to herself, *I must have him.*''

'*What?*'

'She'll probably send word to one of her entourage. She'll say, 'Fit looking steward on door seventeen; have him sent to my second changing room. Put him in a leopard-print thong and tie him to a chair with the cord of my velvet dressing gown. I'll see to him after I've had my bath.''

'*Seriously, what?*'

'Never worry,' I said, as I opened the door to room number twelve, 'If it happens, just relax and go with it.'

Still confused, I let him walk in first; he made a bee line for the vending machines. I was following when a loud voice boomed from the further down the corridor.

'There's the *man!*'

I stepped back out of the doorway to see Sohail wandering down the corridor towards me. He stopped in front of me and slapped me hard enough on the shoulder to knock me sideways back into the break room.

'So?' he began, delight written all over his face, 'Are you going out with yer woman?'

'What woman?' I asked, knowing rightly, while at the same time hoping desperately the news hadn't travelled so far.

'The woman you asked out in front of everybody at the car park in Ballycastle?'

There was no denying it.

'It was Ballyclare.'

'Where's Ballyclare?'

'Em, north of Belfast, towards Larne ... it doesn't matter. How the hell do you know about that?' I asked.

'Lisa told me.'

'Who's Lisa?'

'She's on the SIA rover team, expert in Tae Kwando, you wouldn't mess with her.'

'How does she know?'

'She was at Ballycastle, sorry, Ballyclare. She was searching anybody that looked like they were bringing in alcohol, she told me about you and yer woman earlier tonight. She didn't know your name, but she pointed you out at the sign-in.'

'Right.' *So that's how it works,* I thought, realising this could be a long night, 'Well, she isn't my woman.'

'She said no?' Sohail asked, putting a massive arm round my shoulder.

'She didn't say anything,' I explained, 'We got interrupted by the debrief.'

Sohail literally bent over laughing.

'I've only a few minutes left for my break,' I said, 'I'm going to sit down.'

I moved towards the ring of chairs.

'Have a good one buddy,' Sohail replied and slapped me again, this time on the back, propelling me towards a vending machine.

Recovering my balance, I sat down next to Stella who had a cup of tea in one hand and a twin Twix in the other.

'Ah, it's Casanova,' she said brightly.

'*God,* you know too?'

'Robbie,' she said with a deep sigh, 'This is Safe & Sound, if there's a good story going round, *everybody* knows it. In fact, sometimes a story is so good, it changes in the telling, and then you have two slightly different stories going around about the same thing.'

I groaned.

'How do you know?'

'A wee bird told me.' I made a face. 'A certain supervisor might have mentioned it, just in passing.'

'Leanne?' I asked, stupidly, as there was only one supervisor at the festival.

'Lives next door to me. She gave me a lift in tonight.'

Stella popped the end of her first Twix finger into her mouth. I put the Boost I was holding in my hand back into my pocket; I had lost my appetite. Stella noticed this.

'Ah, don't you worry,' she said, patting me on the arm, 'The good thing about Safe & Sound is that another story will come along pretty soon and replace yours and, what's her name's?'

'Alison.'

'Aye, Alison.'

There was a long pause during which I tried to think of something else to talk about, but Stella wasn't done yet.

'*Did* she agree to go out with you?'

'Well, she never really had a chance to answer, so I suppose I could say, 'not yet.''

'That's the spirit! Never give in, Robbie. Though,' Stella dropped her voice to a conspiratorial whisper, 'A wee word of advice: when you ask a girl out, it's best not to be yelling at her.'

She began to laugh, which was really more of a wheeze, as she rocked back in her chair and some of her tea splashed out of her mug. Paul, and another steward seated opposite us, looked up from their mobile phones with quizzical expressions, but I wasn't going to explain. I glanced at my watch. For the first time ever, I decided to end my break early and head back.

'Stella,' I said, 'It's been a pleasure as always.'

'Take care, Robbie,' she replied, grinning through a mouthful of chocolate and biscuit.

*

Paul and I agreed that I would start at the far end of the vomitories and work back, while he would start at the near side and work up. Halfway down the last vomitory, I found Ciaran leaning idly against the wall, tapping his foot in time to 'It's All Over Now', which I had to admit sounded good with the string section of an orchestra providing tension behind the vocal.

'I'm covering breaks,' I said, 'Unless you're really into this and you want to stay put?'

'I've heard worse,' Ciaran replied, before singing along, 'I used to love her, but it's all over now.' And then he added, 'It's like they're playing it for you, Robbie.'

'*Ha bloody ha.* How do you know?'

'Ricky told me earlier; he was there.'

'Who's Ricky?'

'Short, squat steward, shaved hair, got a story for every occasion.'

Been There. My heart sank. If he knew, everyone knew.

'Is he on tonight?'

'Yeah, door two.'

I looked across the concert hall and could see the unmistakable rectangular shape of Been There at the end of the vomitory.

'Just out of interest, exactly *what* do you know?'

'You and a female steward called Alison had a blazing row in a car park in Ballymena ...'

'Ballyclare.'

'Ballyclare?'

'Yes.'

'I thought he said Ballymena.'

'Not important, carry on.'

'Well, at the end of the argument you asked her out. Is that even close to what actually happened?'

'Yeah, that's pretty much it.'

'That's good,' Ciaran said.

'How so?'

'It's not gossip, it's an accurate retelling of what took place. It restores your faith in human nature, doesn't it? Right, I'm off for a quick fag.'

Ciaran strode purposefully down the vomitory, into the concourse and away, leaving me to reflect on the information learned so far. While the majority of stewards probably knew, the silver lining might be that not everyone knew it was specifically me – unless of course I had been pointed out by some eager storyteller like Been There. I sighed loudly, shoulders sagging.

An elderly, rasping voice beside me said, 'It makes you wish you were young again, doesn't it?'

I turned to find a wrinkly senior citizen who wouldn't have reached five foot standing at my elbow.

'Where are the nearest loos love?' she asked. I directed her down the vomitory and to her left. I couldn't help thinking, *she is definitely too old for me.*

I didn't know the older, male steward on the next vomitory, and thankfully, he made no effort to make himself known to me. His break time passed off peacefully and allowed me to thoroughly enjoy 'You Little Thief' which sounded damn good with the brass section blasting out the main riff.

In the vomitory after that, however, was Niamh.

'Hiya,' she said. 'How's you?'

I closed my eyes and sighed again.

'At least I don't have to ask how you know. You had a ring side seat.'

'Yeah,' she agreed, 'And I got a lift home with Alison.'

I had forgotten about that.

'What did she say?' I asked without thinking.

Niamh pulled a face.

'It wouldn't be right ...'

I wanted to beg her, I wanted to pull in a favour, but damn it, I had integrity. I cursed my solid upbringing and two moral parents with their loose affiliation to a local Methodist church.

'Sorry, shouldn't have asked.'

Niamh looked away for a few seconds.

'To be honest,' she said, looking back at me, 'She actually didn't say much about you, she was just so scundered that it all happened in front of the rest of us.'

'I know how she feels.'

'She was a bit cross that you didn't say anything.'

'What like, *'they're behind you?''*

'It's not funny. She was beetroot all the way to Belfast.'

'It was the heat of the moment,' I said, 'When you're in the middle of an argument, you don't always think sensibly.'

'Yeah, I know,' she said, 'Right, I'm away.'

My mind raced with the realisation that Niamh had information no one else had. I wasn't going to ask her about what happened in the car, but I could ask her about what to do. Over the next ten minutes, I thought about this very carefully.

'Niamh?' I said, when she returned, 'If I was to ask Alison out ...'

'You already did,' she said.

'I wasn't really.'

'You said, *'I'm asking you out'*, really loudly, how is that not asking someone out?'

'I was trying to prove a point in an argument, I wasn't really ... Look, it doesn't matter, what I'm saying is, if I was to ask Alison out, sometime in the future, you know, properly, not yelling at her in a car park ... Do you think I'd have a chance?'

Niamh looked me straight in the face.

'Robbie, that's a conversation you need to have with Alison.'

'Right. So there's enough there to have a conversation?'

'Robbie.'

Her tone was firm, but she gently put her hand on my arm.

'Alright, alright,' I said, backing off, 'But you can't blame me for trying.'

Niamh smiled. I set off down the vomitory before turning back to her.

'Are you alright for a lift later? I can drop you off if you want.'

'I've got a lift lined up,' she said, 'But thanks.'

I didn't know either of the next two stewards, who merely thanked me and went for their break. Feargal Sharkey's set drew to a close with 'A Good Heart' and there was a long interval to prepare the stage for Kylie. My streak of not talking about my exchange with Alison came to an end however, with Wee Myrtle.

'Robbie, isn't it?' she said as I approached her. I nodded. She clicked her tongue. 'You're more famous than Kylie these days.'

'It seems that way. I'm not even going to ask how you know.'

'The rumour mill has really kicked in on this one,' she said, laughing, 'I've heard it from three different sources.'

'All the same story?'

'Pretty much, although the place keeps changing. It's a good story, you don't really need to add anything to it to make it better.'

I groaned.

'Don't worry about it, son,' she said. 'As the saying goes, if you love something set it free,' she paused.

'Then there's another bit that I can't remember, sorry. To be honest, it was all shite anyway. Right, I'll be back shortly.'

She laughed again and wandered off towards the concourse.

I considered trying to explain to her that I hadn't really wanted to ask Alison out, but quickly gave this idea up because, if I was honest, I couldn't really explain it to myself. Did I want to ask her out? Yes. Did I actually ask her out? Yes – there was no denying it. Did I actually mean it at the time? Well, yes and no. Yes, I did want to ask her out, but no, it wasn't supposed to come out like that, and I was simply trying to prove my point that there were alternatives to Andy.

Mildly distracted by the orchestral strains of 'Can't Get You Out of My Head', a new thought occurred to me; what if I had said no, or even just said nothing? Would that have been better? Would it have ruled me out? Can you really say to someone that you wouldn't ask them out and then, at a later date, come back and say, actually, I've changed my mind now that nobody else is listening and we're not having an argument?

Mildly irritated by this train of thought I moved on to the next door which was manned by Ryan – someone familiar with the Safe & Sound limelight.

'How's it going?' he said, smiling.

'I'm fine,' I said grumpily, 'No smart comments, you wee bollocks, go and have your break.' Ryan's face fell and I repented instantly.

'Sorry,' I mumbled, 'I thought you were going to say something about ...'

'About what?'

'About an argument in a car park,' I started, before adding, 'It doesn't matter.'

'Oh that was you,' Ryan said, raising his eyebrows. 'Ricky was telling me something about that earlier on, but I didn't really get it. Something about you asking a girl out after shouting at her?'

'I didn't shout at her.'

'Did you ask her out though?'

'Yes, I did. Now piss off to the break room.'

Watching Ryan leave I swore that if I ever caught up with Been There, I'd find a subtle way to kill him.

At least Ryan seemed to have recovered from his involuntary crowd-surfing incident. I genuinely wasn't certain if someone as nervous as he was would come back from that. I asked him about it when he returned.

'Do you know what?' he said chirpily, 'I think it was the best thing for me.'

I was confused.

'How so?'

'Well, I was always nervous of, well, everyone really. I used to worry about what might happen to me. And then that night, I got dragged into the crowd. Everybody keeps telling me that's never happened to a steward before, so I figure it's probably not going to happen to me again, is it?' I shook my head. 'And if that's the worst thing that can happen, and I survived it, everything else should be alright, shouldn't it?'

He looked up at me with the cheerful eyes of a young Labrador.

'That's a good way of looking at it, Ryan,' I said.

The next door was staffed by a less than cheerful looking Bleedin' Obvious.

'You were on a shift in Ballyclare,' he said, straight off the bat.

'Yeah, I was.'

'And you had an argument with a girl in front of everyone and then at the end of it, you asked her out.'

'Spot on.'

Bleedin' Obvious looked at me without speaking for what I considered to be an uncomfortably long period of time. A weird version of 'I Should Be so Lucky' played in the background. I was about to ask him to stop staring at me and take his break when he said,

'She really likes you, you know.'

I didn't expect that.

'How do you know?' I asked. He shrugged.

'Isn't it bleedin' obvious?' he said, as he walked off to take his break.

*

When Bleedin' Obvious returned, the whole arena was on its feet dancing along to 'Spinning Around.' I wanted to ask what he meant before, but it didn't seem to be the right moment, so I let it be and walked away taking my curiosity with me. All the stewards on tiered seating had now been given a break and so I headed back downstairs to stand with the others at the exits. The gig ended in good time, and the slightly under capacity audience didn't take long to file out. With no slips, trips or falls to report, we debriefed and made our way out of the building.

Checking my phone, I got a message through from Shirley and panicked a little; the last late-night message had been about Paula. However, this one said, 'I know it's weird to wish your ex-husband a happy anniversary, but I still think about the good years we had. Happy Anniversary. Sx.'

I hadn't forgotten the date; I just didn't know what to do with remembering it. I smiled; it was a nice text to receive. The jagged edges in the past can't be undone, but having them smoothed over in the present is a good place to be. I was just about to reply when a female voice called from behind me.

'Robbie!' I turned around to see Niamh running up to me. '*Can* I get a lift with you?'

'Yeah, of course.'

She didn't explain her sudden change of heart, in fact she didn't say much as we walked to my car. All my attempts at conversation were met with little more than monosyllabic answers.

Springsteen's 'Downbound Train' came blasting out of the car radio, and I quickly shut it off. We sat in silence for several minutes, until we pulled out of the car park and drove through the city centre.

'Seems like we're the only car on the road that isn't a taxi,' I said.

'Yeah,' she agreed. 'I caught Damian cheating.'

The car in front slowed down and I nearly drove into it.

'I was on a shift, an outdoor gig, and the crowd size was smaller than expected, so they offered to let a few people go home early and I was knackered because I'd worked all day, so I volunteered.'

I tried to focus on driving. And on Niamh. And not so much on the echoes in my head of Shirley telling me there was someone else. I felt the moment all over again. Adrenaline. Sweatiness. Dizziness. Turned out the edges weren't as rounded off as I thought they were.

I didn't ask any questions. Niamh kept talking and looked straight ahead.

'He was upstairs in bed with her,' she said simply, before taking a long pause.

'It was such a shock. I mean, I knew all along. *I knew it.* So many things didn't add up. But it was really traumatising to see the man I'm going to marry, in bed, naked, with someone else.'

She turned away from me, to look out of the passenger side window with her head resting on her left hand. She wiped her eyes with her other hand.

'I asked him to move out, and he did, but he moved back in a few days later.' She looked at me briefly, before staring straight ahead again. 'He's told me he's sorry and he's promised it won't happen again. He wants another chance.'

The traffic thinned as we left the city centre. The few cars on the road meant I would be dropping Niamh off very soon.

'Robbie?' she suddenly said, urgently, 'Could you pull over somewhere?'

'It's ok, I can drop you to your door,' I replied.

'I don't want him to see me talking to you,' she said quietly. I nodded.

I turned into a side street broad enough to park on and light enough for us to see each other. I let the engine idle, and inclined my head toward her, but without looking at her directly.

'Nobody else knows about this,' she said quietly, 'Except Damian ... and her, obviously.'

'I won't be repeating this,' I said.

'I know you won't.' She took a deep breath. 'And I know you'll be honest with me. I want to know what I'm supposed to do.'

I let her statement hang in the air.

I knew it would be the easiest thing in the world to tell her what to do. Especially in this case. I wanted to fix the world for her, but I knew I couldn't. And my response to a similar situation, couldn't be her plan. I fought hard not to let my own experience leak out.

Niamh turned to look at me.

'Robbie,' she said, *'What am I gonna do?'*

I left a long pause.

'What do you think your options are?' I said gently.

Niamh didn't hesitate to answer.

'I can marry him like we planned. I can *not* marry him and tear up all our plans.'

'Maybe you could postpone things for a while,' I added, 'See how it goes.'

'Damian would never agree to that.'

'Why not?'

She shrugged.

'It's Damian. He wants everything now. All the plans are in place, the wedding, the house – there's no way he'd ever agree to changing them.'

We sat in silence for a moment, each of us looking ahead.

'So, there's two options then, isn't there?' she said.

I nodded.

'It seems that way.'

'That thing in the car park with Alison was mad.' She looked over at me. 'You just told her what you thought. Just like, bleurgh, there it was.'

'Yeah,' I said, 'I just threw it up and left it there, like a good boke at the end of a long night out.'

She smiled. I smiled.

'I can't see two options,' she said, 'I can't see how I can walk away now.'

I let that sit for a moment before speaking.

'How long is it until the wedding?'

'Four months. It's at the beginning of December.'

'You've got time to ask some questions then,' I said.

'Like what?'

'Like, what would I need if I was going to walk away?'

Was I telling her to walk away? Was I manipulating her to do what I thought was best? To do what I did? Trapped in a car next to someone in emotional turmoil, there was no space to sort out my motivation.

'So, you think I should walk away?'

'No, Niamh,' I said quietly, 'Only you can make that decision, it's not for me, or anybody else to say. But what you can do is give yourself the choice to begin with.'

It was the best I could do, given the circumstances.

Niamh put one hand briefly on my arm.

'Thanks for the lift,' she said, 'I'll walk from here, it's not far.'

'Ok ... As long as you're ok.'

It felt like I'd said the right thing, but it did not feel good.

'I'll be fine. Thanks for listening.'

She got out of the car and just as she was about to close the door, she leant back inside it again.

'Robbie,' she said, 'I know I'm not the best person to be giving advice, but Alison was scundered, I'd say she's going to be avoiding you like the plague. So, if you are serious, you're going to have to chase her.'

8. Fine food and foul weather

The outdoor catering facilities – I was specifically told not to call them food trucks – had been fired up for at least a couple of hours before I weighed in just before nine o'clock. Fragrant aromas of roast meats, freshly baked breads, vegetarian ... vegetables, I suppose, and who knew what else, hung in the air. We had parked our cars in a slight dip in the corner of what was well-looked after grass, but still undeniably a field, and gathered at the gate into the next, more elevated field, where all the cooking was being done.

'I love the smell of Hillsborough in the morning,' Tony said, probably the only time anybody has ever used that sentence.

I hadn't expected much stewarding work to come my way in August, but with the BBC gig already done, and an early season football match in the diary for later on, it was shaping up nicely. Then, out of the blue, Tony phoned mid-week to ask if I could do a full Saturday at a food fair. Three signed-up stewards had been able to get a cheap week together in Magaluf and pulled out. Helen had not been best pleased, and Tony, supervisor for the shift, offered to phone round.

'Do you fancy doing the Posh Nosh Fine Food Festival?' he asked me.

'In Lurgan, is it?'

'Very drole. It's in Hillsborough.'

'Of course it is.'

'Nine to five. They want us to look after car parking, and they've offered to give the staff food vouchers for lunch time.'

'Sounds good.'

'Hm, maybe,' Tony replied, 'Depends *how* posh. I haven't seen the list of caterers; we might be up to our oxters in oysters. Don't be expecting a pastie supper.'

Tony's fears did not appear to be confirmed, however, as the smell of hot food was making everyone hungry, even so early in the day.

With just over half the stewards assembled I was busy keeping an eye out for Alison, who I knew was coming.

'How many stewards are there going to be?' I had asked Tony.

'There'll be about a dozen of us.'

'Anybody I know?'

'How would I know who you know?' he replied, 'But if you're asking is Alison going to be there? Then yes, she's on my list.'

'Right, right,' I replied, trying to sound like I wasn't really that interested, but Tony was having none of it.

'So, if you two could sort out your lovers' tiff beforehand, that would be great. Failing that, keep any spectacular arguments to late in the day. It would be entertaining, but best not to do it in front of the food snobs of County Down.'

Without Alison's phone number, no 'sorting out' was possible. Even if I'd had her number, I wasn't sure I would have had the guts to call her.

Next to arrive after me was Sam.

'Ah, it's young Robert,' he said, with a hand on my shoulder. I turned around and smiled warmly, genuinely pleased to see him.

'Are you well sir?'

'I am,' he replied, nodding slowly, 'All things considered.' I was uncertain whether I should ask, and so I only raised my eyebrows slightly. 'First shift after a wee bit of illness,' he added, but didn't give any more details and I didn't ask.

'Good to have you back,' I said simply.

Sam smiled and bowed his head in acknowledgment.

Looking around the group again, I realised Alison had arrived and chosen to stand almost as far away from me as she could, at the other end of the semi-circle gathered around Tony. She did not attempt to make eye contact with me, and I assumed she knew I was there because it wasn't a large group. Similarly, I did not make any effort to get her attention. The avoidance tactics made me feel like I was fourteen again.

'Now that everyone has their sexy yellow vests on,' Tony began, 'Welcome to Posh Nosh Fine Food Festival, the finest collection of almost-English accents outside of Bangor and the Malone Road. Thankfully, we'll be coordinating the car parking today, so we shouldn't have much interaction with the elite.'

I looked around me, it wasn't difficult to see the order of things to come. Traffic would arrive from the main Hillsborough Road, cars would be parked in the

202

bottom field, and the cooking, eating and general revelry would take place at the top of the slope.

'The organisers are estimating up to two thousand people, with around a thousand vehicles.'

'In there?' someone asked, referring to the field below us.

'Not just there,' Tony replied, 'We can use another field as an overflow if we need it, but it's a good deal lumpier, so we'll try to pack as many in as we can. We're going to leave a route down the middle, which we'll tape out in a minute, vehicles will then all park facing into the middle in double lines. Watch what you're doing; no triple parking please!'

A few sniggers were heard in the group.

'Were you there the year that happened at the Balmoral show?' asked one older man. Tony nodded. 'F-type Jag, gleaming, surrounded on all sides by other cars,' he began to laugh, 'He was ripping; he had to stand around for a couple of hours until some of the other cars moved.'

I could hear Sam chuckling to himself beside me.

'I was there that day,' Tony said, 'Thankfully I wasn't supervising. I believe he threatened to sue, but nobody could figure out what for.'

Our instructions were to keep the traffic moving and thus keep festival goers happy by not having them stuck in a queue for an hour. I was assigned gate duty. Stella, looking distinctly out of place away from the Auditorium, was my partner. We settled into our post on either side of the entrance. She looked around uncomfortably, before staring down at the grass with an expression of personal offence.

'The outdoors isn't your thing, is it?' I asked.

She shook her head.

'I like walking, but I also like a good solid pavement under my feet, none of this soft, damp nonsense,' she turned her nose up at the ground. 'I don't like things that move when you step on them.'

'Escalators?'

'They're fine. Solid, inflexible. You know where you're at with an escalator. But this stuff,' she poked at the turf with a toe, 'Slippery, slimy ... you couldn't trust it.'

'All those cow pats mulching back down. Worms and creepy crawly things swarming all over it.'

'Stop it.'

'How long have you worked for Safe & Sound?' I asked, changing topic.

'A few years now,' she replied vaguely, 'It was Leanne who suggested it to me.'

'And you've always looked after the store?'

'Sort of,' she laughed, 'It didn't happen at first, but it's easier to have the same person on all the time and no one else really wanted it. Most stewards like to hear a bit of the gig, but I have a wee touch of tinnitus, and the concerts were leaving me a bit deaf the next day, so I was happy to stay in the break room.'

'Are you a big music fan?' I asked, thinking back to Stella's previous revelation she had seen the Stones in Belfast in the sixties.

'More so in my spotty youth. I have the radio on a lot at home, but I didn't take the job for the music.'

I didn't want to ask directly, and I waited.

'My husband died a few years back,' Stella said simply, 'Not long after he retired. I stopped work too. We had plans. Not big plans, but we were going to buy a caravan with part of his pension and tour Ireland. So ...' she stopped for a few seconds, 'So I was left with a lot of time on my hands.'

'Aw, I'm sorry.'

Once again she reminded me of my mother, now not just in looks, but also in experience.

Stella shrugged.

'Life goes on. It's a cliché, but it's only a cliché because it's true. You have to get up and do something the next day. A few months later I was talking to Leanne over the back hedge and she suggested giving stewarding a go, and I found I quite liked it. It keeps me busy, it's good company and a wee bit of extra money too.'

'Yeah,' I agreed, 'I imagine it suits a lot of people for those reasons.'

Stella nodded.

'There's a lot of single people in Safe & Sound – it fills a night or two in the week. Of course, there's other reasons too; some people really need the extra income.'

'I can identify with that.'

'You broke?'

'No,' I laughed, 'But it gives me a little leeway.'

'And then there are the people who just can't sit still, have you noticed that?' she asked. I shook my head. 'You'll find some stewards work every shift they can get – they just hate being in the house with nothing to do.'

'What's wrong with a bit of television?' I joked, but I knew exactly what she meant. The TV could help you pass the time, but ultimately it couldn't prevent loneliness.

'You know,' she said, quite seriously, 'Some don't watch TV at all; there's a whole range of people here. Dolly Mixtures.'

'True enough.'

'No, do you want a Dolly Mixture?' she said, holding out a bag of sweets to me.

'Oh, sorry. No thanks, still a wee bit early in the morning for me.'

'Never too early for sugar. I've got a bag of cinnamon lozenges for the afternoon.'

*

There were patches of blue sky overhead, when, shortly after ten o'clock, the festival PA system cranked into gear and began to play Van Morrison's greatest hits. The instantly recognisable riff of 'Brown Eyed Girl,' arguably the most over-played recording ever to come out of Northern Ireland, rolled down the slope. By ten o'clock a trickle of cars had started to make their way into the field, building to a steady stream by eleven. There was a predominance of

Range Rovers, BMWs, top-range Audis, and estate cars in general. I didn't spot a Corsa or Fiesta among them.

'A gathering of the well-heeled, for sure,' I said to Stella.

'No chance of a poke man and a bouncy castle up there,' she replied, nodding at the top field.

There was some occasional reluctance to drive on the grass.

'Is the drainage sufficient?' one male driver in a checked shirt asked me from beneath the brim of his 'McQueen' baseball cap.

'Sufficient for what?'

'Sufficient to sustain the mass of my Audi so that it doesn't sink into the mud. It's an A8, you know.'

Not knowing how to respond, but feeling I should do something, I took a step back and gave the car a thorough glance up and down. Because that's how you establish a car's weight relative to the solidity of a field of grass.

'Should be alright,' I said, with as casual an air as I could manage.

'Should be alright?' the driver responded, 'I need better than 'should be alright'?'

I shrugged.

'Best I can do,' I said, smiling, 'It's not really my field of expertise, excuse the pun, I'm just here to help you park your wee car.' I don't normally say 'wee', but it felt good to downgrade his hulking estate. 'Straight down the middle there and turn left up at the top. The next set of stewards'll keep you right.'

He muttered something to the equally unimpressed woman in the passenger seat and then, without so much as a 'thank you' for the high level of customer service I had provided, he sped off up the field in disgust. Or at least he tried to. Halfway up his front left tire caught a hollow in the ground causing a loud 'thunk' and a synchronised 'Oooh' from Stella and me.

He drove the rest of the way more slowly.

There were also queries about having to walk over the grass to the festival.

'I don't want to get my Birkenstocks wet on the damp grass,' one woman in a Mini Clubman explained to Stella.

'Did you not bring your wellies?' Stella asked, with a completely straight face.

'No,' the woman replied, 'My wellies are in the Range Rover I use when I'm down with the horses.'

Touché.

By midday the festival was in full swing and the aromas filtering down the hill were also at peak output. I began to feel hungry. It had been a relatively early start for a Saturday, and my breakfast bowl of Special K seemed a long time ago. I guessed our field was about two thirds full, but despite the steady influx of vehicles, some had now begun to leave and so I reckoned that with careful traffic management, we might get away without having to use the overflow.

The hits of Van Morrison continued on endless rotation. 'Full Force Gale' played, as the sky clouded over in a threatening manner. A lull in cars coming through the gate allowed me to dreamily stare up the hill to the food stalls, when Stella interrupted my thoughts.

'You keep looking up the field,' Stella said, 'Are you really interested in what food is on offer, or is there something else on your mind?'

I grinned.

'Mostly food,' I replied, 'I'm definitely feeling peckish.'

Which was true, some sort of nicely cooked meat in between whatever kind of nicely baked bread was available, was dominating my thoughts. It had been a busy morning, and Alison had been hidden from my view behind a few hundred vehicles

Stella looked at me with scepticism.

'Alright,' I responded, 'And maybe a few thoughts about Alison.'

'You've not given up?' Stella asked.

I took a moment to answer.

'That's hard to say. I never really had a plan – it all just kind of ... happened.'

Stella frowned.

'This isn't making sense?'

'Not to me,' she admitted, shaking her head.

'Alison and I don't really know each other that much,' I explained, 'We've just talked a few times on shifts. We get on well, you know what it's like when you meet somebody and there's a bit of a connection.'

'I haven't flirted with anybody in near enough half a century,' Stella mused, 'But I imagine the feelings haven't changed.'

I grinned.

'That day in Ballyclare ...' I began.

'The world-famous incident?'

'Let's not call it that, but yes, that day, we were just chatting, and then things took a weird turn. Before I knew it, something I had kept very firmly inside my head was out in the open.'

'With a dozen stewards listening in.'

I rolled my eyes.

'I never even had a vague hope of something,' I paused to think, 'Not really. It was just a ...'

'Happy daydream?' Stella volunteered.

'Exactly. And now it's out there, and I can't just pretend it didn't happen and carry on.'

A strange moment occurred. For the first time since Ballyclare, I realised that, despite all the embarrassment, I was essentially happy that what had been inside my head had escaped.

'Have you seen each other since the ...' Stella tailed off.

'You really want to say world-famous incident, don't you?'

'I do, yes. It has a nice ring to it.'

'No, I haven't spoken to her since.'

I couldn't say anything more because a string of cars approached the gate, separating us. The festival PA system began belting out 'Days Like This' and just as the second verse started the heavens opened and it began to pour so hard the rain bounced upwards off the vehicles around us, drumming on their roofs.

Having checked the forecast early doors, and in expectation of at least some rain, I was wearing my waterproof trousers and a thick black raincoat. I put up my hood, pulled the zip as high as it would go and hoped for the weather to break soon. Stella, however, wasn't wearing waterproof trousers and her light raincoat clearly had not been built for this kind of deluge.

It took ten minutes for the downpour to ease to a gentle drizzle, by which time I was soaking, but, as far as I could tell, still dry below my layers. It was obvious Stella's trousers were saturated and I wasn't going to ask about her top half. I suggested she ask Tony about going home, but she wasn't for giving in. She said she had a change of clothes in the boot of her car, asked me to cover for her and toddled off to dry herself as best she could.

A lot of surface water had collected on the ground. Most of the field was covered by thick grass and the rainwater ran down the slope in rivulets, collecting at the bottom, pretty much where I was standing. I looked down at the puddle that had formed around the thick Vibram soles of my walking shoes, and while I was grateful they were waterproof, I was also regretful I hadn't thrown my wellies into the car too.

Tony came by before Stella returned and I explained what had happened.

'Most of our guys have waterproof gear on so we're not in bad shape,' he said, 'Not so much the punters though, there's very little cover up there,' he nodded towards the food stands, 'So it was every middle-class fop for himself. I thought there was going to be hand-to-hand combat over who got the last awning.'

Tony decided that, if Stella could continue, he would send her up to the festival. The organisers had asked if a couple of stewards would be available to help control the queues at the stalls and she might find a warm heating vent to stand near. Another steward would be sent down to help me on the gate. Cars continued to arrive in fits and starts, and with some continued concern for the parking arrangements.

'Park *here*?' said one elderly male in a Merc – who was actually wearing a cravat – 'You can't possibly expect us to walk through that.'

I was amused he used the word 'through', as if walking across wet grass was akin to the parting of the Red Sea. I couldn't see what he was wearing on his feet, but I guessed it wasn't wellies.

'I have no expectations at all,' I replied, 'But if you want to go to Posh Nosh, this is where you park.' I smiled my most exaggerated, friendliest smile, the kind of smile you had as a six-year-old when granny had just opened her purse. I stood back to let him drive on.

Ten minutes later, Sam ambled down the field to join me.

'It's time for your lunch, youngster,' he said, 'I'll hold the fort on my own and then stay here to help get these clampets back out again.'

Delighted to have the opportunity to eat, I didn't hang around. I ditched my steward's vest in the car and set off for the food stalls merrily clutching the now-sodden lunch voucher Tony had given me earlier.

The dark grey rainclouds had largely rolled on leaving some blue sky. It didn't take me long to locate a hog roast and come away with a pulled pork baguette with stuffing and apple sauce splurging out the edges. I noticed Stella drying off in the lee of a van that was deep-frying brie in batter and was conveniently placed next to a Foster's chocolate trailer. She looked well pleased with herself.

Sitting myself down at the end of a picnic table, I let the sporadic sunshine soak in while I stuffed my face. I was so happy to be off my feet and filling my stomach, I didn't even think about Alison. At least until I accidentally walked right past her at the top of the field on my way back down to the gate.

'Hey,' I said, not having prepared anything better.

'Hey,' she returned, looking startled. There was ten seconds of uninterrupted awkwardness.

'Do you think we could ...' I began, but before I could finish, we both became aware of another steward standing near us.

'Not here and not now,' Alison muttered and turned her attention back to a car driving into the space where we were standing.

*

Back at the entrance, Sam was leaning casually against the gate with both hands in his pockets.

'I see you've been rushed off your feet,' I said.

'I think we've reached tipping point,' he replied, 'There'll be more going out now than coming in.'

I glanced at my watch. It wasn't far off two o'clock; with the festival winding up at four I reckoned he was right. Three cars drove past to emphasise the point.

'It feels like the day has flown in,' I said, 'We'll be away in three hours.'

'That's what happens when it's busy.'

'You holding up all right?' I wanted to show friendly concern, but not pry.

'Oh aye. Back on my feet.' We stood quietly for a moment, before he added, 'That's a grand day now.'

I agreed it was, and together we discussed the forecast for the next few days, the wetness of the ground, the muddy tracks forming as more cars left and our shared love for stuffing in a sandwich, even though it was technically bread in between more bread.

My thoughts drifted back to Alison, however. We were here together, with only a small group of stewards in a relatively small venue. She had said 'not here and not now', so did that mean somewhere else at another time? Could that mean later on? I chose to remain hopeful.

Sam noticed I wasn't paying full attention.

'Something on your mind there, fella?'

I smiled awkwardly and decided to plunge in.

'Bit of woman trouble.'

'Ah, that's the best sort of trouble.'

'We had a bit of an argument,' I tried to explain without getting into the details, 'There are some things still to be said.'

'Remind me again, what stage you're at.'

'Divorced several years back, this is the first, em, attempt at someone else.'

'What's stopping you?'

I shrugged.

'It's complicated.'

'Do you still want a relationship with her?'

I nodded.

'What's complicated about that?'

I looked down at my feet and made a few squelching noises in the mud before I answered.

'Well, the relationship wasn't really a thing, you know,' I began, 'It was, sort of just a beginning, and then there was someone else, though I think they're not in the picture so much, if you know what I mean.'

'Clear as mud.' Sam took a deep breath and looked at me directly. 'If I've learnt anything,' he said, 'If it's important, say it.'

'I'm not sure it's that simple.'

'It's exactly that simple. The confusion comes because you can feel very vulnerable being honest.'

We waved out several cars. I decided to move the conversation on rather than try to explain more. I commented on how the turf at the gate was really starting to cut up, but Sam was not so easily distracted. This intrigued me; I'd never seen him so serious before.

'I've spent my life watching people come and go,' he said, 'I used to think it was great, getting paid for checking names on a clipboard, opening a barrier for a vehicle and most of the time staring off into space. Money for nothing.'

I might be wrong, but I thought I heard a hint of anger creep into his tone. A grey cloud shut out the sun overhead.

'But then it became a habit.' Another car passed between us, but Sam did not take his eyes off me. As soon as it passed, he continued. 'Life moved on around me and I only knew how to smile and laugh and wave. But there were things to be said.'

He looked away from me as a BMW 7 series ploughed past us. I had a sense that, unfinished as the thought was, he had expended a lot of energy saying it.

'Thanks, Sam. Maybe you're right. Maybe I just need to work out what I want to say.'

He looked back and nodded. Another two cars exited the field and Tony stopped to talk to us about arrangements for getting the vehicles away as smoothly as possible. After he left, I watched the sky clear a little and the sunlight return.

What *did* I want to say to Alison? Was I asking her out or not? I wanted to, but it really depended, on what was happening with Andy. Or did it? Surely convention dictated you didn't ask someone out when they were in a long-term relationship with someone else. Especially when you hardly knew the person to begin with. And yet, if that person was looking for an alternative, what could be bad about offering one? Aside from the vulnerability, like Sam said.

'I *was* in the hospital with stomach pains.' Sam interrupted my train of thought. 'Caused by the amount of pills I'd taken.' He looked hard at me, making sure I understood what he was saying. I nodded.

'It had all become too much of a strain, you know?'

'I understand.'

'Everybody expects you to be happy, to chat away, to be alright,' he paused, 'And I just couldn't do it anymore.'

A Range Rover rolled past breaking our view of each other. It sloshed through the mud at the gate and we both watched it trundle down the hill until it joined the main road.

'But when you waken up,' Sam said quietly, 'When you didn't expect to waken up, and you see the pain in your wife's eyes, and in your children's eyes, you have to say something. You have to let them in.'

Several more cars were making their way down the slope. Mud gently splattered our trousers as they passed us.

'In some ways,' Sam went on, 'That bottle of pills was what I needed, though I wouldn't recommend it to anybody,' he added with a rueful smile. I let his words hang in the air for a moment before I spoke.

'How are you now, Sam?' I asked.

'I'm a lot better,' he replied, 'I'll be seventy-three later this year, and in some ways, I feel like I'm starting all over again. I'm learning to say the things that need to be said.' He looked me full in the face, holding eye contact for several seconds.

'I know,' I said, 'I hear you, Sam.'

*

Despite the increasingly muddy conditions and with only a little congestion near the end, we managed to safely escort the visitors' cars off the site and stood down just before five. Tony thanked us all for a fine day's work. I was hoping that Alison might make eye contact or stand somewhere near me, but she made no attempt. Niamh's words were still ringing in my ears, but having been put off by Alison earlier, I decided to swallow my disappointment and leave things be for now.

I unlocked my car and sat down on the passenger seat to take off my waterproof over trousers so that I didn't coat the driver's seat in mud. As I was putting my boots back on, I could hear the revving engine of Stella's Fiesta, parked next to me, the wheels spinning in the mud. Tony came over to offer advice on driving slowly and trying to pull away in second gear, but every time Stella tried, she stalled the engine. Tony slipped into the driver's seat and gave it a go, but the car remained stuck fast and only seemed to be sinking further into the mud.

'I think we may have to give it a push,' I said, walking round behind the car.

I stood behind one wheel and another steward stood behind the other. Alison joined us in the middle and we looked at each other very briefly.

'I think I'll stay well out of it,' Stella said.

'Alright,' Tony yelled from the driver's seat, 'On three ...'

The first attempt yielded no movement from the car, and so another couple of stewards joined us at the back end, wherever they could get a hand on the vehicle. For the first few seconds it seemed like nothing was happening, until the front wheels caught a little bit of traction and the Fiesta suddenly shot forward. It took us all by surprise and we fell forward in a heap.

The back wheel I had been standing over caught a patch of mud from where the front wheels had dug in. A spray of dark, wet soil was flung behind the car, hitting me full in the face. Most of the stewards laughed, myself included, even though I couldn't see, but Alison responded with 'Oh, Robbie,' and began to scrape bits of mud off my face before she grew self-conscious and stopped. Stella opened the car boot and offered me a handful of baby wipes to clean myself with and a fun-size Milky Way for my trouble. She thanked me, while also laughing at me.

Tony came over to check I was ok, and his concern would have been more touching if he hadn't been crying with laughter. I gave my face one last wipe, assured everyone I was fine and dug my car keys out of my pocket.

It was then I noticed Alison walking away to her car. My heart sank. It had seemed like there had been a perfect opening for us to laugh together, say something and move on. But the moment seemed to have passed.

I wiped myself down as best I could, wishing I had gone to help Stella with my over trousers still on. I got into the car and turned over the engine. Thankfully, it pulled away easily, to the gentle strains of Springsteen's 'I'm on Fire.' It lumbered over the ruts in the mud and made it out to the junction with the main road. Before I pulled away, I briefly checked my mobile phone. There was one text message from an unknown number. The message simply said 'Starbucks at Sprucefield after stand down. A.'

9. Food and water of both kinds

The journey to Sprucefield, whose name is taken from the ancient Irish phrase for 'soulless selection of car parks and chain stores', only took a few minutes. I parked up quickly and hurried into Starbucks with an erratic heartbeat pumping a cocktail of adrenaline, nerves, hope and confusion. Alison was seated at the back wall, in a large red leather chair that had the effect of making her look rather small. She already had a steaming mug of coffee and a flapjack in front of her, and was studying her phone.

She looked up as I approached.

'I was starting to think you weren't going to come,' she said.

'Why?' I took a seat in the equally large green leather armchair opposite her.

'I texted you at lunch time and you didn't reply.'

'Yeah. Sorry. Only caught the text a few minutes ago when I was leaving. I didn't look at my phone all day.'

'One of Safe & Sound's finest,' she said, with a hint of a smile.

'Not really. Just forgot about it, that's all. It was a bit of a strange afternoon.'

Alison looked at me quizzically, but I couldn't explain.

'I feel like I'm still covered in mud.' I rubbed at my face.

'Yeah,' Alison agreed, 'You've got a thin layer of it left; it's really pronouncing the wrinkles round your eyes. You look like you've used one of those apps that ages you.'

'Thanks.'

I looked around the shop. There were few seats left as shoppers sought to end their day out with a hot beverage and a ridiculously priced variation of baked flour, sugar and butter before heading home. Silence fell between us as we ran out of preliminaries. I used the space to go and get a pot of tea and a chocolate muffin.

'So, how are you?' I asked when I returned to my seat.

Alison didn't rush to reply.

'Ticking over,' she said eventually. 'I was back up home for a week there; that was nice. But now I'm back down here to work and ...' She wrinkled her nose in an expression of disgust.

I desperately wanted to ask what the current status with Andy was, but held my tongue.

'I'm missing Coleraine,' she said simply, 'Missing Dad, missing the beach, missing friends. I still don't know that many people down here.'

My internal tension subsided. She was inviting me into her world.

'I'm spending a lot of my time out walking, listening to music. Not that I mind, I like doing that, but I miss my stereo, it's still in Coleraine.'

'Can't you bring it down?'

'Scared to. It's a late-eighties Hitachi I was given by my uncle when he upgraded. One of the first machines to have a CD player. It's never been out of my room and I'm worried that if I ever move it, it'll fall apart.'

 'Impressive length of service.'

 'It's like an old friend.'

 'I know what you mean. A vintage Thorens turntable has pride of place in my living room.'

 'You're a vinyl man?'

 'Very much so.'

 'I really don't get it.' She shook her head. 'Records scratch and skip, that used to frustrate the life out of me. I'm a CD girl all the way.'

 'You don't get the same smell from a CD.'

 'Is that important?'

 I ignored her.

 'Or the same feel, or the proper size of the album art ...'

 'I just need to hear it,' she said. 'As long as there's a good sound.'

 'But it's about the experience, too,' I replied, 'Every time I take a disc out of its sleeve, it takes me back.'

 Alison nodded and took a long drink.

 'That much I understand,' she conceded, setting the mug down and folding one leg under herself. There was something about it I found endearing, maybe because this was new; we had never sat together casually before.

 'I've been playing records on that turntable since the late seventies,' I continued.

 'I'm assuming you weren't the first owner, even though you now look old enough.'

 I shook my head.

'No. It was Dad's – his baby. The TD124, 'a marvel of German precision engineering' he used to say. In the early days, I only got to use it under close supervision.'

Alison sat back in her chair and let her head rest on its high back.

'I take it he's not around anymore?' she asked, quietly.

'No. He died a while back. When Mum moved house she didn't want to bring it with her. She doesn't listen to music that much anyway. She'd sooner have the TV on.'

'It's funny how people interact with music,' Alison said, lifting her coffee mug again. 'Some people don't seem to notice it, some people like it in the background. Some of us totally obsess about it, it's like a ...' she stopped to find the words.

'Religious ritual?' I asked.

'Yeah.'

There was a long pause.

'Of course, when I took the turntable, all of Dad's old LPs came with it too. There was no point in Mum keeping them. I traded them for a new radio; I think I did better out of the swap.'

I topped up my mug from the teapot, mostly hitting the target, but some of it bled down the side and leaked across the table. Alison lifted a serviette and mopped it up.

'That's when I think about Dad most,' I said quietly, 'Every time I let one his records roll out of its sleeve, place it on the turntable, wipe it down and drop the stylus. It's an act of remembrance.'

Except it's not, I thought, *not really; it's like he's there in the room.* I took a sip of tea to help smooth out the tension in my throat.

'Yes,' Alison said simply.

'Well that got serious quickly,' I replied, trying to make the moment lighter, but she ignored my comment.

'Certain music takes me to a place and time,' she said, breaking her flapjack into smaller pieces, 'But the beach is where I feel closest to Mum. She loved the beach.'

'Castlerock?' I asked, thinking of Coleraine.

'Downhill,' she replied, 'A little further along the coast. You can drive your car onto the beach and walk for miles.'

The coffee shop was busy and noisy, but the space between us had become a little oasis of tranquillity.

'Have you made it out to Crawfordsburn?' I asked.

She laughed.

'Once, yes. But it's not quite the same.'

'No,' I agreed.

'The north Atlantic has a wildness to it. Miles and miles of open sea and a hell of a lot of sky. Usually with big, threatening rain clouds in it. Belfast Lough seems ... much tamer.'

'Good view of Kilroot power station,' I added flippantly. I instantly wished I hadn't, but she ignored me again.

'Downhill makes you feel completely small and insignificant and wonderfully free all at once.'

'I can see why you miss it.'

I so desperately wanted to talk about everything that had and hadn't been said in the car park at Ballyclare, but, despite our reconnection, I had no idea how to do it. I didn't want to be the one to go there first as I thought maybe Alison might do so in her own time. On the other hand, I was beginning to worry that if I didn't try to talk about it, maybe Alison would think I was avoiding the topic.

Our conversation turned to what the shift had been like, but there wasn't very much to say about parking cars in a field. Yes, she got wet too. At lunch time she'd had a grilled halloumi and salad sandwich. And then the conversation ran dry.

We broke the silence together.

'Things are still up in the air with Andy,' she said, just as I said, 'I'm sorry I asked you out.'

'You're sorry you asked me out?' she replied, at the same time I said, 'How do you mean?'

If only I could have held back just a little longer.

'Yours would be the easier conversation to have,' I said, 'But I get the feeling we're going to have mine.'

'Damn straight.'

Shit and bugger, I'd done it again.

'Do you want another coffee?' I asked.

'Robbie.' Her tone would not have been out of place in a puppy training class.

'Things got heated,' I explained, 'I didn't mean it to come out like that.'

'Didn't mean it to come out like *that*, or didn't mean it to come out, full stop?'

Our oasis had disappeared, and I was standing in the desert with the hot sun beating down on me.

'Eh ...' I began, trying to figure out the better option. 'I didn't mean it to come out like *that,* although, I didn't really mean it to come out at all. I mean, I would never have asked you out, at that point.'

Alison looked at me blankly.

'When you asked me out, did you mean it or not?'

'I meant it. In the sense that I liked you and I would have asked you out, perhaps in time, but given all that you said about Andy beforehand, I didn't think it was the right time and we were talking hypothetically post-Andy. So, no I wouldn't have asked you out then, even though I actually did, but I would definitely, or at very least most likely, have asked you out at another point ... definitely when we weren't having an argument.'

'Everything you just said was in past tense,' she said.

'That's because it happened in the past,' I said.

'Don't be a smart ass.'

This irritated me, because, despite my ham-fisted attempts to explain, I was making a genuine effort to answer her questions.

'Do you not think what I just said was complicated enough without having a variety of tenses in it?'

'God, Robbie!'

She was loud enough for the two women at the table next to us to look over. 'Sorry,' Alison muttered, smiling sweetly at them. We both pulled our chairs in to the table so that we could irritate each other at closer range.

'Let's do present tense,' Alison said, tension in every syllable, 'Are you asking me out or not?'

I reviewed the options. To say yes might result in a favourable outcome, but it also left me open to rejection. Saying no foreclosed the possibility of rejection, as well as a favourable outcome. Anything else, such as 'maybe', 'perhaps' or 'I might be' was likely to be read in a negative light. I estimated that no woman was ever likely to respond positively to the sentence, 'I might be asking you out.'

Hesitation can also prove costly, as it did in this particular case.

'Robbie,' Alison said, 'It's a simple question, and you haven't said anything for about a minute now, so I'm taking that as a 'no.''

'It depends,' I replied, in a stroke of what I considered genius.

'On what?'

'On how things are with Andy?'

'What's he got to do with it?'

'You're sort of in a relationship with him. Maybe.'

'I don't see why that should stop you.' Her tone was sharp.

'Well, convention would dictate you shouldn't ask someone out who's going out with someone else.'

She shrugged.

'That's a stupid rule. If it even is a rule; I mean, it's not written down anywhere, is it?'

I couldn't argue, but I did think this was unreasonable.

'Look,' I said, slightly louder than I had intended, causing the two ladies beside us to glance over. I lowered my voice. '*I like you.* If you weren't with someone, I would probably have asked you out by now.'

'Probably. Every girl loves a probably.'

'Because I don't know.' I could feel heat coming into my tone and face, 'In an alternative universe somewhere you weren't with someone and I did ask you out, but in reality you are and I didn't, so I can't say for certain. What I can say for sure is that I'm not going to ask you out now until I know there's a chance you're going to say yes.'

She sat back and folded her arms. I leant back and breathed out slowly, feeling like I had dodged a bullet.

'I need to pee,' she said standing up, 'Do you want another drink?'

'Not if those two things are connected.'

She glared at me.

'No, I'm grand,' I said, 'I need food more than water.'

'Do you want to go to McDonald's for a burger?'

'Are you asking me out?' I said, because it was too funny not to.

'You're an asshole!'

The two women next to us physically jumped. And then, suddenly, she laughed. I wished I could have recorded the sound so I could play it again whenever I wanted.

'All right,' she said, 'That actually was funny. I'll be back in a moment.'

She made her way to the toilets, while I waited at the door.

*

The clientele of McDonald's consisted almost entirely of noisy groups of teenagers, along with a few families; hassled parents trying to herd their offspring to tables while balancing trays of food and drink. Alison and I were distinctly out of place.

'This was a mistake,' she groaned, raising her voice to be heard.

'Let's get something and take it outside,' I suggested.

'To the car park?'

'We can eat in my car if you want.'

'Inviting me back to your place already?'

We ordered separately, paid separately, and made our way back to where I had parked.

'Fuck,' Alison said suddenly, getting into my car.

'What?' I asked, but she didn't need to reply.

Wee Myrtle had been putting something into the boot of the car parked opposite to mine, and now, making her way to the driver's door, she had seen us both. Directly in front of us, we were literally only a few feet away. She looked over and raised an eyebrow.

'I've seen nothin',' she said, 'My lips are sealed.' She mimed zipping her lips before getting into the car and driving off, giving us a wave and laughing as she did so.

Alison groaned. I took a huge bite out of a burger that allegedly had chicken breast in it and chewed thoughtfully.

'If they're talking about us, they're leaving somebody else alone,' I said. Alison glanced over at me. 'My mother says that, though I'm not sure it logically follows that if you're talking about one thing, you can't go on to talk about something else at a later stage, but there you go.'

'Robbie?'

'Yes?'

'Shut up.'

'Ok.'

We ate in silence for a few minutes, during which I think Alison chose her words.

'Andy's mother's health isn't great,' she said eventually, 'It's not life-threatening; she's just older and weaker and her arthritis is slowing her down. In time she'll need more care than Andy can give her, but he's not at the stage where he can talk about that yet.' She ate a few more French fries. 'He's moved in with her, more or less permanently. I am not going to move in with her, nor have I been asked to. Truth is,' she took a deep breath, 'That even if Andy's Mum wasn't a factor in all of this ... well, I don't know where we'd be. There's no parallel universe to know for sure, is there?'

She looked over at me.

'Maybe it took moving down here to test whether there was enough in our relationship for it to keep going. You strip away a familiar job, familiar places, friends, family and you see what you're left with.'

That made sense. Hope was rising, though there was also the possibility that she was about to tell me that she was heading back north. It felt like our relationship, at whatever stage it was at, hung in the balance.

I would have given it more consideration if I had not been really hungry. I was right there, hanging on every word, but I was also holding three quarters of a chicken burger that was getting cold, and I had hardly touched my fries. It seemed simpler for her, she had chicken nuggets, which were much easier to nibble on, whereas a burger takes you to really open your mouth wide to get a proper ratio of bread, burger and salad. I opted for a drink of my strawberry thick shake instead. I'm not sure what the protocol was, but I think a sip of a drink is more acceptable at moments like this. The straw was not fully inserted into the cup and so as I sucked hard, I made a massive slurping noise. Alison looked at me.

'Sorry,' I said, 'I am listening. Really.'

'We chat maybe once a week,' Alison said, 'Trade a few texts. I can't really give it an official status because it started out with Andy calling in and sometimes we'd go out, then we stopped going out and then he stopped calling in, and now we hardly talk. I think that means it's dying,' she concluded.

I risked a handful of French fries.

'You can talk, Robbie,' she said, 'I'm releasing you from the order to shut up.'

'Oh, right,' I said with my mouth full. But I couldn't think of where to start.

'What do you think?' she asked.

'Do you really mean that?' I had been there before.

'What?'

'I can now say *anything*?'

'Anything. But be gentle.'

I set the chicken burger down.

'Yes,' I said, 'It sounds like it's dying. But then, I don't have all the information. You've got ten years' worth of detail; I've just got a few conversations, so it's not for me to say.'

'Fair enough.'

'I have a question,' I added, 'I use it all the time, for myself, and for the young people I meet in work.'

'Go on.'

'If you were giving advice to someone in your situation, like you weren't involved at all, what would you advise that person to do? And you don't have to answer. You don't have to tell me anything.'

'I'd tell them to bring it to an end now,' she said simply, without thinking time. 'I'd be understanding that it was a long-term relationship, but I'd say there was a point where you have to look at the future, even though it's uncertain.'

I thought the right moment had come.

'Would you, come out with me sometime, for a meal, not fast food in a car park, a proper meal?'

'A date?'

'Yes.'

'No.'

'Oh.'

'I really like you,' she said quickly, 'And in that alternative universe somewhere, I might have said yes, and we would go out and I might be really happy. But right now, I need to have a proper talk with Andy and then I need some time to figure out if I want to stay in Belfast.'

'That all makes sense,' I said, but still feeling like I had been pushed away. 'I can't really compete with the north Atlantic,' I added, trying to bring some levity.

'I miss my Friday afternoons,' she said quietly.

I didn't ask, I just held the silence until she was ready to say more.

'After work, I always drove out to Mum's grave and sat there for a bit. Not every Friday, but most Fridays. It wasn't far. I can't do that here.'

She folded the lid of the box with the last couple of chicken nuggets inside and turned to me.

'She's been gone for such a long time, but it's still something I need to do. I've never told anyone about that before. Does that make me sound mad?'

I shook my head.

'I mean,' she added, 'People know that I visit Mum's grave, but I don't think anyone knows how often. Not Andy. Not Dad.'

All of a sudden, we were a long way away from a bland retail park, in a space of our own, sharing love and grief and beauty and frailty together.

'I don't think it's mad,' I said simply, 'We all grieve in different ways. I never visit Dad's grave, but I talk to him all the time in my head. I don't think I'm mad. At least, no more so than anyone else.'

She smiled.

'Thank you,' she said.

'What for?'

'For what you just said. But also for asking me out.'

'Twice.'

'Don't push it.'

'Ok.'

'I have a counter offer,' she said. I raised both eyebrows. 'How about doing this again?'

'Sprucefield really made an impression on you, huh?'

'Robbie!' she said loudly, 'You can be so lovely one minute and so bloody exasperating the next.'

'It's a unique selling point. Sorry, I'm not making this easy.'

'No, you're not!' But she couldn't keep the smile off her face. 'A coffee shop sometime, maybe something to eat, but no big thing, not a date, just a chat and a catch up. I need it to be uncomplicated. Does that sound alright, or does that sound like I'm stringing you along?'

'That sounds good,' I said. The most understated response ever.

'Ok,' she said, 'Well, that's that cleared up, so ...'

'So what?'

'So you can finish your chicken burger.'

*

I drove home, showered, changed, put a heaty-up thing with pasta in the oven and made a cup of tea.

I took Elton John's 'Honky Chateau' LP from the Elton section in the rack, slipped the disc in its liner out of the sleeve, and then the disc from the liner and put it on the turntable. I set the stylus to the second last track on the second side. I nodded at the other empty armchair before sinking into my favourite one with the large red velvet cushion.

'You've good taste, old man,' I said, before I started to sing along quietly.

And I thank the Lord there's people out there like you.

10. Stand and stunned

The late August evening was warm and pleasant. It wasn't a long walk to East Side Rovers' tiny ground, so I didn't take the car. The new football season had kicked off and East Side, thanks to their miraculous run in the Cup, had qualified for the preliminary rounds of a European tournament. The concept of East Side Rovers, whose average weekly crowd was three hundred, playing in Europe left local football fans both excited and bemused.

East Side were a long way from playing major opposition. To make it to the *next* qualifying round, they had to beat the mighty juggernaut of Albanian football, Futboll Klub Kukësi. The tie was held over two legs, the first of which had already been played in Kukës. East Side had gallantly lost by two goals to one, and now, with home advantage, the club's board were desperate for a decent gate to offset the cost of the team's excursion to Albania. Extra stewards had been drafted in, in the hope of a crowd large enough to require stewarding.

I arrived a few minutes before six o'clock and joined the gaggle of stewards in the car park – a patch of waste ground, part of which was still charred from July's bonfire. We put on our yellow vests and signed in with the supervisor, Diarmuid. New to me, he was a tall bloke with unkempt hair, who seemed rather distracted. There were about eight of us in total, Wee Myrtle and Paul being the only others I knew by name.

On the stroke of six, Diarmuid called us to order.

'Thanks for turning up on time,' he began, 'Tonight's game is East Side Rovers versus the Albanian side Kukësi. It's the return leg and I'm told that East Side actually have a chance. I wouldn't know, I don't take anything to do with sport, I don't even like walking to the shops. I mention it because the game has received a lot of local publicity and the club are hoping for a decent crowd, which is why we're here to support their own stewards.'

He stopped momentarily and gazed off into space. One or two of us looked around in case there was something we should be aware of, but Diarmuid only sighed slowly, and then continued on with the briefing.

'The club are particularly concerned that UEFA rules for European games are enforced. If the club fails to comply, it can be fined. Right now, the biggest fine East Side could afford would be paid in pound coins, so we have a job to do tonight.'

Diarmuid began to allocate tasks. Those with an SIA qualification were put on the gate for searches, at least to begin with. The rest of us were allocated around the pitch or to the one stand.

'UEFA stipulate that anybody in a stand must be seated. East Side's stand holds about a thousand people, but even if there's only a couple of hundred in it, they must all be in their seats.' He looked at me and asked my name.

'Robbie, I want you at the back of the stand where the burgers are being sold. Fans can queue up for hot

238

food, but once they've got their order, they have to sit down.'

I nodded. It seemed simple enough.

I noticed Niamh and another female steward arrive just as the briefing was finishing. Diarmuid spoke to them separately as the rest of us wandered off to our positions. Doors wouldn't open until seven; kick-off was at eight.

Much as I like stewarding, there's a lot of time to kill, doing practically nothing. I climbed slowly to the top of the stairs in the stand and stood with my back to the shuttered kitchen hatch where hot food would be sold later.

The sun had already begun its long descent in the west. Somewhere just before nine o'clock it would drop in behind Black Mountain and leave the sky a washed-out blue. The slate-grey roof tops of east Belfast stretched out before me, pierced by the occasional church tower or spire, remnants of a time when the majority of Belfast's citizens sat in the pews every Sunday.

To the east, the land rose to become the Castlereagh hills, farmland progressively eaten into by housing developments as so many of Belfast's citizens preferred life in the suburbs. I like the idea of more peace and quiet and the chance to go see cows at will, but I'm a city-dweller at heart. I like people. I like knowing my neighbours. I know it's weird, but I like hearing the muffled sound of next door's TV coming through the wall. It lets me know I'm not alone.

I stared across the empty pitch, with nothing to look at save for the other stewards who were also staring into space. I thought about work, which was picking up pace again. Let's-not-rush-this June and July were gone, and August was building towards another oh-shit-there's-lots-we-have-to-do September.

Over the summer I had met Paul only once. The storeroom job hadn't lasted, and his plans to enter the world of snooker were never mentioned again. But he was now in his fifth week selling mobile phones in a large shopping mall. Every day, he was face-to-face with the public, and seemingly enjoying every minute of it. There he was, across the pitch, affably chatting to another steward; somehow Safe & Sound had changed him completely. It was nothing short of a miracle, and I still didn't really understand what had happened, but one brave plunge into something utterly different had totally reoriented his life.

Aside from Pathway, the diary was starting to fill up with stewarding shifts – perhaps more than I really wanted. Out of the blue Aaron had called to say he had booked a flight home for a few days at Halloween, conveniently coinciding with the Northern Ireland match should I want to get tickets. Mum was the same as ever. She was only shopping in Sainsbury's these days because she nearly had enough Nectar points for a free travel kettle, which I knew would never leave her house. I'd seen very little of Paula; she was never available for any length of time, and it was really starting to get under my skin.

And then there was Alison.

Two 'non-dates' in coffee shops doesn't count as a major incursion into the leisure time, but you also have to factor in the period spent in anticipation beforehand and in happy reminiscence afterwards. Another non-date had been planned for the following week; an informal evening meal in a Korean café I had never heard of on Botanic Avenue. If that went well, I was planning to suggest we keep a Saturday free to drive down to the Mournes and go for a walk before autumn lost its warmth.

Alison and Andy remained officially attached, while not really having much in the way of meaningful contact with each other. I don't think Facebook has a status for that. In her more candid moments, Alison recognised things had run their course, but Andy was still recalibrating life in the light of his Mum's worsening health. He had asked for a little more time to think things through and Alison, not fully ready to walk away herself, had agreed. The sitcom 'Friends' has prevented anyone seriously using the phrase 'on a break' ever again, so they were on pause; in a lull; currently inactive pending further development.

This left me happy to be spending time in Alison's company, but slightly gloomy that I might suddenly become the third wheel on the bicycle. I couldn't see any way that my friendship with Alison could survive in its current form, should her relationship with Andy revive. I tried to remain upbeat, however, by thinking about this as little as I could.

My thoughts were rudely interrupted by the metallic roll and smack of the kitchen shutter flying up to reveal Fat Sandra standing behind the counter. The middle-aged woman was nearly as wide as she was tall – and she was my height – and wore a navy apron with the words FAT SANDRA printed across them in white.

'How you doing?' I said, 'Sandra, I assume.'

'Fat Sandra,' she replied, 'I don't object to my full name.'

I laughed.

'I can't possibly call you Fat Sandra. We've only just met.'

'Oh I'm big enough to take it. Literally.' She hauled a large bag of burger baps onto the counter. 'They used to call me Big Fat Sandra, but I objected. I mean, that's excessive. It's like saying 'Old Aged Pensioner'; you don't have to hit people over the head with three words that mean the same thing.'

I laughed again.

'So, is this your regular spot?'

'Every home game. Usually just Saturdays, but tonight's a big night.'

'So I hear. What do you make of their chances?'

She leant forward with both arms on the counter and her chin resting on one hand.

'Depends,' she said, thoughtfully, 'If we get a good crowd in and they make a bit of noise, and our tails are up, and the boys get the first goal … anything could happen. I think the Albanians have a couple of weaknesses in their defence; dodgy centre-back for a start, bit of a ball-chaser. Let's just say I'm quietly optimistic.'

She deftly sliced open the bag of rolls with a bread knife.

'I'm very impressed with your analysis,' I said.

'Well. My husband is one of the coaches and he never shuts the fuck up about the team. My mistake, after all these years, is still listening to him.'

Fat Sandra began to stack burger baps onto a plastic crate.

'So you're the poor bastard they've put up here?' she asked.

'What?'

'Is it your job to make sure people don't stand along the back after they've got their food?'

'Yeah ...'

'Good luck with that.'

I thought about this for a minute.

'Why is that difficult? Surely people want to go back to their seats?'

'Aye, you'd think. Not this lot. It's an East Side tradition to get your burger and then stand around talking in the space up here. Most match days that's not a problem, because there's not really that many fans, but when it's a big game, the IFA get very sticky about it; fans have to be in their seats.'

'So what normally happens when a steward asks them to move?' I asked, but I already knew the answer.

Fat Sandra looked me straight in the eye.

'The steward gets called names associated with female bits of the body, and nobody goes anywhere.'

'Right.' I tried to figure out what to do with this new information. 'So what's my best approach?'

'The only way you can avoid an argument with this lot ...'

'Yes?'

'Is to let them stand where they want.'

'So, I just need to not do my job, and everything will be fine.'

'You're learning fast kid.'

Fat Sandra turned away and threw a dozen frozen burgers onto the hot plate.

*

I spent the next short while pondering my two options. I decided it would be helpful if I checked things out with my supervisor, however the closest he came to me was a thumbs up from the other side of the pitch.

The crowd started to trickle in just after seven, with most supporters leaving it until much nearer eight. The ground certainly wasn't at capacity, but there was enough of a crowd to create a good atmosphere. The flood lights were on and the pitch was fully lit, the teams were warming up, and the smell of fried onions was wafting past my nose. There were worse ways to spend a Thursday evening.

My position at the very top of the stand meant that few supporters came past me on the way to their seats. One or two said hello, but I would have been completely without company if one fan hadn't cheerily approached me.

'Hiya! How are you!' he hailed me loudly, 'You're Paula's dad, aren't you?'

'Yes, I am,' I replied, allowing him to grab my right hand and shake it vigorously. 'Deano, isn't it?'

'That's me!' he replied enthusiastically. 'So what are you doing here then?'

I looked down at my hi-vis luminous yellow vest that had 'steward' written in large letters across it.

'I'm a steward.'

'Right, right,' he said, frowning as though I had tried to explain nuclear fusion to him.

'Are you getting a burger?' Deano asked, nodding towards the hatch.

'Not just now. They're not very keen on us eating in our uniforms.'

'The players?' he said, looking down at the pitch.

'No, the supervisors,' I explained, 'It doesn't look too good when you're supposed to be working and you've got a big dirty burger hanging out of your mouth.'

'Right, right, it's like the Doritos then, isn't it?'

'Em ...'

'I'm not allowed to eat them when I'm out with a client. Or in the car. Or in the office, actually, you're not allowed to eat food in the office; break room only.'

'Right, right,' I replied, realising I was parroting Deano.

'Well, I haven't had tea, so I'm going to get a burger now, good seeing you Mister, eh ...'

'McKittrick, same as Paula. But you can call me Robbie.'

'Robbie. Right, right.'

Like a puppy in human form, he bounced off to join the short queue at the kitchen. Not for the first time I tried to work out what possible overlap there was between him and Paula, but I had to give him credit for attempting to call me Mr. McKittrick. The boy had some class.

The match kicked off bang on eight and I settled into watching a scrappy but energetic game without goals, with raucous home support. The best moments were probably the sporadic singing of 'we've never heard of you,' which I am reliably informed goes to the tune of 'La Donna é Mobile' from Verdi's 'Rigoletto.' I've never heard the opera in my life, but someone once told me the name of the tune and I stored the information away so that every so often I could drop it into conversation to make people think I'm a lot smarter than I am. The irony of East Side Rovers fans, whose ground capacity is 2500, singing 'we've never heard of you', was not lost on the fans themselves. This is part of the charm of Irish league football; nobody thinks it's the English Premiership. This was further evidenced by one brief chorus of 'we're shit, and we know we are.'

The burger queue began to grow at the end of the first half. By the time the half-time whistle blew a long line had formed across one half of the stand. Having learned from my previous experience at the Irish Cup Final, I decided that trying to assert authority wasn't the way to go, on the basis that I didn't have any. I could ask people to move, and if they didn't, I could only ask them again. If this is all you've got, it's best to avoid confrontation.

I also implemented a cunning plan. I chose to mingle with the group that now had their burgers and were standing chatting at the other side of the stand. I merrily said 'hello' and asked them how they thought the match was going. I didn't ask anybody to move, but hoped that, based on my friendly nature, I would be able to gently nudge them back to their seats later.

When the space at the top of the stand had filled up, I knew the moment had come when I needed people to move on, otherwise I'd be getting it in the ear from Diarmuid. Keeping this area clear of standing fans was, after all, the one job I had been told to do. I smiled brightly and asked each group politely. Some moved on, most just ignored me. I upped my game and tried to be more assertive, which yielded little movement. One old geezer told me to fuck off, but he was smiling as he said it, so that was alright.

It properly kicked off, however, just as the second half kicked off.

Just after the whistle, Diarmuid appeared on the touch line pointing and yelling up at me.

'Get them the fuck out of there!'

The whole stand heard him; sections of the crowd went 'Ooooh!' sarcastically. I promptly did as I was told.

I tried a jovial, 'Folks, can I ask you to return to your seats for the second half?' thanking them in advance of their cooperation. When that was met by a large round of indifference, I approached each cluster individually. The first group, to my surprise, moved away; the second ignored me; the third, a collection of men I figured were well into their seventies, opted for confrontation.

'Are you saying I can't stand here to eat my burger?' one man said, with both hands in the pockets of his anorak.

'You're not actually eating a burger,' I replied.

'I've finished now, I'm letting it get down,' Anorak replied, 'You shouldn't do exercise so quickly after eating.'

'I don't want you to do any exercise,' I replied. He leaned in.

'My seat's away down them stairs. That's the most exercise I'll do this week.'

The other men laughed. I laughed too, even though it wasn't that funny.

'I'm just being told I have to clear this area; no one's allowed to stand in the stand when the game is in progress,' I explained, realising how ridiculous the sentence was and hoping they didn't notice it. No such luck.

'*You can't stand in the stand?*' said the smaller man wearing a duncher. 'That's political correctness gone mad.'

'That's not political correctness,' said a third man in a woolly hat.

'Well what is it then?' asked Duncher.

'I don't know,' Woolly Hat replied, 'But political correctness is when you can't call someone something.'

'What like?' said Anorak, screwing up his face.

'Like a fucker. You can't call someone a fucker these days,' Woolly Hat explained, 'That's political correctness.'

'No,' a younger voice from just outside the group chipped in, 'You have to be discriminating in some way for it to be not politically correct. Like, you can't call him a gay fucker.'

'Hang on, you can't say that,' I interrupted, feeling I should seize the initiative, 'There's no need for that here.'

'Well I know that,' the younger man replied, 'I wasn't *calling* him that, I was just saying that he'd have to use a discriminatory word for it to be non-politically correct.'

'Like specky bastard?' another voice from outside the group said.

'No, not really,' the younger man said, 'That's just an insult.'

'Look,' I interrupted, 'What I need everyone to do is ...'

'Or retard?' said Anorak.

'Yes, that is another word we definitely shouldn't be using,' I said. I was trying hard not to, but I could feel myself losing it.

'Health and safety!' said Woolly Hat loudly and proudly, 'That's what this is. Not being able to eat a burger here is *health and safety* gone mad!'

There was a murmuring of agreement from the whole group and a handful of bystanders who had stopped to listen in.

'It is health and safety,' I agreed, 'And the rule is that you can't stand here during the game *whether you've got a burger or not!*' It came out in a more tense manner than I had intended.

Duncher took a step towards me.

'We don't like health and safety around here,' he said in a manner that wouldn't have been out of place in a Western where the dialogue had run off at a tangent. Menace dripped from his tone. If he had been fifty years younger, I might have been more concerned.

'There's nothing I can do about that,' I said, 'It is what it is.'

Duncher took the duncher off his head, rolled it up and put it in his coat pocket, before poking the index finger of his right hand hard into my chest.

'Now you listen, big bird...' he began, but he got no further.

'*Lads, lads!*' an enthusiastic voice called from the edge of the group, 'The nice yellow man's just doing his job, there's no need for aggro here!'

Deano, for it was he, slid between myself and my seventy-something adversary and addressed the whole gathering.

'The second half has started, and the boys need our support! We need to get back down there and make a bit of noise, c'mon!'

Sticking his arm around the now-capless bald-headed older man, Deano guided him away from me and towards the stairs. Everyone else followed. Deano glanced over his shoulder and gave me the thumbs-up, grinning. I returned the gesture and caught my breath.

'Do you want a free burger, love?' a voice from behind me hissed.

Fat Sandra was leaning out of the hatch holding out a white paper bag. The queue had vanished.

'There's only a couple of them left and I hate throwing them out.'

I thanked her and surreptitiously took the bag, stuffing it inside the black fleece I was wearing beneath my vest. I knew I'd get a break at some point; it could keep until then.

*

Thankfully, the match became an absorbing affair and I had little to do for the rest of the night. East Side scored early in the second half, which meant they would make it into the next round.

In the last few minutes, all the stewards changed position to stand near the touchline in order to ward off any attempt at a pitch invasion. With my back to the play, I watched the intense, excited faces in the stand urging their team to defy the odds and hang on in there.

The pressure got to the home team however and, despite some resolute defending, they conceded in injury time. The energy in the ground evaporated at the final whistle. The East Side players were applauded off the pitch and the supporters headed home quickly in a general state of melancholy having again come so close but not made it over the line.

They filed out past me with little said bar a 'goodnight' or an 'alright now.' Only Deano, as enthusiastic as ever, came over to speak to me.

'Sickening, man, sickening,' he said, shaking my hand for the second time that evening, 'We came so close! But it was a cracking game; the boys did well.'

'They did,' I agreed, 'They certainly didn't disgrace themselves.'

'They did not.' Deano nodded furiously.

'Thanks for, eh, thanks for stepping in earlier. It made my job a whole lot easier.'

'No worries, no worries.' Deano smiled from ear to ear. 'Happy to help.' He leant in closer to my face than I wanted him to. *'Some of our guys, they get a bit intense.'*

'I noticed.'

'But they mean well, and most of the time they're harmless.' I didn't ask for details on what they were like the minority of the time. 'Right! I'm off to the pub!'

I smiled.

'Will it be a late night?'

'No, no. Just the one. I'm a total dick when I'm drunk, and I need to take it easy because I've an early morning appointment. I'm heading away out past Bangor. I've a couple of boxes of Poppin' Jalapeno flavour to drop off; that's a big step for Ballywalter.'

I laughed, even though I don't think he meant it as a joke.

'I'll see you around,' he added.

'See you.' I held up my arm in mock salute.

Deano took several steps away, stopped and turned back.

'You haven't seen Paula much lately, have you?'

My eyes widened. I was not expecting that.

'Er, wee bits and pieces. But not this last few weeks, no. She's a tricky woman to pin down.'

He nodded his head as if he was thinking hard about what I had just said.

'Paula's funny, you know,' he said.

'How so?'

'She gives off about you when you do see her. And she gives off about you when you don't see her.'

The stand had emptied; there was only us two left. As the last of stewards left, Diarmuid called my name from the other side of the pitch. I waved back to let him know I'd heard him, but there was no way I was going just yet.

'What do you think that means?' I asked Deano.

He put both hands on his hips and pursed his lips, which I took to mean he was putting a lot of thought into his answer.

'That's a good question,' he replied, his face still screwed up. 'I think,' he began slowly, 'That if she didn't care what you did, she wouldn't say anything at all.' He paused. 'And I think, she would like to see more of you, even though she is still pissed off at you. Does that make sense?'

'Yes, I think it does.'

It was my turn to pause. I was completely unprepared to have this conversation, and not totally convinced Deano was the person I wanted to have it with, but there we were. I made the snap decision to make the most of it.

'It's just hard, Deano, to figure out where I fit in to Paula's life.'

He nodded.

'Yeah. I can see that.' He took a step towards me. 'My advice, if you want it ...'

'Deano, come on!' Two other blokes roughly Deano's age stood at the end of the tunnel into the stand, waving him towards them.

'I need to go,' he said, moving away.

It seemed mad, but I took a step towards him and looked at him full in the face.

'I do want it. Your advice.'

Deano drew breath to speak, but he was interrupted by another shout from his mates. He lifted his wallet from his back pocket, opened it and gave me a business card.

'Call me tomorrow lunch time,' he said, 'Between one and two.' And then he ran off.

I looked closely at his name, number and the tiny picture of a bag of chilli heatwave Doritos printed in the corner. I slipped it into my trouser pocket. I felt like I had been spun round several times and staggered off to find the other stewards.

*

We gathered in the car park to leave back our vests and tell Diarmuid about any incidents we were aware of. I decided my brief encounter with a cloth-capped man with anger issues wasn't worth the telling and set off for home, falling into step with Niamh as I did so. She'd had a quiet night in her section of the ground, save for one older woman who'd fallen down a step in excitement when East Side Rovers had scored. Niamh had spent most of the second half chatting to her while a paramedic strapped her sprained ankle.

We arrived at Niamh's car and, on realising I was walking, she offered me a lift. It hardly seemed worth it, given that the walk home wouldn't have taken that long, but I wanted to let Niamh return the favour.

As she pulled up outside my house, I half expected her to tell me something about Damian. I wasn't wrong.

'I've called off the wedding,' she said simply. She turned to look directly at me.

'Ok.' I'll admit it, there was cheering in my head, but I don't think this showed on my face.

'I've ended it with Damian. I've bought him out of the house. I borrowed some money and re-mortgaged. We've talked and fought and argued, and there's nothing more to say. I don't want to see him again.'

She looked out of the front of the car and sighed.

'How are you doing?' I asked.

'Fucking awful.' Her tone was matter of fact. 'I've been a total mess this last couple of weeks, just so upset. I've taken everything I dreamt of and worked for and planned for years, and torn it all up. I mean, have you any idea how much I have talked about the wedding?'

Before I could even begin to think of an answer, she laughed out loud.

'Alright, you probably do,' she said, 'Everybody does.'

I smiled. We sat in silence for a moment.

'It's grief,' I said at last, 'It's the loss of what you thought was going to happen.'

'That figures,' she said slowly, 'But it was never going to work. It's grief, yeah, but there's also a little bit of relief. You have to look at the way the future is shaping up and ask if that's what you want. That's the only thing that lets you tear up the present.'

I nodded. She looked at me again.

'You asked me what I would need if I was going to walk away,' she said, 'That night after Kylie.' I remembered. 'That was a good question. Thanks Robbie, I owe you one.'

I admit it, that moment felt good. Not that Niamh was hurting and trying to put her life back together, but knowing that I helped. Niamh had taken stock, made a decision and figured out for herself how to get it done. In some ways, I was a little envious.

'So,' I said, 'You're managing things on your own?'

She shrugged.

'Yeah. I've nearly paid this car off, once that's done, things'll be a little easier. Paying the mortgage is a stretch, but I can do it. No nights out for a while though.' She smiled ruefully. 'Not that I'm really feeling like it at the moment. I might let a room out to a friend, that would help. But not yet, I want my space right now.'

'That makes sense.'

'And I'm not going to do any more shifts for Safe & Sound, not for a while anyway.'

'Oh?'

'My aunt manages a catering firm. She's offered me a part time job as a supervisor at events. I'll still be working at the weekend, but it'll be a little more money,' she paused, 'And it'll take me out of the Safe & Sound rumour mill. There isn't anybody I haven't told about the wedding, I just can't face telling them that ... none of it's going to happen.'

Her throat tightened and she wiped her eyes.

'So this is our last car journey then?'

'God, Robbie,' she said, sniffing, 'Are you trying to make me cry *more*?'

I grinned as she leant across the car to hug me.

'Thanks again.'

She wrapped her arms briefly around my neck, and then we parted. We looked at each other in the face.

'Any time. When I say, 'I'm happy for you', you know what way I mean it, right?'

She smiled.

'I do.'

I opened the passenger door and lifted one foot out.

'In a weird way, I'm going to miss our car journeys,' I said, 'They were never predictable.'

Niamh laughed.

'No. From your side of things, I suppose they weren't.'

I grinned.

'Take care, Niamh,' I said, from outside the car, 'I hope I see you around.'

I watched her drive off down the street. In my head, I replayed what she had just said to me.

'You have to look at the way the future is shaping up and ask if it is what you want.'

Too true, I thought, before I stuck the key in the door of the empty house and went inside.

11. Concert, car and contentment

September went by in a blur. Work went up a gear and the last of the outdoor gigs combined with a more densely packed line up at the Auditorium led to more late-night shifts than I wanted. I wasn't really complaining though, the nights out were good craic and my week was filled nicely. By the end of the month however, I was feeling the pace, and knew I needed to slow down.

When Helen phoned me up mid-week to ask if I could steward at an all-day event on Saturday, my immediate reaction was to say no. I was already working late on the Friday night and I had a busy day of loafing planned, before eventually going out for a few pints at the local. Helen's pleasant telephone manner was hard to resist, however. There was no pressure from her, but I still felt trying not to do the shift. It was only when I caved, I found out the location was Slane Castle in County Meath, an hour and half's drive outside Belfast.

Security Ireland were covering the gig, but a variety of simultaneous events left them short of manpower; Safe & Sound had been asked to cover one of the entrances. At least it was Coldplay; not in my top ten bands of all time, but still very listenable and one of the biggest live acts on the planet. The other silver lining was that Alison – who didn't want to go either but also couldn't say no to Helen – suggested that we car shared.

'Are you sure about that?' I asked her during a quick phone call on the Thursday night beforehand. It seemed too good to be true.

'Makes sense. No point in bringing two cars, is there?'

'No, it just seems ...'

'What?'

'A bit *couply*, doesn't it?'

'Couply?'

'Yeah,' I searched for words, 'You and I arriving together in front of the Safe & Sound crew. That's going to raise eyebrows isn't it? You'll have to spend all day explaining our non-date arrangement.'

This arrangement had been working rather well. Up to that point, we had met for coffee a few times and been out for a couple of informal meals – straight after work with no extension to another venue such as a cinema or home – and once for a short walk and an ice lolly in Botanic gardens where I lamented that even though the Tropical Ravine had been beautifully restored, it just wasn't the same without terrapins. Alison enjoyed the walk, but didn't understand my disappointment at being unable to relive my childhood by looking at swimming reptiles.

'I can live with whatever sad interest other stewards might have,' she replied, 'Besides, if you drive, I can take full control of the stereo and broaden out your musical tastes.'

'My musical tastes are already broad.' I tried to hide my irritation. 'Anyway, I've had a copy of 'Born in the USA' stuck in my CD player for ages.'

'Ain't that the metaphor.' I sighed forcefully but didn't answer. 'Does the car have Bluetooth?'

'Don't think so.'

'Does the stereo have a three-mil jack?'

'A what?'

'A three point five mil jack input? A wee hole where you put a wee lead that lets you play your phone through the car stereo.'

'I don't know. I'll have a look.'

As it turned out, it did. I'd spent a whole year either listening to the radio or Bruce – or nothing – when I could have listened to anything I wanted with the cunning use of a short lead linking my phone to the car.

I spent all of Friday morning in happy anticipation of driving to and from Slane with Alison beside me. In my fantasy world, we'd listen to and talk about music intensely and share a little more of our lives with each other. At the end of the day, there'd be a greater bond between us. Getting out of the car in the early hours of the morning, while Alison wouldn't kiss me goodnight or even invite me in for coffee, she'd look at me wistfully, realising there was a path to a perfect life lying right there, with me. In that moment, she'd know that at some indefinable point not too far away, she would say, 'Robbie, enough of this non-dating crap, let's go out together; *let's make this work*.' And then we'd be together, forever and always.

'So I said to Leanne it wouldn't be any bother if she travelled down with us,' were the exact words Alison used to shatter my dream, when she called back on Friday lunch time.

'Oh, ok.'

'I mean, she could use her wife's car, but then Gemma would have to borrow her Dad's car, and he's in Glenavy, and it would just be simpler if we helped her out.'

'No bother,' I said, noting how my lunch-time donut from Tim Horton's had turned to dust in my mouth.

To round things off, Helen was waiting for me at the Auditorium when I signed in on Friday evening.

'Robbie,' she said, holding my right arm with both her hands, 'I heard from Leanne that you were able to give her a lift and I was wondering if you had room for one more in your car?'

Helen's in-person charm was every bit as effective as her telephone manner.

'I couldn't refuse you,' I replied, 'I can take one more.' I was just about to ask where I had to pick her up when she gave me further details.

'Alan lives in Lisburn, and he'll make his way to one of the car parks at Sprucefield; you can pick him up there.' She handed me a post-it note with his phone number written on it, before adding, 'If you could give him a wee bell tonight and firm up arrangements, that would be great. Thank you so, so much! I owe you one!'

*

I tried to hit the sack as early as I could after the Friday night gig. The ringing in my ears from Def Leppard's full-on set, however, and the adrenaline levels that come from manning a capacity crowd concert floor of well-lubricated eighties metal fans, did not promote sleep. I think I dozed off somewhere after three but even though I got up at around ten, I didn't feel well rested, or enthusiastic about doing it all over again just outside Drogheda. I sat at the kitchen table with a strong cup of coffee and a toasted bagel dripping in butter, looking at the footie fixtures on my phone and dreaming of what might have been.

I left the house just after eleven, driving across town and then north to pick up Alison. It was the first time I had ever been to her house. Not that I was actually *in* her house, she bounced out as soon as she saw me pull up, laden down with a coat over her arm and three bags.

'How long do you think we're going for?'

'Shut up and open your boot.'

She deposited her coat and two of the bags and got into the car beside me. 'One bag is my usual gear for outdoor shifts, one is a few food items for breaks or when we're coming home. I made some sandwiches with chicken in them, so I thought I'd better put in a few ice packs to keep them from spoiling. And there's a flask in there as well.'

'Do you want to run back and get the windbreak and a rug?'

'You will thank me later, Robbie McKittrick.'

I didn't argue with her because I knew I would want some variation from my pack of Wagon Wheels – courtesy of my mother who had seen them on offer at the Vivo round the corner.

'And this,' Alison continued, holding up a small, black, square-shaped package, 'Is a few CDs, in case this,' she held up a short audio cable, 'Doesn't connect my phone to your car.'

'Right,' I replied, thinking I had put considerably less preparation into the day.

There was no problem with Alison's audio cable, however, and so we set off toward Leanne's house to the songs of Waxahatchee's 'Saintcloud' album.

'I'm not going to recognise a single song today, am I?'

Alison smiled and looked away.

'Not for the first while,' she replied, 'Maybe on the way home we could fall back on a few old favourites, now that they're all stored on here.' She lifted up her phone and, not for the first time, I marvelled at how, for a small monthly subscription you could have virtually every song ever written playing in your car at the touch of a tiny screen.

Leanne was ready to go too and appeared at the front of the house while I was still parking the car. She threw her bag in the boot and jumped into the back seat.

'Just the one bag I see,' I muttered to Alison.

'I have a lot of chocolate. If you're going to carry on like this, you don't get any.'

'Hi guys,' Leanne said, fastening her seat belt, oblivious to our exchange, 'Thanks for the lift down, Robbie, much appreciated.'

'No worries. You're not too far away from Alison, so it's no bother.'

'I did offer to walk down,' Leanne said.

'But I said you wouldn't mind driving up,' Alison added.

'Not at all,' I replied, thinking how we sounded like an old married couple, and liking it. 'Now, just Alan to pick up and we're on our way.'

'Alan?' Leanne asked.

'Yeah, younger guy who needed a lift. Lives in Lisburn; we're picking him outside McDonald's at Sprucefield.'

'Ok,' Leanne said, but in one of those indefinable ways that meant she was clearly thinking something she wasn't saying.

'What?' Alison beat me to it.

Leanne shrugged. 'I think I know who you mean, that's all.' I could see Leanne begin to smile in my rear-view mirror, and then she burst out laughing.

'What?' Alison and I both said together.

Leanne regained her composure and took a deep breath.

'Alan, if it is the Alan I'm thinking about, is *interesting* ...' she said.

'How so?' Alison asked, 'Come on, spit it out.'

'He talks fast and he talks about cars.'

'Ok.'

'He has the nickname Motormouth.'

265

'He goes by the nickname Motormouth, or gets called Motormouth behind his back?' I asked.

'Good point,' Leanne replied, 'I'm not sure. Best just to call him Alan.'

*

Alan, skinny, slightly spotty and barely looking eighteen, was also ready and waiting, horsing his way through a box of chicken nuggets outside McDonald's. He didn't have a bag with him and jumped straight into the car.

'Hiya Ricky!' he said.

'Robbie. And this is Alison beside me here and Leanne, beside you.' Alan looked at neither.

'Ford Focus 2015,' he said brightly.

'I think so, yeah,' I replied.

'Oh, it is, aye,' Alan assured me, 'Zetec TDCI five door, 118 brake horse power, four cylinders and six-speed gear box. Decent wee bit of poke on her. Anybody want a chicken nugget?' No one did. 'You should've been here five minutes ago,' he went on, 'A new Jag XE came out of the drive through.'

'Who would eat chips in a brand new Jag?' Leanne asked, but Alan continued.

'Two-litre, four-cylinder, turbocharged petrol engine.'

'Right.'

'Were you working last night, Leanne?' Alison asked, changing the subject.

'No, thank goodness, I was out on Thursday night at Bangor sea front, there was a string of local bands.'

'Quiet shift?' Alison asked.

'Not bad. Good crowd at it, but some were a bit young and excitable. Highlight of the evening was one girl who had so much WKD in her that she clambered on top of a police Octavia to dance.'

'How old was she?' Alan asked. Leanne shrugged.

'Seventeen or eighteen probably.'

'No, how old was the *Octavia*?' Alan continued, 'The PSNI are starting to replace their older models at the minute.'

Leanne looked at him blankly.

'Really couldn't say. Octavias all look the same to me.'

'Well, you got to start with how the bonnet tapers, or, if you prefer, the height of the rear bumper ...' Alan began, but Leanne cut him off.

'Don't worry about it, kiddo, I'll live in ignorance.'

'Are you driving yet?' I asked.

'Not really,' Alan answered. I could see his face turn glum in the rear view.

'Not really?'

'I passed the theory ages ago, but I'm still taking lessons.'

'You got a test coming up?' Alison asked.

'Failed my second one last week,' Alan replied, throwing the last of his chicken nuggets into his mouth and crumpling the box. 'I keep being told I'm driving erotically.'

'Erratically,' Leanne corrected, but Alan didn't seem to hear.

'One examiner said my driving made him go rigid.'

'Maybe he did mean erotically,' I said quietly, but Alison shushed me.

'The other examiner said I was coming at things too fast,' Alan added.

'Again ...' I began, but Alison's glare made me stop.

*

It was a longer drive than I thought it was going to be, but not so much in actual time. There wasn't a single topic of conversation Motormouth couldn't turn to cars, and if we didn't talk, he gave us a commentary on the year, make and models of the cars around us. In the end, Alison put on a compilation of Ben Folds tracks —totally new to me, but as close to Elton John as you can get, without actually being Elton John — and gradually turned the car stereo up. Bit by bit we drowned him out.

I parked up in a field in the village. Getting out, Alison glared at me over the car roof.

'What?'

'You agreed to bring him,' she hissed, 'I'm blaming you for the most torturous ninety minutes of my life.'

Alan and Leanne got out of the car after us.

'2014 Audi A4,' Alan said, looking at a car parked in the next row, before going off for a closer look.

Leanne had a similar expression to Alison.

'And we get to do it all again later,' I said, as I opened the boot. Both women glared at me.

'If there's a small wood with soft ground,' Leanne muttered, 'I say we kill him and bury his body.'

'Aw,' I replied, 'And deny him a last road trip in a hearse? That's just cruel.'

Following the signs, we made our way to Entrance 2, where a dozen Safe & Sound stewards had already gathered; Sam, Kettley and Sohail among them.

'Young fella!' Sam greeted me with an exaggerated salute. I grinned.

'Sam! Sohail ... Kettley ... well, what weather is in store for us today?'

'Cloudy, some chance of rain, but nothing we can't handle,' Kettley replied, 'A heavy weather front is on its way, but we should be back home by the time it hits.'

We settled into small talk about recent shifts before Brian, our supervisor, called us to order. He and Leanne were in charge together, but he took the lead with the briefing.

'Simple stuff today. Half of you will be on tickets, half of you will be on searches. We're south of the border, so you don't need to be SIA to search. The list of banned items has been posted on large signs at the entrance, they're also on display in the car parks and it's the same list that's on everybody's ticket. Nobody can say they didn't know they couldn't bring a folding chair to the gig.'

I glanced back at the sign. Sure enough, folding chairs, folding stools and shooting sticks all had a large red 'X' through them.

'Dining room chairs aren't on the list,' I muttered to Kettley, 'So technically, we can't turn one away.' He grinned.

'True,' he whispered, 'Nothing about sofas, recliners or bean bags.'

'Or a futon,' I added.

'Or a pouffe,' Sam joined in and made us both laugh.

Brian paused momentarily and Leanne raised her eyebrows. She didn't punish me however, sending Motormouth out on tickets and putting Sam and I together on male searches.

'I'm getting too wrinkly for searches,' he said, as we dragged the last of the barriers into position.

'Hard labour is it?'

'You never done them before?' I shook my head. 'They're murder on the knees and the hamstrings. You've got to check down the back of the legs of every single person. That's a lot of bending over.'

I confessed I hadn't thought about that.

The lull between setting up and gates opening was spent standing around chatting and eating lunch, while trying to not look like we were eating lunch. The concert promoters wanted us at our posts and there wouldn't be another break time until the evening, so we knew, without it being said by either supervisor, this was the time to get something into us, as long as we didn't make it look too obvious.

I joked that we should adopt Coldplay's song 'Yellow' as a company anthem, but Sam seemed confused. Firstly, he knew nothing about Coldplay. Secondly, he couldn't get his head around a song being called 'Yellow.'

'*Yellow?*' he asked, 'What is it about?'

I struggled to explain.

'Not really sure to be honest.' I literally scratched my head. 'The singer writes a song called 'Yellow' – in the song called 'Yellow' – and at other points looks at the stars, swims and draws lines.'

'And did people buy this song?' Sam asked, frowning.

'In their millions, yeah.'

'Nice work, if you can get it.'

I stuffed a mini Mars bar into my mouth and drained the end of a bottle of diet Sprite.

'You don't have to answer, but I couldn't not ask,' I said, 'How have you been?'

Sam crammed the end of what very much smelled like a tuna and onion sandwich into his mouth and chewed it thoughtfully.

'The short answer, youngster, is that I'm alright.' He sipped at a bottle of water. 'The longer answer is that I've gone from feeling sad and empty and pointless, to having so much to think about, there are days I think my head might explode.'

'We've time on our hands,' I replied, 'But no pressure.'

Both of us tucked away our empty bottles into the bags at our feet, and I left space for him to say as much as he wanted to.

'I'm seeing a counsellor,' he began, 'That took a lot of persuading, and I only intended to go once to prove how stupid it was so I could tell everyone who kept nagging me to leave me alone. But it turned out to be ok. He asks good questions and I end up thinking about things I never thought about before. I've come to the conclusion that I've done a lot of not thinking about stuff. In fact, I'm a fucking genius at it. I've been *not* thinking about things all my life.' He smiled.

'In what way?' I asked, 'If that's not too personal a question.'

'It's a personal question all right, but I don't mind answering it.' He looked away from me, across to the hillside where the concert would take place and the green hills far beyond. 'I've started thinking about the hand I was dealt. My parents, my grandparents, two brothers, are all gone now, but they each had an effect on me, for good and bad. I've never properly thought about that before.'

His eyes returned from the hills and he looked at me directly.

'I've carried stuff around with me for years, and never stopped to think about the effect it was having not just on me, but on others in turn. On my wife, my children, my grandkids. The choices I made in life ...' he paused for a moment. 'I thought I was in control, but now I think, a lot of the time I wasn't really making choices, I was just reacting to things because that's the way I was made. Is any of that making sense or are you thinking about calling the funny farm?'

I smiled.

'It all makes sense,' I replied, taken by how open and honest his answer had been. 'I'm no expert, but we're all shaped by the experiences we have, and sometimes, maybe even quite often, we don't recognise it.'

Sam nodded.

'I never knew that I could stop and say, 'is this how I want it to be'?' he said quietly.

'Are you better off for knowing?'

He looked at me and raised both eyebrows.

'That's a good question. Are you my counsellor in disguise?'

I smiled again, as did he.

'I am better off,' he continued, 'But it's sad too. I wish I'd made better choices. They say regret is a waste though, so I try to focus on now.'

'True.' I recognised the wisdom of his words.

'And pretty soon I'm going to hear a millionaire rock star sing a song about things that are yellow, so it doesn't get much better!'

That was as much as he wanted to say. The depth with which he had spoken was more than I had expected. I tried once more to explain the Coldplay lyric, but it didn't make things any clearer and Sam continued to take the piss.

Shortly afterwards, the gates opened, and ticket holders began to stream in, eager for a spot as close to the stage as possible. Sam gave me a crash course on how to wipe my hands over men I'd never met before and then we felt up blokes until seven o'clock.

*

With the second of two listenable local support acts almost at the end of their set, and the crowd coming in having almost dried up, Leanne sent Sam and I off for a break. We made our way to the stewards' hot food stand for a burger and chip and collapsed into plastic chairs that sank slowly into the damp ground. Not that we cared, as we complained about the amount of knee pain we were experiencing.

Returning to our post, Brian announced that we were being hastily reassigned.

'They haven't provided enough toilets inside,' he said, 'So there are big queues.'

'Do you want us to get people to pee faster?' Sam asked, grinning.

'No,' Brian replied, 'I want you stop blokes from pissing up the outside of the toilet enclosure because they can't be arsed waiting. Consider yourselves the first recruits to Willy Watch.'

'Conscripts more like,' Sam muttered as the three of us made our way into the arena.

'And it was all yellow,' I sang quietly.

Sam just looked at me.

Our number grew, until there were well over a dozen willy watchers on our patrol. Our job was simple; whenever a slightly pissed bloke made his way to the canvas covered barrier and unzipped his fly, our job was to kindly ask him not to urinate in front of approximately eighty thousand people, but to queue

274

up for a few minutes and point Percy at the plastic piss pots inside the toilet area.

It took a while to make it clear to the inebriated punters that we really weren't going to let them pee wherever they wanted, but after what became something like an x-rated game of 'Whackamole', most people took the hint and stopped trying. It helped when, just after half eight, Coldplay came onstage and demand for bladder-voiding facilities suddenly dropped.

The sun had already set around seven, and the last remnants of light in the sky had all but disappeared. It very much looked like Kettley's forecasted downpour was out there somewhere, but the rain stayed away, and the cloud cover provided heat. The floodlights were now on full power, illuminating the crowd of thousands who covered every square metre of the hillside that forms the natural amphitheatre at Slane. The sea of faces was never static; always shifting and moving, mesmerising to watch.

Like them or loath them, Coldplay live were superb, working the crowd and leading them in anthem after anthem. Yellow, sadly, did not receive an airing, but in a quieter part of the set they played 'In my Place', which I remembered from an early album. The lyrics hit me with fresh meaning: *'In my place, in my place, were lines that I couldn't change; I was lost, oh yeah.'* I looked along the barrier, Sam was several stewards away, but he wasn't paying any attention to the music.

As the song continued, I spotted Alison at the top of the hill, clearly visible in the bright light of the first aid area. She was sitting beside a girl bent over in her seat, holding a paper bag. Alison was holding the girl's hair back. The song drifted on into the third verse; *'If you go, if you go, leave me down here on my own, then I'll wait for you.'* It was a beautiful moment listening to a world-class band play such a tender song, while watching someone who had become enormously important to me, whom I did not want to lose, yet at the same time, never really had.

And then the moment was ruined by having to tell a thirty-something bloke, 'You can't piss here, put your dick away.'

*

The concert finished just before curfew at eleven, with the promoters thanking everyone for their good behaviour and requesting that they leave the venue as quietly as possible because this was, after all, a residential area. Then they set off a firework display that lasted fifteen minutes.

Stewards of all persuasions united to sweep the hillside until the last of the concert goers had left and only the vendors remained to clear up and then dismantle their catering stalls. The weary stewards of Safe & Sound met up back at Entrance 2, where Alison informed me that while Leanne was genuinely grateful for the lift down, she had been offered a lift home with Brian.

'She thought the supervisors might have to stay late to speak to the organisers, and she didn't want to hold us back.'

'Course she didn't,' I said, 'Very thoughtful of her.'

Alan saw us from a distance and made his way over.

'Maybe he'll be too tired to talk,' Alison said, but neither of us really believed it.

Alan began his commentary as we crawled out of the village itself, giving us the lowdown on the vehicles we passed. Alison distributed various types of chocolate-covered biscuit, which slowed him down a little. By the time we hit the motorway, the back of the car had gone strangely silent.

I glanced over my shoulder.

'*Is he asleep?*' I whispered. Alison looked back.

'Yes,' she said, 'With half a Twix still in his hand.'

'He'd better not get it all over the upholstery.'

Alison looked at me.

'Who the hell refers to it as 'upholstery'?'

I shrugged.

Alison plugged her phone back into the car stereo, reducing the volume to a level where we could listen and still talk.

'How was your day?' I asked.

She didn't answer and I became aware that she was looking at me.

'*What?*'

'Andy never asks me how my day was,' she said, 'I mean, he'll listen when I tell him, but you have to volunteer the information.' She paused. 'My day was fine. I was on ticket scanning, then they sent me over to first aid where I mainly sat with young girls who had vommed, were vomming or thought they were about to vom.'

'Nice.'

'S'alright. Most of the time they were quiet and I got to listen to Coldplay. What about you?'

'Fine. On searches; knees are killing me, as are my calves. Way too much bending down. Then I was sent to guard the outer barrier of the men's toilets to protect it from being pissed on.'

'I'll take the vomit thanks.'

'What did you think of the gig?'

'Loved it. Especially the last four or five songs before they went off, they really built it up.'

'Yeah, I always thought Coldplay were a bit bland, but they were spectacular tonight.'

'A bit bland?' Alison replied, 'This from the man whose tastes don't expand much beyond classic rock.'

'That is totally unfair,' I responded with a little volume. Alison motioned with her head.

'Shush, you'll waken the baby.'

'I have broader tastes than you think.'

'Alright, let's put this to the test,' she said. 'None of your clothes are in bright colours.'

'Men don't wear bright colours.'

'Every fleece you own is either blue or grey.'

'I have a green one.'

'Bright green?'

'Dark green. And I have a bright yellow one.'

'Work clothes don't count. When you pick up a book it's either a thriller written by someone like Lee Child …'

'Nothing wrong with Lee Child.'

'Or a rock biography. The number of books you have on the Beatles runs into double figures.'

'Maybe.' I have exactly seventeen.

'You love the 'Star Wars' films.'

'Everybody loves 'Star Wars.''

'Somewhere in your house, I'm certain there will be a plastic teddy bear thing from one of the early films.'

'An ewok.'

'And a soldiery thing with the white armour and helmet.'

'A stormtrooper. Yes I do have a stormtrooper figure, but no ewoks.' Which was true. What I did have was two Gammorrean guards from Jabba's palace guarding a shelf of rock biographies.

'You also love Monty Python, especially the 'Holy Grail', 'Ferris Bueller' and still have a soft spot for the 'Police Academy' films.'

'Not 'Ferris Bueller.'' But doesn't everybody have a soft spot for the films of their youth?'

'You love football and still support the same team you did as a child.'

'Most men do – that shows how loyal we are.' I could feel my internal temperature rising, but she kept going.

'Your living room is painted cream.'

'Everybody's living room is painted cream.'

'And you love a good spreadsheet.'

'Ha!' I said triumphantly, 'That is where you are wrong. I hate spreadsheets, they're horrible things.' I should have stopped there, but I got carried away demonstrating how much I hated spreadsheets. 'I make lists. I am the king of lists.'

Alison looked at me.

'Yeah, 'cause being king of lists proves how rock n roll you are!'

I wished she had stopped there, but she kept going. 'Face it, Robbie, you are lovable, but completely predictable. An off-the-rack fifty-something bloke.'

I should have focussed on the 'lovable'; instead I chose to go on the offensive.

'Alright, so I may not be the most original in my tastes, but you've got your own ruts too.'

'How so?'

'Andy is the obvious one.'

Shit. Again.

It was out of my mouth before I had thought it through. I glanced to my left. Alison stared straight ahead. We had been listening to an album called 'Come on up to the house – women sing Tom Waits.' A beautiful version of 'Ruby's Arms' played without interruption for a moment.

'Sorry,' I said, breaking the silence, 'That was uncalled for.'

She turned her head towards me.

'It's alright,' she said, quietly, 'I asked for it. And it's fair enough I suppose.'

'Ruby's Arms' came to a close and Alison decided it was time for a different approach.

'Pick any song you like, but it has to be something important to you.'

'All my favourites are from the seventies, so you'll just make fun of me.'

'I promise I won't. Any song you want.'

I pretended to think about it longer than I needed to think about.

''You're gonna make me lonesome when you go', Dylan, from 'Blood on the Tracks."

She looked at me, before she looked for it on her phone. I thought she was going to pass comment, but she didn't.

To my surprise, she chose 'Blackbird' from The White Album and then I chose Springsteen's 'Brilliant Disguise.' We worked our way through 'Bell Bottom Blues', 'May you Never' and 'Here Comes the Sun' – all mine – as well as 'Tiny Dancer', 'Scenes From an Italian Restaurant' and an obscure Stevie Nicks track called 'Imperial Hotel' – all hers – which I had long since forgotten about. This prompted us to think about how critical Fleetwood Mac's 'Rumours' album had been to our teenage years and so we cruised into Lisburn listening to the bass riff from 'The Chain.'

We woke Alan up during 'Second Hand News.' He came to with no idea where he was and was initially quite panicked until we assured him we hadn't kidnapped him; we wanted to leave him home as quickly as possible. It turned out he didn't live too far away, so we dropped him off at his door. Alison thought this was a very kind gesture and 'lovely of me' and I let her believe it. In truth, I was just trying to make the journey last as long as possible.

We listened to another few tracks from 'Rumours' as I held my speed at a steady sixty on the motorway. I made the excuse I was tired. I was, as well as being under-slept and still up at twenty to two in the morning. I could have driven all night, however. The sky was heavy, but the road was dry and clear. I had good music, good company and what seemed like a lifetime supply of chocolate. I had a good feeling too; a warmth in the centre of my chest. If I'd had a mug of tea in my hand, I could have said I was completely content and at peace with the world.

'Ali?' I said.

'What?'

'Find Mona Lisas and Mad Hatters.' I knew she was smiling without having to look at her. A few seconds later we were immersed in the opening lines, *'And now I know, Spanish Harlem are not just pretty words to say.'*

We reached her front door before the end of the song, but Alison didn't make any move to get out until it was over. When the last chorus faded completely, she unplugged her phone and picked up her bags from the footwell.

'You called me Ali.'

'Yeah ...'

'Only Mum ever called me Ali.' She looked directly at me for a moment and I desperately hoped she would lean forward and hug me or kiss me. I would even have settled for a touch on the arm, but she opened her door instead, got out and went to the boot to get her other bag. I rolled down the window to say goodnight.

'Thank you for driving,' she said, 'And your song choices. You've got good taste in music.'

'Even though ...'

'Don't spoil the moment. Just accept the compliment.'

I smiled.

'Thank you for your company,' I said, 'I like being around you.'

She smiled back, but suddenly there was tension in her face.

'Robbie,' she began, and something about her tone made me feel that the world might come off its axis. 'The Elton John gig at the Auditorium next week ... I bought tickets ages ago. I wasn't going to go with Andy, what with the way things are. But he's asked to go with me. He says he's had a chance to think and he misses me. He wants to give things another shot.'

'Ok,' I said, nodding and maintaining what I hoped was a neutral expression. Inside I had just been pushed off the top of a building, while snipers took shots at my falling body and prehistoric winged creatures ripped off pieces of my flesh with their talons.

'I just thought you should know. Sorry. That's a bit of a weird ending to the day. A good day.'

'That's alright,' I said, forcing a thin smile, 'We were always non-dating, remember?'

We said goodnight, and I pulled away as fast as I reasonably could, without looking like I was trying to get away as fast as I reasonably could.

Five minutes before I reached home, the heavens opened. Rain fell so hard it bounced back up, a foot in the air. I got soaked on the short journey from the pavement to my front door. I set my bag down on the kitchen floor and put the kettle on. I was tired, wet, and fucking miserable.

12. Apartment and a plan

The front door closed firmly behind him as he left, and I remained standing in the middle of the living area. It was enormously trusting of him to leave me here and I wanted to respect that, but I couldn't resist the lure of the shelves. You can tell a lot about someone from what reading material they have on show. In this case, however, there was no reading material, nor was there a single CD, let alone any lovely vinyl. This was the flat of someone from an age group content to stream.

The top shelf held several football trophies, some dating from several years ago. One small plaque was inscribed with 'Best Beginner 2008' from a local Taekwondo club. Judging by the lack of any further awards, I assumed the interest in Taekwondo had been short-lived.

The second shelf held a variety of unrelated miniatures; a mini figure of Robin van Persie, Artoo Detoo from Star Wars, a Lego Dobby the House Elf from Harry Potter, a cheap plastic replica of Gonzo from the Muppets, which might have come from a Happy Meal, and last of all, a rather dog-eared stuffed rat from the film 'Ratatouille.' Remy, if I remember correctly.

The shelf below held a Lego model of the Millennium Falcon, of which I heartily approved. I squatted down onto my hunkers to get a better view. Ten-year-old me badly wanted to lift it off the shelf, but fifty-two-year-old me feared it might break apart in my hands.

Standing up again, with a crack from my left knee, I considered the best way to keep myself out of mischief was to sit down on the sofa and not move.

The walls of the flat were sparsely decorated. Three posters had been blu-tacked with absolutely no sense of spacing around the room. The first was an action shot of Cristiano Ronaldo, from the first time he played in Manchester. The second was a montage from the 'Iron Man' films. The last was an advertising poster for Cool Ranch flavour Doritos. Talk about taking your work home with you.

I readjusted my position on the sofa, the faux leather squeaking under me. The thought that my daughter and her boyfriend had probably done unspeakable things on these cushions popped unbidden into my head. I screwed my face up in an effort to not think about it.

I glanced over the small pile of DVDs beside the TV. Mostly Marvel universe films, which held no interest for me, but the box set of 'Band of Brothers' right at the bottom earned marks for taste.

I stared out the window and down to the street below. It was a small but compact new flat and, I reflected, much nicer than the two-up two-down, slightly damp terraced house Shirley and I had started out with in our early twenties. Not that Paula and Deano were starting out, at least I hoped they weren't. I had warmed to him. He was generous and good-hearted, but he had a long way to go to convince me he wasn't a bin lid.

I immediately felt guilty for thinking that. If they did end up together, I knew I could make my peace with it. I was pretty confident he treated her well, which, at the end of the day, is all any parent should really be concerned about. And beneath his surface Muppetry, he also understood people.

I didn't phone Deano the day after the East Side game; it seemed too weird. Who phones their daughter's boyfriend to talk about the complexity of their father-daughter relationship? Especially when you've only met three times. But I spent another week trying to pin Paula down to a meal out at the Korean place Alison had brought me to. Despite my misgivings, and inability to understand much of what was on the menu, the food had been amazing, and I was keen to go again. Paula however, kept fobbing me off with excuses. I had hoped our conversation in the hospital was a turning point, but this proved not to be the case, and I couldn't understand why. Eventually I phoned Deano out of desperation, because if the answer to your problems is to consult Deano, then it has to be out of desperation.

It was unkind to think that, however, because Deano not only understood the problem better than I did, he also knew the solution.

'You're her Dad; she loves you,' Deano said simply, surprising me with his directness, 'But things have been off between yous for a long time. I think she would like that to be put right.'

'You think?'

'Yeah. It's hard to say because she doesn't come right out and say it. It's awkward like, isn't it?'

'Yes,' I said, referring to both my relationship with Paula and the excruciating nature of the phone call.

'How do you stop things being awkward?' he asked, and I wasn't sure if he was being rhetorical. Turns out he wasn't. 'For something to stop being awkward, you have to, I don't know, like, get past the awkwardness, and that can be really awkward. I think that's why Paula keeps avoiding you. Does that make sense?'

I thought about it.

'Yeah,' I said, 'I think there's wisdom in that.'

'Ha ha!' he laughed loudly down the phone, 'Somebody thinks I'm wise. That's fuckin' hilarious!'

His solution was simple; the only way to get beyond awkward was to work through the awkwardness. I just needed to keep chasing and meeting up and talking, until my relationship with Paula was in better shape.

'I have been trying,' I said, trying not to sound whiney, 'But the best I ever seem to get is half an hour in a coffee shop before she has to go to somewhere.'

Deano's solution, at least in the short term, was simple, but daring. Paula was coming over to his flat for pizza and what he referred to as a 'Netflix-bender' a couple of nights later. His plans had changed, but he hadn't had time to tell her yet.

'Her night is free,' he said, 'So you can be there when I go out.'

I thought about this.

'Won't she be really pissed off that I'm there and you lied to her?'

'Aye, probably. But maybe yous'll have a really nice night in and it'll be alright.'

'You're optimistic,' I said, but I agreed to it anyway. In the end, what was there to lose? I wasn't being given much, so it seemed fair game to risk what little I had.

I glanced at my watch. It was now just after half seven, the time Paula had told Deano she'd be over. There was no sign of her car in the street, although I realised she might be on foot as it was only a ten-minute walk from our house. Her house. Her's and Shirley's house. Screw it, *our house.* It was where we had all lived; it was always going to be our house.

Second thoughts began to make their voices heard. There was still the opportunity to slip out and run away. But what would that do for me? And I'd have to tell Deano I chickened out, and he'd have to explain to Paula why he wasn't at home and then she'd know as well. And she'd probably tell Shirley too. No, I decided, I was fully committed to staying the course. If nothing else, it was the route of least embarrassment.

I glanced around the room again, but there was nothing else to look at, so I did what everyone does when they have time on their hands and took out my phone. There were no new Facebook updates, nothing in the various irritating WhatsApp groups I had been added to and no new text messages.

Absently, I opened up the messages from Alison. The last ones were related to the Slane trip five days ago, and there had been nothing since. Not that I had expected anything. The Elton John gig was the following night and, although I'd said I was available, I hadn't been offered the shift. It was probably just as well. At least now I could go to the pub, or watch a film or do anything to distract me from ruminating on how someone I loved being with, and whom I had secretly hoped would be the other half of a long-term relationship, was going to be 'starting over' with someone else.

Modern media is a funny thing. You would think, with the amount of connectivity we have at our disposal, that all our relationship problems would be solved, whereas it seems like we're worse than ever. I could call Alison or send an instant message any number of ways. I could type the simplest sentence like 'Please don't get back with him' or 'Let's give *us* a shot' and she'd know exactly where I stood in a heartbeat. And yet I knew I wouldn't do it. There was nothing I could type she didn't already know.

Except how strongly I felt.

It might have started on a whim, a passing shine to someone, a 'fancying' as we used to say in primary school. But it was more than that now; it was fully formed attraction. I knew exactly what I was losing.

The lock turned in the door; Paula had her own key. I would have given more thought to what that said about her relationship with Deano had my heart not been pounding so loudly. Palms already sweaty, I stood up and faced the door.

'Hiya! I ordered from the Pizza Perfection web site before I left,' she called down the hallway, 'It should be here any minute.'

I didn't know how to answer. 'Did you get me pepperoni?' seemed a tad presumptuous, so I said nothing. The living room door swung fully open, and Paula walked in.

'Dad?'

'Yes,' I said, because there's no way I could deny it. 'How are you?'

She looked at me blankly and ignored the question.

'What are you doing here? And where's Deano? Is he alright?'

The last question threw me. Was she concerned I'd killed him and taken his apartment?

'He's fine, he had to go out,' I said, wishing I had rehearsed my opening lines. 'We were talking earlier in the week. He said I could come over and have pizza with you.'

Paula's face was a mixture of confusion and disbelief.

'What do you mean, you were 'talking earlier in the week?' Since when do you and Deano 'talk'?'

There was an edge to her tone, and I knew I was on dangerous ground.

'We met a week or two ago, *accidentally,* at a football match. I was in yellow, I mean, I was stewarding.'

'And?'

'And we were just chatting. He's very nice. I've, er, decided I quite like him now.'

'Chatting about what?'

'The match mainly ...'

'Dad ...'

'He asked me about you.'

'A likely story.'

'No, really,' I said, holding my hands out to emphasise my honesty. 'I don't think he meant anything by it. Out of the blue he just asked if I had seen you much.'

'And?'

'I said I hadn't.'

The bungee cord of Paula's patience snapped.

'Would you please tell me what you two were talking about that ends up with him being out and you being here?'

I took a deep breath.

'I said I wanted to see you more, but it was difficult to catch up with you,' I took another gulp of air. 'He said he thought you would like to see me more, but that it was really awkward, and it was hard to get past that. And I think he's right, he's actually quite an in-depth thinker, you know ...' I didn't get any further.

'You two don't get to play me, behind my back,' Paula replied forcefully, 'I'm not having any of this!' She turned on her heel and walked swiftly back down the hallway.

It would have been a dramatic exit if the pizza delivery guy had not been blocking the doorway. As Paula flung the door wide, he walked in and deposited two gigantic pizza boxes in her arms. Two drinks sat on top, one bright red and the other bright blue.

'There you go love,' he said, 'The Thursday night special. One giant pepperoni and one giant barbecue chicken with two free slushies. Enjoy.' And then he was off back down the stairs.

Unable to turn around, Paula reversed back down the hallway and into the kitchen. She set the pizza boxes carefully onto the small table in the middle of the floor. I stood in the doorway.

'Nobody is trying to manipulate you,' I said, 'Don't blame Deano, he was only trying to help.'

She glared at me.

'But don't blame me either. You're my only daughter and I'm just wanting to spend more time with you.'

She continued to glare without blinking.

I took a step back towards the living room so that her way out of the kitchen wasn't blocked.

'You can go,' I said, 'I'm not trapping you here. I'm just asking you to stay and have a slice of pizza with me.'

Ten seconds passed with neither of us speaking or moving. It felt much longer. They say your life flashes before you when you're dying, but I think whole sections of your life flash before you all the time, especially in moments like this.

Vignettes of Paula flicked through my head. Five-year-old Paula wobbling along on a purple bike with stabilisers. Nine-year-old Paula dressed up as an elf in the school Christmas play. Eleven-year-old Paula in a secondary school uniform that looked like it was eating her. Six-year-old Paula with her arm stuck in the railings at the local library. Fourteen-year-old Paula singing loudly at the reception after her great aunt's funeral because she had been helping herself to the wine and neither Shirley nor I had noticed. Twelve-year-old Paula crying uncontrollably because her goldfish had died after she had added pink bubble bath to the water in an effort to 'make it look nicer.'

Paula sighed dramatically.

'One slice,' she said, flouncing onto a seat on the opposite side of the table and folding her arms.

'Should I get plates?' I asked. She shrugged viciously.

'If you need one, they're in that cupboard.' She pointed. 'I'm fine with my hands.'

'Ok,' I said, 'I'll probably be fine too.' I looked at the food and drink on the table, never having felt so much pressure on such a simple task. I lifted the two slushies.

'Red or blue?' I asked.

She shrugged again, which, when added to how she closed her eyes and looked away simultaneously, radiated her distaste for me.

'I'll go blue then.'

I set the red drink down in her front of her and the blue one in front of me. I opened the lid of the first pizza box and watched the steam unfurl to reveal pepperoni.

'That thing's huge,' I said, 'Do the two of you really get through one each?'

Arms still folded, Paula glared at me.

'Is it not a bit late for lessons on healthy eating?' she said.

And then I think she caught the petulance in her voice. I've seen it so many times before at work; there's only so long people have the energy required to keep up annoyance in the face of someone being nice to them. Eventually they sag into begrudging communication.

'Deano can put away a full one. I only ever eat half and he usually eats the end of it for lunch the next day.'

'Oh, ok,' I said, 'Is pepperoni alright?' I pulled off a slice; she pulled a face.

'It's alright, but the chicken is much nicer, it has barbecue sauce.'

With one hand holding a large slice of pepperoni, and nowhere to set it down, I tried to close the lid and lift up the whole box so Paula could access the box below.

'I'll do it,' Paula said, unfolding her arms, standing up and taking the box from me. She pulled off a slice of pizza for herself and we sat opposite each other eating in silence.

'Could I give you some money for the pizza?' I asked.

'No.'

There was another long pause.

'Can I ask you if it's good?'

'Yes. It's good. It's always good, that's why we order from there.'

'Fair point.'

I tried a variety of topics to elicit conversation; how work was, how her Mum was, how Deano was. This last one was met with, 'I think you know, you seem to be talking to him as much as I do.'

I asked her about friends, spare time and TV. I even tried to initiate a conversation about music, but I didn't recognise a single artist she mentioned, so that one was dead in the water. Our attempts to talk were excruciating, but somehow we managed to get to a third slice each and finish our slushies. Paula set down her empty plastic cup.

'This is why I avoid meeting up,' she said.

'What?'

'*This*. The awkwardness of *this*. Trying to have a normal conversation, like that's what we do now. It's such a ...'

'Strain?'

'Yes.'

'Yeah,' I said, 'My intestines are pretty tight too. And the pizza probably isn't helping.' Neither of us spoke for a few seconds.

'But this is what we have,' I said, 'The choice is this, and to keep doing this, until hopefully it becomes something better. Or we can have next to nothing; no awkwardness, no annoyance, no anger over what's happened in the past. But I don't want that. I don't think you want that.' I expected a shrug in response, but Paula stared down at the pizza box so hard I thought it might catch fire.

'No, I don't want that. But this, this is hard work.'
Her eyes flickered up to meet mine before settling
back on the pizza box.

'Sometimes,' I said, 'It's easier to get to know people
when you do something together. Sitting eyeballing
each other can be very uncomfortable. In work, not
that this is work, but, sometimes, when I'm meeting
someone who's really nervous, we don't do coffee
shops. We go for a walk, or play pool or crazy golf.'

'You want me to play crazy golf?'

'Do you like crazy golf?'

'No.'

'Then, no. But we could go for a walk, or even a run?'

'What?'

'Deano says you've started using a couch to 10k
app.'

'Bloody Deano. He can't shut up for two minutes.'

'It's a good idea though, we could do Park Run
together?' Paula shook her head and then inexplicably
she laughed.

'What?'

'It's hard to have such a serious conversation with
someone while the inside of their mouth is bright
blue.' I smiled.

'What the fuck is that stuff anyway? It doesn't taste
of any fruit I've ever come across.'

'I think it's meant to be bubble gum flavour.'

'I wasn't getting that. But then I haven't eaten
bubble gum since I was about nine. I feel like there's
been a chemical spillage in my mouth.'

She laughed again; a glorious, happy sound that made some of the tension in our conversation evaporate. At least, it did for me.

'Do you want a cup of tea?' she said, already knowing I would say yes and reaching for the kettle. It was only a cup of tea, but it was an invitation, and a start.

Paula stood with her back to the sink and looked directly at me. She sighed.

'This is *nuts,*' she said.

'What is?'

'This. You, scheming with my boyfriend, who you hardly even know. Lurking in his flat.'

'I wasn't lurking; I was standing in the middle of the living room.'

She ignored me.

'Who does that?'

I shrugged.

'There was nothing to lose. I wasn't seeing you anyway.'

The kettle reached the boil. She put tea bags in two mugs and poured in the water.

'How did you think this was going to work out?' she said.

'I had no idea. I sort of thought we might get something to eat, but the film was always pushing it.

'What?'

'Deano said you were going to watch TV. So I thought maybe we could watch a film.'

'You're crazy,' she said, but there was no heat in it.

She set the mug on the table in front of me and asked me if I wanted a biscuit. I declined because the sugar content of the slushy was already enough to induce a diabetic coma.

'I put a lot of thought into a film,' I said. 'Since going to the cinema was something we used to do a lot as a family … you and I have a lot to catch up on.'

'Are you wanting us to watch every film from the last several years?'

'No, no, but I did look at the biggest films of 2015.' The summer I moved out. 'I thought there would be something there to start with.' She looked over the top of her mug of tea in disbelief.

'The big summer film was 'Jurassic World.''

'Big dinosaurs, no thanks.'

'There was 'Inside Out,' which I have never seen.'

'Way too emotional, bawled my eyes out at that.'

'I think we can both agree 'Fifty Shades of Gray' is off the table.' Her eyes widened slightly and she didn't answer.

'Which leaves 'The Martian.''

'Sci-fi?'

'Sort of.'

'No way.'

'It's not your normal sci-fi, it's very human. Quite funny in parts.'

'Deano and his superheroes is bad enough,' she said, 'But I don't do spaceships.'

'At least have a look at the box.' I got up to retrieve it from the living room.

'You brought it with you?' Paula called after me, '*I don't believe you.*'

When I returned, she unwillingly took the box from me and half-heartedly scanned the cover.

'I promise you,' I said, 'It's a really entertaining film.'

'It's got Matt Damon and Kate Mara. It can't be all bad.'

We moved to the living room, mugs of tea in hand, and I watched a film with my daughter for the first time in years.

I've seen 'The Martian' several times, but it's funny how watching a film in a different context can give it a whole new meaning. In this case, the film's central storyline, the challenge of rescuing something lost, was not wasted on me.

As the credits rolled, Deano returned.

'You're still here,' he said happily when he saw me. 'And so are you,' he said to Paula.

'I think it's time for me to split,' I said, getting up, but Deano wasn't having any of it.

'No, no, man, you don't have to go. I'll put the kettle on.' He went into the kitchen. 'Is there any pizza left?' he called over his shoulder, 'I'm starving.'

Paula smiled at me. For that split second, we were on the same team. *I could get used to that,* I thought.

'Looks like I'm staying for a while longer,' I said, 'Sorry.'

Paula rolled her eyes.

'What's another ten minutes?' She lifted our mugs and took them into the kitchen.

Paula brought me another cup of tea while Deano returned with four slices of pizza stacked on a plate and a packet of Caramel Rockys.

'Help yourself,' he said happily, stuffing the end of a slice of pepperoni into his mouth. 'So, did you two actually talk to each other then?' he asked.

Paula sighed.

'Subtle as ever. Yes, we did.'

'Thank you Deano,' I said.

'No worries,' he replied. Then, seeing the DVD cover sitting beside me, he asked about the film. I gave a brief overview of the plot; man gets stranded on Mars and has to be rescued.

'Is it a true story?' he asked. Paula set him straight while I busied myself unwrapping a Rocky.

'So, do you live on your own then, Robbie?' Deano asked. I nodded. 'You haven't picked up with anyone else?'

'Deano!' Paula exclaimed, eyes wide.

'What?' Deano responded through a mouthful of pizza, 'Just making conversation.'

'This would actually be a good time for you to talk about football,' Paula suggested.

'No,' I said, 'There's just me, for now anyway.'

'For now?' Paula asked sharply, but with interest, rather than distaste.

'You working on it?' Deano asked.

'I'm not about to live with someone, no,' I said, trying to clear things up, 'I'm not even dating someone, not properly.'

'Not *properly*?' Paula asked.

'Er, no.'

'What's 'proper' dating?'

'When you actually call it a date.'

'What do you call ... whatever it is you're doing?'

'A non-date.'

'So you've been non-dating someone?'

'Er, yes.'

'I don't really understand,' said Deano.

'I think you need to tell us the story,' Paula said.

I hesitated.

'Are you going to be alright with it?' She raised her eyebrows. 'I mean, the idea of me seeing someone else?'

'Yes. I'm over the idea that you and Mum are going to get back together again,' she said sarcastically.

Wondering how I had stumbled into this, I summarised, as best I could, how things had started with Alison, and where they stood now. When I finished, both Paula and Deano sat with their mugs of tea in their hands, leaning forward in their seats and nodding deeply. Somehow this had turned into therapy.

'You need to do something,' Paula said.

'Definitely,' said Deano.

'Like what?'

'I don't know,' Paula said.

'That's great, thanks.'

'But you need to do something,' she said again.

'Yes, we've covered that.'

'It sounds like she's waiting,' she said.

'Waiting for what?'

'Waiting for you to ask,' she replied.

'I have asked. More than once.'

'Maybe it needs to be more than that,' she said.

'More than what?'

'More than just asking her out on a date.'

'You need to get her attention,' said Deano, starting on a second Rocky. 'Don't just let her go off with yer man again.'

'Any ideas?'

'I don't know,' Paula said, 'But you need to do something.'

'Thanks. You've been very helpful.'

I left soon after.

The walk home should have been bathed in a happy glow created by how my relationship with Paula had turned a corner. Instead, my mind was unsettled by Paula and Deano's reaction. Was I standing back from Alison at the very moment I should be stepping up? And if I did 'something', if I 'got her attention', what would that involve?

I was too perturbed to sleep but made myself go to bed anyway. At two in the morning I was still awake. I put on my headphones and selected a Spotify playlist to help me get over. Somewhere in my semi-consciousness I resolved to do something.

By the time I had finished breakfast the next morning, I had a plan. Not a good plan, not a well thought-out plan, and not a very sensible plan, but a plan, nonetheless.

13. Farewell and formal declaration

I phoned Helen at the office just after ten.

'I need a favour; is there any way you can add to me to tonight's shift at the Auditorium?'

'Elton John fan, huh?' she said.

'Yeah, I don't have a ticket for tonight, but I might get to hear some of it.' Technically speaking all of this was true.

Helen checked over the rotas.

'Sorry Robbie, we're full at the minute.' I groaned inwardly. 'But don't despair yet, it's not unusual for someone to drop out over the course of the day. If someone does, I'll give you a call.'

I thanked her and hung up, then busied myself at home, washing dishes, doing laundry, hoovering, even an unnecessary trip to Tesco's to put the time in, while being constantly distracted pondering how I might best overcome each of the flaws in my plan.

I checked my phone every ten minutes all morning; by four o'clock I had all but given up. Just as I was settling down on the sofa with a large mug of tea and an episode of 'Homes Under the Hammer', Helen rang back.

'Sicknote's pulled out,' she said happily.

'The lad is consistent.'

'Apparently he's a lump.'

'That's a bit harsh.'

'No, he … has … a … lump.'

'Oh dear,' I said, becoming more serious. 'That's never good.'

'On his face,' Helen added.

'Ok.' I thought about this. 'So it might be a spot?'

'That's what I was thinking. Be in for six as usual.'
She hung up before I could ask what position I'd been
given. Maybe that was for the best however, it
doesn't pay to stretch favours too far.

*

With excitement and tension building, I parked up at
the Auditorium a little before half five, earlier than
any other shift I'd ever worked. I signed in, bought a
one-shot and discovered I had been put on tiered
seating, which is usually my favourite, but wasn't
going to work for me tonight. I loitered in the foyer
until I saw Tony.

'Hey, I need a favour; is there any way you can
switch me from tiered to tickets?' I asked.

He looked at me suspiciously.

'Calf muscles are killing me,' I explained, 'Pushed it a
bit harder than I should at Park Run last week.'

None of this was true; there are people pushing fat
kids in buggies who run faster than me at Park Run.
He agreed to make the change, but I felt bad lying to
Tony.

With twenty minutes to go until the stewards'
briefing at six o'clock, I made my way down the
concrete steps and along the corridor below the
auditorium. Trying to look as nonchalant as possible,
while also feeling guilty, I trotted past the series of
dark-grey steel doors, and then on past the room with

the spray painted '12' on it. A set of imposing red steel double doors blocked my way, as did the steward guarding them. Sohail.

'Hi there,' I chirped, 'How's it going?'

'I'm every bit good,' he replied.

'I just need to slip past you,' I said, when he made no move away from the door.

'Sorry, Robbie. You're not allowed in there.'

'Tony sent me down,' I said, deploying my well-rehearsed line, 'I have to go and find the backstage supervisor. He has a question about security.'

This, I knew, was a risk. I needed a reason to get backstage. It needed to be a strong enough reason to get past the beast at the threshold, in this case Sohail. For that reason, I had thrown in the word security. I was playing with fire, however. 'Security' can imply a whole range of possibilities, including things that in this day and age can get a whole building evacuated and shut down.

Sohail looked at me suspiciously. I could feel myself reddening.

'No he didn't,' Sohail said confidently, seeing right through me.

'Alright, no he didn't,' I conceded, deciding that honesty was the best policy – at least when the other policy didn't work. 'I need a favour. I just need back there; five minutes, tops.'

'I can't do that, man,' Sohail replied, 'I'd like to. You know me, I like to help everybody. But if I let you back there, and you get caught, they'll come looking for me and then I'll get fired. Or worse.'

'Is there something worse than being fired?'

'Yes. Tiered seating.'

'What if you said, I rushed at the door and forced you aside?'

Sohail started to laugh, insultingly hard.

'I'm sorry man,' he said, 'If it was up to me, I'd let you in, but I like this job. I'm good at this job and I don't want to lose it.'

'Alright. No sweat.' I clapped him on the side of an expansive bicep and retreated back down the corridor.

It was nearly ten to six. I decided I had time to sit down for a moment and console myself, so I slid into Room 12 and slumped down on a plastic chair in front of the vending machines. Normally I'd be thinking about what kind of chocolate bar I wanted, but at that moment I was only experiencing the bitter taste of failure.

The two other stewards in the room cleared out, leaving only Stella and myself.

'You look like the scoop just fell off your poke,' she said.

I tried to smile.

'Yeah, a little. It's hard to explain. I had a plan and it fell apart.'

Stella nodded.

'Was it an evil plan?'

'No. It was pretty innocuous, in the broad scheme of things. Just a wee idea.'

'Has this got anything to do with Alison?'

'How could you possibly know that?' I asked, startled. Stella chuckled.

'I saw her in the car park earlier, before I came in. She was going to get something to eat before the gig. Along with the guy she was holding hands with.'

I felt like I had run into a concrete bollard at speed. There was nothing in what Stella had said that I couldn't have imagined, but hearing it said out loud made it more real.

'She's a big Elton John fan. I knew she was coming ... and I knew she was bringing Andy.'

'And that dashed your plan?'

'Actually, Sohail dashed my plan. I was trying to get backstage ...'

Stella's eyebrows shot up and her smile disappeared.

Another two stewards came into the room to sign out torches and Stella moved away to make sure the paperwork was completed. When they left, I went to follow them.

'Robbie,' Stella said, 'What was your plan?'

'Are you sure you want to know?'

She looked at me hard.

'You're sure it's not an evil plan?'

'Positive. Scout's honour.'

'Are you a scout?'

'Em, not anymore. It's been a while, but I'm still honourable.' I grinned, as did she.

'No,' Stella said, 'I don't want to know.' Then she took a long breath. 'I think it's going to be a long, long time.'

'What?'

'Every gig, there's a different pass phrase. That's why Sohail didn't let you through. I always get told because sometimes I hear things that a supervisor should be aware of. My closest supervisor is through the big red doors.'

'And tonight's phrase is, 'I think it's going to be a long, long time?''

She nodded. I made to leave.

'Robbie?' she said, urgently.

'Yeah?'

'Do you know what you're doing?'

I thought about it.

'Not in the slightest. But I've been told that sometimes you just have to do something.'

'Fair enough. Here's a mini Mars bar for luck.'

*

'Sohail,' I said, leaning in, 'I think it's going to be a long, long time.'

He raised his eyebrows, looked carefully at me, and stood aside. I opened one of the red steel doors and let it shut behind me as quietly as I could. My sweaty hand slid off the handle as I moved away.

The next section of the corridor was the same size and shape as before, curving gently round to my left. But this side of the red door was a different world. The paintwork was fresh and bright, the floor was carpeted and the lights above me were glass domes hanging from the ceiling. The smell of freshly cooked food wafted down the corridor. Nice food, not the boiled-up hot dogs available on the concourse.

I proceeded along the corridor, it curved gently away to my left, which meant I was unnoticed, but also meant I couldn't see who was coming until the last minute. This was the part I hadn't been able to plan because I didn't know what I was going to find.

The first two doors I came to were labelled as stores. Two blokes with long hair tied back, black combat trousers and carrying rolls of cable over their shoulders walked past me. I noticed the three passes on the lanyards they wore round their neck and instantly felt exposed without one. They kept on walking and vanished into one of the stores.

The next two doors were dressing rooms five and six. A little further along were the doors for dressing rooms three and four. Two young women, probably in their twenties and wearing what looked to me to be waitress uniforms, scuttled past paying me no attention whatsoever.

I was now panicking at an elite level. I had no idea what I was looking for, but I reckoned that dressing room one was the place to head. Still no one approached me as I stood between the doors of dressing room one and two. Briefly, I checked for the small note in my pocket and placed my hand on the door handle of dressing room one.

'*Robbie?!*' the voice made me jump. I looked up to see another young woman in a waitress's uniform, walking towards me.

'*Niamh!* You're working here?'

'Yes. But what are you doing backstage?' she asked. Not for the first time that night, I reddened. I also pulled my hand back from the door like it was red hot. 'You weren't going in there were you?'

I shook my head. And then I nodded.

'You *cannot* go in there,' she said, 'Get in here!'

She grabbed me by the arm and pulled me further along the corridor and into the kitchen. It was a hive of activity with food cooking under noisy fans and three chefs scurrying to and fro. They completely ignored us as Niamh led me into a small store off the main kitchen.

'*What the hell are you doing?*'

I puffed out my cheeks and struggled to hold her gaze; what I was about to say sounded ridiculous.

'Were you trying to meet Elton John?'

'No. Definitely not.'

'Then what?'

'I was hoping to leave a note.'

'*A note?!*'

'A request for a song.'

'You can be fired for being back here, let alone being in there! And all for a song?'

I shrugged, like a petulant schoolboy caught eating gum in class.

'It wasn't for me,' I said.

Niamh looked at me closely, and then her demeanour softened.

'I'm guessing Alison comes into this story.' I nodded. 'Where were you going to leave it?'

I shrugged again.

'Don't know. Somewhere obvious. On his mirror maybe.'

'Oh Robbie,' Niamh said, in a mixture of sympathy and exasperation, 'For a start, Elton John's dressing room will be either three or four, they're the biggest ones. There's a few of his staff in there now, if they had found you ...' She sighed, 'Look, you need to get out of here.'

I glanced at my watch; it was now two minutes to six. I needed to get back to the front of the Auditorium fast. I turned to go, but Niamh grabbed my arm.

'I'll check the coast is clear,' she said. She disappeared out of the kitchen and into the corridor, returning twenty seconds later. 'Let's go!' she hissed.

She insisted on walking me to the red doors as she thought it would be less likely a steward accompanied by the catering manager would attract attention.

'Thanks, Niamh,' I said, slipping through the crack in the doors.

'Robbie?' she said, suddenly, 'Give me the note.' I hesitated. 'No promises; but if there's a chance ...'

'Are you sure?' I asked. She held out her hand impatiently. I handed it over.

*

Almost running, I made it back to the foyer by six, thankful the briefing hadn't started. I joined the edge of the gaggle of stewards and stood beside Been There.

'Big gig tonight,' he said. I agreed. 'I was on the last time he was here, a few years back. You'll never guess what happened.'

Jittery from a day's anxiety and the last few minutes of adrenaline, I said the first things that came into my mind.

'You saw one of his kids.'

'No.'

'You met one of his kids.'

'No.'

'You got to keep one of his kids?'

'Are you taking the piss?'

'Not at all.'

Been There leant towards me and whispered.

'I saw one of Elton John's roadies wipe his piano down. With Pledge.'

'Pledge?' I replied, 'As in the spray polish you can buy in Tesco's?'

Been There nodded solemnly.

'Goes to show,' he said meaningfully.

I had no idea what it went to show, and I never found out because Tony started the briefing.

'Capacity crowd tonight folks, so we're going to need to keep the lines moving nice and steady as they come through the doors. Now, has anyone not used a scanner before?'

*

While it was an all-age crowd, it tipped massively towards the over-forties who arrived ahead of time and took their seats in an orderly manner. Once the rush was over and Elton had taken the stage, Tony split us into two groups for breaks. My group went first. I sat down beside Stella in Room 12. She said nothing, but she raised her eyebrows and paused her consumption of a Curly Wurly.

'It's all under control,' I said, 'Nothing to worry about.'

'That's good,' she said.

But I *was* worried. The risk I was taking had now been transferred to Niamh. I could survive being fired from my few shifts in the month, but Niamh really needed her job. What if something went wrong?

Ryan took a seat on the other side of me.

'How's it going?' I asked.

'Bloody tiered seats,' he said, 'People who want to stand; people who want to sit and can't see because others are standing; people who can't find their seat because they can't remember which door they came in. The usual.'

'Older crowd though; less boke.'

'True,' he said, munching on a Double Decker, 'But more arse-pinching. I've been felt up twice tonight already.'

'Take it as a compliment, kid.'

After the second group's break had been covered, I was delighted to be sent upstairs into the auditorium to cover other stewards in the vomitories. This gave me the opportunity not only to hear some of the gig, but also to keep an ear out for the unlikely possibility of 'Mona Lisas and Mad Hatters' being played.

I made my way round to the far side of the building and released the first steward. Tony had let me see his copy of the set list and I knew the show was roughly a quarter of the way through. Elton had reached a quieter phase and was playing through 'Sorry Seems to be the Hardest Word' and then 'Someone Saved My Life Tonight.' Not upbeat, but songs with so much poignancy they held the audience spellbound. I looked across the auditorium at the faces soaking up the experience in rapt attention. It was only disrupted by knowing that somewhere out there, though I had no idea where, was Alison. With Andy.

By the time I had made it to the next vomitory, Elton had moved on to 'Daniel', which I knew was another of Alison's favourites. *She'll be loving every minute of this,* I thought, and I hoped again for the inclusion of 'Mona Lisas,' but there was no sign of it yet. A calm, reflective mood swept over me induced by the synth solo in the middle of the song. *You just tried to add a song to Elton John's set list in order to get a woman to leave her boyfriend and go out with you,* I thought. The darkness hid the surge of blood to my face. It had been a ridiculous idea brought on by desperation and lack of sleep. It was also a ridiculous idea that a song might prompt someone else to make a life-changing decision.

The reflective atmosphere continued at the next vomitory. Elton was playing 'Candle in the Wind' and I was stuck on the lyric, 'I would have liked to know you.' My ridiculous plan was never about the song, I realised, it was about the gesture; it was about doing something. The set moved on from 'Candle' into 'Don't let the Sun go down on Me' and I began to consider that an Elton John concert is not where you want to be if you're tired and emotionally raw. Just as my mood was descending, however, the song was interrupted by a 'wet spill' and a well-lubricated elderly woman who had lost her mobile phone. I located it quickly with my torch, and I was off again.

You can tell the end of a gig is coming when, somewhere after the seventy-minute mark, the set slowly begins to rise in tempo. 'I'm Still Standing' was the first of the upbeat songs that signalled we were probably into the last fifteen or twenty minutes before the encore. Lyrically, it's quite a defiant song, but 'looking like a true survivor, feeling like a little kid' never seemed more apt.

I leant against the vomitory wall, in a slovenly posture stewards are not encouraged to adopt, and sighed wistfully. *If nothing else happens with Alison*, I thought, *at least I can say I tried.*

'I'm Still Standing' gave way to 'The Bitch is Back' and I knew then that 'Mona Lisas' wasn't going to make the set; Elton and his band were building towards a grand finale. All hope of a grand gesture was gone.

I had to suffer almost all of 'Crocodile Rock' at the next vomitory before I was finally released to go back and stand at the exits for egress. The barriers and turnstiles had already been removed and there was nothing left to do but stand at a gap between doors, smile sweetly and bid everyone a goodnight. Only a few spectators were leaving yet, however. This was Elton John's farewell tour, and while he had stated he was quitting touring many times in the past, age and family commitments had now caught up with him and this was almost certainly the last time he would entertain a crowd in Belfast.

And then the music stopped. No sound came from the auditorium, aside from the sustained applause and roar of the crowd seeking an encore. Niamh came walking across the foyer towards me, her face downcast.

'I'm so sorry, Robbie,' she said. I smiled and touched her on the arm; I felt like it was my turn.

'It's fine. It was a completely stupid idea and I should never have done it. I don't know what came over me.'

'No, you don't understand.' She took a deep breath. 'I couldn't leave your note somewhere; I knew that would cause trouble if someone complained. But just before the show he asked to meet the waitresses, and me.'

'Elton John?'

'Yeah.'

'Wow.'

'It was only for a minute,' she went on, 'Just to say hello and thanks. He was really nice. We were just about to go when I blurted out that I had a favourite song. He seemed a bit amused and he asked me what it was.' Niamh's face reddened and she looked down at the ground. 'That's when I realised that I hadn't looked at your note. I had to take it out of my pocket

318

and read it to him. *Oh Robbie, it was so embarrassing!'*

'What happened?' I asked, not being unsympathetic to Niamh's experience, but wanting to know how this ended.

'I think I made it sound like a question.'

'How do you mean?'

'I think it sounded like, 'Mona Lisas and Mad Hatters?''

'And then what?'

'Well ...' she hesitated, 'He started to laugh.'

Laughter is good, I thought.

'And then he said, 'You've never heard that song in your life, have you?''

'What did you say?'

'I said no, but I had a friend who really, really liked it and would love to hear it live.'

'And what did he say?'

'He said it was few years since he had played it live and he laughed again. And then his team asked us to leave because he was due on stage very soon.'

I couldn't help but smile.

'It's not funny,' Niamh said, 'I just wanted the ground to swallow me whole.'

'It'll be funny tomorrow. Or maybe the next day. Either way, thank you Niamh.'

'Your Song' had started to play as we had been talking and I realised, with Elton returning to his breakthrough song, that we had probably reached the end of the gig. The doors of the concert hall were now fully open ready for the mass exodus, and I could now see the stage in the distance. Despite the chatter of a few stewards, who obviously didn't appreciate a master at work, I could hear the song reasonably well.

The last notes rang out and Elton took a moment to shake hands with a few people at the front of the stage before sitting back down at the piano. It seemed he wasn't finished yet.

'Someone reminded me of this song earlier on tonight,' he said, 'I haven't played it for a few years, but it's still one of my all-time favourites and one of Bernie's finest lyrics.'

And then it happened.

Elton John played 'Mona Lisas and Mad Hatters.'

The chatter of others melted away, as did the background rumble of traffic noise from outside and I became enthralled in the music made by one man and one instrument.

I'll admit it's a strange lyric:

'Subway's no way for a good man to go down,
Rich man can ride and the hobo he can drown,
And I thank the Lord for the people I have found,
I thank the Lord for the people I have found.'

But there's something that Elton's melody brings to the fore; the words and music so perfectly complement each other they produce an enormous emotional resonance.

And I thought of Alison. Somewhere inside I knew this would be the high point of an amazing evening. No matter what, this was my gift to her. Well,

Niamh's gift to her, and to be fair, Elton definitely had a hand in it too.

He finished with 'Goodbye Yellow Brick Road' which, being a farewell tour, took the audience to a whole new level of emotion. I wondered if there was a dry eye left in the house. The song ended and the whole band came to the front of the stage to take a bow together, before leaving Elton on stage and alone for a sustained ovation. Then he was gone, the house lights came on and the spell was broken. The exits filled with people transferring from one world to another. Conversations that began with 'wasn't that incredible?' segued into 'where did I put the ticket for the car park?'

I smiled and bid people goodnight. I tried to watch for Alison, but found it difficult with so many people coming past at once.

She found me, however.

'Hi!' she said, standing on her own, directly in front of me.

'Hey,' I replied, *'So?'*

'Amazing gig; he's just *so* good. I'm a little bit sad that'll probably be the last time, but, all good things come to an end.'

'As George would say, 'the sunrise doesn't last all morning.''

'Trust you to bring a Beatle into it. Did you get to hear any of it?'

'Yeah, I was covering breaks on tiered, and then I was out here. I heard all of the encore.'

'He played 'Mona Lisas' right at the end,' she said, eyes wide, 'How incredible was that? It was the most perfect ending.'

It was a long time since I had been so happy.

'I had a little something to do with that,' I said, trying to make it sound impressive, but worried that I just sounded smug. Alison looked confused.

'You got it added to the set list?' she joked.

'Kind of. In a very round about way.' She continued to look confused. 'No really, it's a bit of a story,' I began, but she interrupted.

'You can't resist a good wind-up.'

A tall, trim bloke, short hair and Lennon-esque gold-rimmed glasses stepped out of the crowd. He had an open, welcoming expression.

'This is Andy. Andy, this is Robbie, one of my fellow stewards.'

Andy and I exchanged pleasantries as we shook hands.

'Great gig,' Andy said, 'Did you get to see any of it?'

I filled him in, while realising my moment to tell Alison the details of my story had slipped away.

'I'm not a huge Elton fan,' Andy said, 'Not as much as Alison anyway, but so many classic songs with such a great band. Just incredible.'

"Funeral for a Friend' into 'Love Lies Bleeding' made the hairs on the back of my neck stand on end,' Alison said. 'Don't worry, I'll give you a song-by-song analysis next time we're on a shift together.'

'I look forward to it,' I said, deciding that she had just defined our future relationship: two people in bright yellow who steward events.

'We'd better hit the trail and join the queues to get out of here,' Andy said, putting his arm around Alison. They wished me a goodnight together and happily exited the building.

I sagged against the wall; a physical manifestation of going from elation to abject disappointment in a couple of minutes. I had done something, but it wasn't enough. My chance had come and gone.

And then I was visited by three ghosts. Alright, not ghosts, because each of them was still alive. Three memories spoke almost simultaneously. I heard Niamh say, 'You have to look at how the future is shaping up.' I heard Sam say, 'Is this how you want it to be?' And I heard Paula say, 'It sounds like she's waiting.'

And I thought, 'Och, *fuck it*.'

Abandoning my post, I ran off towards the car park.

I caught up with them in the long queue for the payment machine.

'Alison!'

She looked startled by my sudden appearance.

'Robbie?'

'Yeah, I was thinking ...' I began.

There was five seconds of dead air. And then I chickened out.

'You can have my one shot. I'll get another one in a minute.'

I took the car parking ticket from my pocket and held it out to her. Slowly, very slowly, she reached out and took it off me. Our eyes met for longer than anybody's eyes have ever met over a car parking ticket.

'Thanks, Robbie,' she said, 'You're very kind.'

'Yeah.' And then I was torn. I should have moved away, but I didn't. I just stood there. Like an eejit.

'Robbie?' Alison asked.

'Yes?'

'Is there something else?'

I have no idea what she was expecting, but I'm sure it wasn't what came out.

'Yes,' I said, 'There is. Quite a lot actually.' And then I paused, not so much to gather my thoughts, as to quell my sheer panic.

'Ok,' Alison said, uncertainly, 'We should maybe step out of the queue.' But I didn't give her a chance to move.

'Alison,' I began, 'I know we didn't date. I know it wasn't a ... a *thing,*' I turned to Andy, 'We really didn't go out together, even when yous weren't, you know, properly together.'

'Uh-huh ...' said Andy.

'But it changed me,' I went on, 'It's like we were together. Not so much in real life, more in my head. *But that still counts*.'

Alison looked confused. So did Andy. So did some of the people in the queue who were close enough to hear everything.

'You make me a different person,' I continued, 'A better person.'

'Did he say a *bitter* person?' a man in the queue asked the woman beside him.

'A *better* person,' she answered, and then muttered, 'Cloth ears.'

'My life is better when I'm with you,' the words tumbled out, 'I do things I wouldn't normally do. I say things I wouldn't normally say – and some of the time, not really in a good way, but that's alright. I listen to new music, I try new food, I see the world differently ...'

'*Robbie,*' Alison interrupted firmly, 'This is really not the place to declare undying love ...'

But there was no stopping me; the dam had been breached.

'I'm not declaring undying love. I'm declaring undying interest. Interest in your day, your thoughts, your loves, your hates, joys, sorrows, all of it. I want to be there for that. If you want Andy to be there for all of that, and if he can do all of that, well and good. I won't stalk you; this'll be the last time I do this.'

'Have there been other times you've done this?' said a woman in the line.

'No,' I replied, 'This is a special occasion.'

I looked back at Alison.

'But if Andy can't do that, then I want to.'

I ran out of energy at that point.

'That's it,' I said, 'That's all I've got.'

There was a brief period of silence broken by one person in the line who started to clap, but was quickly silenced by someone else saying,

'*Don't be fuckin' stupid.*'

Another voice said impatiently,

'Could we get our car parking tickets now, *please?*'

I turned and walked back to the Auditorium. I did not look back and Alison did not call after me.

*

If anyone noticed my sudden absence on the door, no one mentioned it. Tony saw me returning, but probably assumed I'd gone to help someone and didn't ask. I can remember nothing of the debrief or the journey home, but I made it safely to an armchair with a cup of tea, so it must have been without slips, trips or falls.

I flicked on the TV, but nothing could distract me. I ate more chocolate than I should have and then felt sick. I thought about sending a text, but decided I'd probably said enough for now. More than.

And then at 2am, the first text arrived.

It said, 'You are an asshole.'

I waited barely a minute before replying, 'Yes, I know. Sorry.'

The second text came through fifteen minutes later. 'I had a blazing row with Andy.' This was then followed by 'And then a long talk.' I felt it best not to reply. A few minutes later she sent another text. 'And it'll be the last one.'

It's so hard to read the tone of a text. So hard to figure out if conversation is being invited or shut down. I stared at the screen as another text came through.

'Are you awake?'

'Yes,' I replied. And then I sent another one, 'Adrenaline levels still quite high.'

Suddenly, the phone rang. I answered it.

'Hey,' I said.

'Hi,' she said quietly, 'You just couldn't wait, could you?'

'Wait for ...?'

'A better time.'

'I was seizing the moment,' I said, 'I was worried there might not be another one.'

There was a long pause.

'There would have been another one,' she said. I wasn't certain what she meant. 'Robbie,' she went on, 'When he played 'Mona Lisas ...''

'Yeah?'

'I was thinking of you.'

Acknowledgements

A huge thank you to the people who suffered through early drafts and gave me helpful feedback: Paul Doran (for committing so many thoughts to text and for giving me the chance to hone my writing at tenx9), Neil Sedgewick, Lorraine Thompson, George and Christine Sproule, Caroline and Charmaine Orr and Natalie Gilbert.

Thanks to Jason O'Rourke at typewright (www.typewright.co.uk) for proofreading, editing and a really helpful fresh perspective. Any errors in the text are entirely mine from last minute changes...

Thank you to Brian O'Neill for the cover.

And to the bin-liddery, Muppetry and all-round riotous unpredictability of the general public of Northern Ireland, you never fail to entertain me.

Printed in Great Britain
by Amazon